MURDER AT COLLINS AIRFIELD
A MARGARET AND MONA GHOSTLY COZY

DIANA XARISSA

Copyright © 2024 by DX Dunn, LLC

Cover Copyright © 2024 Tell-Tale Book Covers

ISBN: 9798338426562

All rights reserved.

No part of this publication may be reproduced, distributed, or transmitted in any form or by any means, including photocopying, recording, or other electronic or mechanical methods, without the prior written permission of the publisher, except as permitted by U.S. copyright law. For permission requests, contact diana@dianaxarissa.com

The story, all names, characters, and incidents portrayed in this production are fictitious. No identification with actual persons (living or deceased), places, buildings, and products is intended or should be inferred.

First edition 2024

❦ Created with Vellum

1

"What is that noise?" Margaret asked as she sat up in bed. It was dark, and the clock told her that it was two o'clock in the morning. Katie mewed softly as she climbed up the bed toward Margaret.

"It's the fire alarm," Mona's voice was quiet but still managed to be heard over the incessant ringing sound. "There's a fire. You need to get out of the building."

Margaret was still half asleep as she got out of bed. She pulled on a pair of jeans and a T-shirt and brushed her hair into a ponytail. Then she picked up Katie and held her close.

"It's going to be okay," she told the tiny cat. "We're going to be just fine."

She walked out of her bedroom and into the living room of the large luxury apartment she was currently calling home. Her purse was where she'd left it on the table near the door. After checking that the keycard for the apartment was in the bag, she opened her door. Several of her neighbors were standing in the corridor, looking confused.

"Are we supposed to evacuate?" one of them asked Margaret.

Before Margaret could reply, the door at the top of the stairwell opened. A fireman stepped out.

"Everyone needs to leave the building," he said. "It's precautionary. We're working to get the fire under control. But we want you all to be safe. Please use the stairs if you can. If you can't manage the stairs, please let me know."

He began to knock loudly on apartment doors. "There's a fire. You need to evacuate the building," he shouted loudly as he made his way down the corridor.

Margaret and the others headed for the stairs. In her haste, Margaret had forgotten to put Katie in her carrier. She looked down at the cat, who was smaller than average, and sighed.

"You're going to be good and stay with me, right?" she whispered.

Katie snuggled against her and squeezed her eyes shut. Margaret glanced at her purse. It was large enough to tuck Katie inside if absolutely necessary. The walk down from the sixth floor seemed to take forever. The shrieking siren kept blasting in her ears. When they reached the ground floor, a pair of firefighters urged them to exit the building as quickly as possible.

"Please cross the road to the promenade and remain there until the building is cleared," they were told. "We're working to contain the fire. Please let someone know if you know that there are people remaining in the building."

Margaret followed the small crowd out of the building and across the street. The entire area was lit up by the flashing lights of fire trucks, police cars, and an ambulance. On the promenade, people in everything from evening wear to pajamas were huddled together in small clusters, all silently staring at the building they'd just left. Margaret smiled and nodded at a few people as she found a spot to stand near the edge of the crowd.

"You're Margaret Woods, aren't you?" a woman asked a few minutes later.

Margaret looked over at the woman. She appeared to be somewhere around fifty. She was wearing pajamas, with a bathrobe over the top, and a pair of slippers.

"I am," Margaret admitted.

The other woman nodded. "I thought so. I've seen you going in and out of the building before. I was always going to say hello, but I didn't want to bother you."

"Hello," Margaret said after an awkward pause.

The woman laughed. "I'm American, too, you see. I was always going to introduce myself to your aunt as well, but I never worked up the nerve."

"I'm sure Aunt Fenella would have loved to meet you."

"Maybe. I thought about it when she first arrived on the island, but at that point everyone on the island wanted to meet her. She'd just inherited a huge fortune. Everyone wanted to be her friend."

Margaret nodded. "Except when she first arrived, Aunt Fenella had no idea that she'd inherited a fortune. She was just happy to have an apartment to call home."

"Really? I suppose I'd imagined that she knew all about her Aunt Mona Kelly."

"She'd only met Mona a few times over the years, when Mona traveled to the US to visit her sister, Aunt Fenella's mother. I don't think any of Mona's US family knew just how wealthy Mona was."

"Maybe you'd have visited her if you'd known."

Margaret laughed. "I suspect some of the family would have visited, certainly."

"That came out a bit more rudely than I intended."

"It's fine. It's three o'clock in the morning."

"Everyone on the island knew Mona, and we all knew she was incredibly wealthy, too. She captured Maxwell Martin's heart when she was eighteen, and he showered her with expensive presents for decades."

Margaret nodded. She knew there was quite a lot more to the story than that, but it seemed easier to keep it simple.

"Every time I walk past Mona's car in the parking garage, I'm jealous," the woman continued. "I've always wondered if she really loved Max or just loved his money. There were all sorts of rumors and stories about her and other men."

"And it all happened before I arrived on the island."

"Of course." The woman shook her head. "I'm making a right mess of this. I'm Marcia Baker. I moved to the island twenty-five years ago when I married a man I'd met through a weird set of circumstances."

"Oh? Now you have to tell me more."

Marcia laughed. "I was in my mid-twenties, working as a veterinary assistant in Iowa. Someone brought in a cat that didn't have a tail. The man claimed that it was a Manx cat. My boss, the vet, asked me to see what I could learn about Manx cats, so I did some research. The internet didn't have as much useful information in those days, of course."

Margaret nodded. "And it sounds as if that was lucky for you."

Marcia nodded. "It really was. I found a few books at the local library, but they weren't much help. The vet told me to try calling a vet here on the island. Our little patient had some issues with her tail nub, you see, and we weren't certain how best to deal with it."

"So you called a vet on the island?"

"That was the plan," Marcia said, laughing again. "What I actually did was call the wrong number."

"Oh dear."

"Yeah. When the guy answered, I said I needed information about Manx cats. He said he'd do his best. I just started asking away, never even thinking to check that I had the right person."

Margaret laughed. "And was he able to help much?"

"Oh, he tried. He answered all of my questions, but it quickly became obvious that he didn't really know anything about cats."

Marcia stopped as another ambulance pulled up in front of the building.

"I hope that doesn't mean that someone got hurt in the fire," Margaret said.

"The paramedics aren't rushing inside, so that suggests that they're here just in case they're needed," Marcia said.

Margaret sighed. "Let's hope they aren't needed, then. But you were telling me about your phone conversation."

"Oh, yeah, so I asked a bunch of questions and got answers that I knew were wrong. When I confronted the guy, he said it was obvious that I was American, but even so, it seemed odd that I would just call a random Manx person and expect that person to know a great deal about cats, Manx or otherwise."

"He wasn't wrong," Margaret said with a chuckle.

Marcia nodded. "I got angry with him and said that I'd assumed that a vet on the island would know more about Manx cats than I did. He replied that he expected one would and then offered to find me a phone number for one. That was when I finally realized that I'd called the wrong number. I was so flustered that I simply hung up on him."

"I can understand that."

"Then I called the right number, which was only one number off the number I'd called in error. They were very helpful. We quickly discovered that our patient wasn't a Manx cat at all. Actually, we discovered that our patient's owner was taking ordinary kittens and removing their tails in an attempt to sell them as Manx."

"How awful."

"Yeah, it was pretty bad. The guy ended up getting banned from owning animals for the rest of his life, which he totally deserved."

Margaret nodded and gave Katie a pat. "How could anyone hurt a kitten?"

"So the next day, after I'd shared everything that I'd learned with my boss and he'd called the police to report the abuse, I called the wrong number again. I wanted to apologize for my mistake. And honestly, I wanted to talk to the guy again. He had a very sexy voice, and I loved his accent."

"I think a lot of Americans find British accents attractive."

Marcia grinned. "I understand you've already found yourself a boyfriend. Ted Hart is a very handsome man, accent or no accent."

Margaret felt color rush into her cheeks. "I am seeing Ted Hart," she acknowledged. "And he is very handsome."

"And he's a police inspector. Your aunt married a police inspector from the Douglas unit. I suppose it's only natural that Ted was one of the first people you met when you came to the island."

Margaret nodded. *Except Aunt Fenella didn't introduce us to Ted. We met Ted because we found a dead body,* she thought.

"But where was I? Oh, yes, I called the wrong number again to apologize. I explained the mix-up and then we started talking, and talking, and talking. We ended up chatting for over an hour. By the end of the call, he'd asked for my number and said that he might call me one day. As it happened, 'one day' turned out to be the next day."

Margaret laughed. "How romantic."

"Yeah, I was dating a guy back in Iowa, but I ended things with him as soon as I started talking to Rick. We talked every day for a month, and then my boss got the bill for the calls I'd made to the island, and Rick got the bill for the calls he'd been making to me. After that, we switched to email."

"Phone calls used to be so expensive, especially international calls."

Marcia nodded. "Anyway, we emailed back and forth for a few months before Rick suggested exchanging photos. By that time my family was convinced that Rick was either a sixty-year-old man who was hoping I was underage or a sixteen-year-old boy who was hoping for naughty pictures."

Margaret laughed. "I can understand their concerns."

"I could, too, but this was years ago, before people were using the internet for all things nasty and criminal. It never crossed my mind to lie to Rick about anything, and fortunately, he didn't think to lie, either. When we finally did exchange photos, he looked exactly like what I'd been expecting, all long hair and crooked teeth. My goodness, but he was gorgeous."

"The Isle of Man is a long way away from Iowa."

"It is, indeed, but after we'd seen photos, we decided we wanted to meet in person. I wasn't sure about coming to the island and he wasn't interested in spending time in Iowa, so we decided to meet in London. I've never been more afraid of anything than I was of flying to London on my own."

"You should have brought a friend."

"I should have, but I couldn't find one that wanted to come along. My mother cried buckets at the airport. She was convinced that Rick was going to kill me in my sleep during my visit. He'd booked us a hotel in London and paid for two separate rooms so that I wouldn't think he was just trying to get me into bed. At least, that's what he'd told me. When I got on the plane, I was trusting him to be at the airport and trusting that he'd actually booked a hotel like he'd said."

"What happened next?" Margaret asked as a few firefighters walked out of the building.

The two women watched them stop just outside the door for a conversation.

"Oh, it was all drama," Marcia said with a laugh. "I got off the plane, stumbled my way through immigration with my brand-new passport and then wandered accidentally into the red channel at customs. When they asked me what I wanted to declare, I just stared at them. Eventually, someone kindly took pity on me and sent me over to the green channel. Once that ordeal was over, I walked out into the biggest airport I'd ever seen and simply froze. It seemed as if there were thousands of people going in every direction, and I had no idea which way to go."

"Big-city airports are terrifying."

"They really are. Eventually, I followed the crowd toward an exit. I kept scanning faces, trying to spot Rick, but I couldn't see him anywhere. I finally found a bench and just sat down, clutching my suitcase, while I tried to think."

"Did you have a cell phone?"

"No. Even if I'd had one, I doubt it would have worked in the UK."

"Sometimes I forget how fast technology has moved."

"It's astonishing, really."

"So what did you do?"

"I was mentally adding up the credit limits on my various credit cards, trying to work out how much I could afford to spend on a hotel room, when I heard my name. You know those announcements when they say 'so-and-so, pick up a white courtesy phone?' It was one of those announcements. And I was so dumb, that I sat there, thinking that they were paging a different Marcia Masterson."

Margaret laughed. "I can see myself doing that."

"Eventually, it crossed my mind that Rick might be looking for me and that maybe the page was for me, so I found a courtesy phone. When I told them my name, they told me that Rick was looking for me and told me where to find him. He wasn't even that far away, and he was holding a sign with my name on it. I really don't know how I missed him when I got off the plane, but I found him."

"And was it love at first sight?"

Marcia laughed. "Maybe for him. I wasn't so sure. My mother's warnings were still ringing in my ears, of course, so I took it very slowly. We got a taxi to the hotel, where we did have separate rooms. I took a quick shower and changed before we went out for lunch. Everything felt odd. The language was more or less the same, but everything felt very different. It was like falling into another reality or something. It's hard to explain."

"I understand, though. I felt the same way the first time I traveled to the island. Actually, I still feel that way a lot of the time."

Marcia nodded. "It's weird, isn't it? The UK is as much a foreign country as France or Kenya or Afghanistan, but because the language is the same, we expect it to feel like the US."

"And sometimes it does, but usually it feels very different."

"Of course, I've been here for a long time now. I can't imagine moving back to the US."

"But what happened in London that first day?"

"We had lunch and then we walked around the city. We walked past Buckingham Palace, and we took the tube other places. I was exhausted and jet-lagged, but I didn't want to stop. I only had a week, and I wanted to see everything."

"I can understand that."

"I was falling asleep on my feet when we got back to the hotel. We went to our rooms to change for dinner, and I truly did fall asleep. And I was completely out, too. When Rick knocked on the door a short while later, I didn't hear him. He knocked. He tried calling the room. I was out cold. Luckily, he'd asked for two keys for each room when he'd checked in, so he let himself in to check on me. When he realized that I was just sleeping he went out and got himself some dinner. Then he came back with sandwiches, chips, chocolates, and a cold drink for me. He left them in my room with a note, telling me to eat when I got hungry and sleep as much as I needed to sleep and that he'd be back in the morning."

"How very kind."

Marcia nodded. "He was very kind. I have no idea what time it was when I finally did wake up, but I was starving. I ate everything Rick had left and then went right back to bed. I woke up at seven the next morning feeling almost back to normal."

A police car rolled to a stop near the women. They both took a few steps away from the vehicle before Marcia continued talking.

"Rick spent the rest of the week showing me everything wonderful about London and even a bit farther afield. We ate at fancy restaurants, went for tea one afternoon, and just generally had an amazing time. By day three, we only needed one hotel room. On my last evening in London, Rick proposed."

"That was fast."

"We'd been talking for months on the telephone and over email. I know it sounds fast, but it didn't feel fast. It felt just right. I said yes and then flew home and started making plans."

"But you'd never been to the island."

"I know, but Rick promised me that we could move anywhere in the world if I didn't like the island. I agreed to give it a year before I asked to move elsewhere."

"I suppose that's fair enough."

"My mother did everything in her power to convince me not to marry Rick. When she realized that wasn't going to work, she started trying to convince me to make him move to the US instead of me moving here. The problem with that plan was that he had a great job and already owned a house. I liked my job, but it didn't pay great, and I was still living with my parents. Moving to the island just made more sense."

"What was Rick doing for work then?"

"He worked in the insurance industry. I didn't realize when we met just how successful he was. I was just happy that he had a job and a house. It wasn't until after we were married, and I actually moved to the island, that I discovered that his house was what I would consider a mansion."

Margaret grinned. "What a lovely surprise."

"It was lovely, especially since he had a housekeeper who took care of the place and him. I had no idea."

"Did you get married in the US, then?"

"Oh, yes. My mother wasn't letting me leave Iowa without a ring on my finger," Marcia said with a laugh. "She'd been planning my wedding since the day I was born. I have two older brothers, and she'd been hoping for a girl every time. Anyway, she planned just about everything, and she and my father paid for it all, so I couldn't really complain. We got married less than a year after I'd dialed that wrong number. And then I moved to the island."

"Did you fall in love with it immediately?"

"Sadly, no. I cried myself to sleep every night for the first three months. I didn't know anyone. Rick was working all day. Our poor housekeeper was wonderful, but she didn't have time to entertain me. She had to cook and clean and run errands for Rick. I was terrified of driving on the wrong side of the road. And I'd never lived away from my parents before, either. It was all overwhelming."

"I'm surprised you stayed."

"I was crazy in love with Rick. That was the only reason I stayed. In those early months, I just kept counting down the days until that year I'd promised him would be up. Then Rick persuaded me to take some driving lessons. And he bought me a car. And I started to go out and about a little bit. Even that didn't help much, though. What really helped was when I started taking classes at the college. I'd originally dropped out of college after a year when I decided that I'd rather work than have to take one more test."

Margaret laughed. "I loved college, but my sister, Megan, was a lot like you. She only stayed in school because my parents bribed her to do so. She's glad they did now, but at the time she was really tired of studying and tests and writing papers and everything."

"When I'd first arrived on the island, I'd assumed I was going to have to get a job, but once I discovered that Rick was earning enough to support us both, I realized I had a lot more options than I'd expected. He was the one who suggested that I should go back to school. And that was a smart idea."

"What did you study?"

"Business management. I only took a few classes, actually. What made it so wonderful for me was that I made a few friends. And those wonderful friends made time in their lives to show me the island and help me fall in love with its uniqueness and its history."

"It really does have a wonderfully rich history."

"It does, and the more I learned about it, the more fascinated I became. I ended up taking every history course the college offered and then taking classes through the Open University to learn more about European history generally, but that all came later. What mattered in the short term was that I realized that I wanted to stay on the island, at least for longer than that single year."

"And here you are twenty-five years later."

Marcia nodded. "Rick and I talked about moving several times, but we never did. He was ten years older than me, so we talked a lot about moving once he was ready to retire. I never found a full-time job, but I do a lot of research and teach an occasional class at the college."

"That sounds interesting."

"I have brochures in my apartment if you're interested in taking a class or two on the island's history. I teach college classes, but I also teach short courses for adults with more general interest."

"I'd love a brochure."

"I'll slip one under your door."

"You keep your paws off it," Margaret said to Katie, who was fast asleep in her arms.

"When did you move into Promenade View?" Margaret asked.

Marcia sighed. "Rick and I were still talking about his retirement in the weeks before his fifty-eighth birthday. Two days after that birthday, he had a massive heart attack and died in his office. I was devastated when they came and told me."

"I'm so sorry."

"He was the love of my life. We never had children. It wasn't a conscious choice, it simply never happened. Suddenly, I was all alone in the world."

"And a very rich widow," the man standing nearby said.

Marcia laughed loudly. "Everyone on the island knows everyone else's business," she said. "I don't know that I'd say 'very rich,' but Rick definitely left me well provided for. It only took me a few months to decide to sell the house."

"I'm sure it was a difficult decision," Margaret said.

"Yes and no. It was always far too large for us. Rick and I talked about it all the time. He'd bought it because it was the sort of property that men in his position were expected to own. He'd also always assumed that he'd have a wife and children one day to fill some of the rooms. Once we were married, we both assumed we'd have children sooner or later. Eventually, it became obvious that I wasn't going to get pregnant, but by that time I'd come to love the house. So we stayed there, even though it was ridiculous to have eight bedrooms when Rick and I always shared one. The only time we truly appreciated the space was when my parents came to visit."

Margaret laughed at the face that Marcia made. "That bad?"

"My mother struggled with the cultural differences. My father always had a deep distrust of foreigners, so being surrounded by them made him edgy. And neither of them felt comfortable having a housekeeper. My mother wanted to make her own breakfast every day and keep her own room tidy. After their first visit, we used to give the housekeeper time off while my parents were here. That was easier on everyone."

"So you sold the house and bought an apartment in Promenade View?"

"I sat down with my advocate, and we had a long talk about what I wanted to do next. In the end, buying an apartment in Douglas made the most sense. I also bought my parents' house back in Iowa. They both passed away a few years ago. The house was left to me and my brothers in equal shares. One of my brothers moved in and took care of maintenance, but then he was offered a job in the next town over. He wanted to sell the house so he could afford to buy something in his new town. My other brother lives in Alaska and has no interest in ever going back to Iowa. I couldn't bear to let the house go, though, so I bought out their shares."

"Do you go back often?"

Marcia laughed. "I went back to sign all the papers when I bought the house. It hadn't been long since Rick's sudden passing, and I was seriously considering moving back to the US. After a month in Iowa, I realized that I didn't want to live there any longer. I listed the house with a property management company, and they were able to find tenants almost immediately. When their lease is up, if they don't renew, I'll probably go back for a month or two. If they do renew, I'll postpone the trip for another year."

"So the island is home."

"It's where I feel closest to Rick, which is important to me. I tried dating a bit when I was in Iowa, but we can save those stories for another day. I haven't ruled out the possibility of meeting someone else, but finding someone isn't a priority."

"I'm single," the man next to them said.

"No, he isn't," the woman on his other side said. "We've been married for thirty years."

"She's rich," the man said in a pretend whisper to his wife.

She rolled her eyes. "She's also smart and pretty and twenty years younger than you. You don't have a chance."

The man looked at Marcia. "I don't even know her," he said, nodding toward his wife.

Marcia laughed. "If I were you, I'd hold on tight to her."

He looked at his wife and chuckled. "She's still pretty, and she's smart. Sometimes I forget how lucky I am."

"I'll have to start reminding you more often," his wife said.

"We've all heard all sorts of rumors about you," Marcia said to Margaret. "What made you decide to move to the island?"

"My sister Megan and I came to visit Aunt Fenella in December," Margaret told her. "We'd been talking about coming to see her since she moved to the island, but we were both busy with work and other things. And then my ten-year relationship ended, and I started re-evaluating my life. I decided I wanted to change everything, so I quit my job and sold my house. Megan had just started a year-long sabbatical from her job, so it was the perfect time to visit Aunt Fenella. I decided that I'd sort my life out when I got back after the visit."

"And you fell in love with the island on that visit?"

Margaret looked around and then back at Marcia. "I did, rather. I'd never been to the island before, but as soon as I arrived it felt like home in an odd way. Since I was single, unemployed, and homeless, moving here was an easy decision to make."

Marcia laughed. "You seem to have landed on your feet for an unemployed, homeless person."

"I was all of those things by choice, except maybe single. Things have worked out better than I worried they might, though. Aunt Fenella offered me the use of her apartment while she's off on her honeymoon for the next year. I have to look after Katie, but that seems a small price to pay."

"Meroow," the small cat in Margaret's arms murmured.

"She's adorable. I've been thinking about getting a cat, but I'm afraid that seems too spinsterish."

"One cat is probably okay," Margaret said with a small chuckle.

"Did I hear that you're working for a local company now?" Marcia asked.

Margaret nodded. "Park's Cleaning Supplies. I was lucky that they found that they needed a chemical engineer not long after I arrived on the island."

"So you're working for Park's, living in your aunt's apartment, taking care of her cat, and dating Ted Hart. It sounds as if your life has changed a lot in the past few months," Marcia said.

"It has changed completely, and I'm so much happier here than I was in the US."

"I'm really glad to hear that. I'm also glad to hear an American accent. I miss them sometimes."

"They're all over the telly," the man next to her said.

Marcia nodded. "But that isn't really the same. I can't talk to the telly about the things I miss about the US."

"What do you miss?" Margaret asked.

Marcia named a few food items that had Margaret nodding.

"I was shocked that I couldn't get any of those things over here," Margaret said.

"And I miss space," Marcia added. "The US is just huge. You can get in your car and drive for hours and hours and hours and still be in the same state. Or you can drive for days and cross through several different states. Houses are bigger. Cars are bigger. Cities and towns spread out in every direction. There's just a lot more space."

"Maybe you should have kept your mansion," the man said.

Marcia laughed. "Maybe I should have at that."

"Here we go," the man said, nodding toward the front of the building.

A man in a dark suit had just walked out through the glass doors. He walked across the promenade and stopped in front of the crowd.

"What's going on?" someone shouted.

"When can we go back inside?" another voice yelled.

"In case you didn't know," Marcia whispered to Margaret, "that's the Chief Fire Officer."

2

The man cleared his throat. "Thank you all for your patience," he said. "I'm happy to report that the fire is out. We need a bit more time to make certain that the building is completely safe before we allow you all to return to your flats."

"It's the middle of the night, and we're all tired," someone said. "If the fire is out, we should be allowed to go back inside."

"The last thing anyone wants is to let you all back in and then have to get you to evacuate again because the fire manages to restart," the man said. "We also have to be certain that the gas and electricity are safe for use in the rest of the building."

"Where did the fire start? How many flats were damaged? How much damage was done to the flats in question?"

Margaret looked over and swallowed a sigh. She'd thought she recognized the voice. Heather Bryant, investigative journalist for the *Isle of Man Times,* looked far too bright and perky for the current time of night.

The Chief Fire Officer looked at her and shook his head. "Someone will be making a formal statement later in the day. It might even be me, but it won't be now."

Heather shrugged. "Does anyone want to share what they know

with me? The island's residents have a right to know what's happening on the island. Who knows which flat or flats were involved? Is your flat next door to the fire? Are you standing out here, worrying that you've lost everything to fire, water, and smoke damage? Get your story told."

A few people moved over to talk to Heather. As they did so, Margaret deliberately took a few steps away. Marcia was quick to do the same.

"The fire was on my floor," she whispered to Margaret. "I know the owners of the flat where the fire started. I've been looking everywhere for them, but I haven't seen them out here. I really hope they weren't home or that they're simply staying out of sight for the moment."

Margaret opened her mouth to ask questions, but she stopped as a familiar car pulled to a stop a few feet away.

Marcia grinned. "I wondered what was taking him so long," she said.

Ted emerged from his car and headed straight for the Chief Fire Officer. He hadn't spoken again since Heather's request for information. When Ted reached him, the pair had a quick chat. When they were finished speaking, Ted turned and began to scan the crowd. When his eyes met Margaret's, he smiled and strode to her side.

"Hello," he said, pulling her close.

"I have Katie," she said quickly before he squeezed her too tightly.

Ted chuckled and then released her. "Are you both okay?"

"We're fine. Just tired."

"Yeah, I think everyone is tired. Why can't people accidentally set their houses on fire in the middle of the afternoon?"

"Is that what happened? Someone accidentally set their apartment on fire?"

"I've no idea what happened, actually. I'm not even supposed to be here. I was only notified because the dispatcher knows that you live here and that we're involved."

"It's a small island," Marcia said.

Margaret nodded. "I would have called you myself, but I didn't want to wake you."

"You should have rung. Your apartment building was on fire," Ted said.

"I wasn't even sure if it truly was a fire," Margaret replied. "We were just told to go outside. I didn't see any signs of flames or smoke."

"The fire was on the fourth floor," Ted told her in a low voice. "And that's all that I know."

"I would have told you all about standing outside in the cold in the middle of the night over lunch tomorrow," Margaret said. "Now I might just want to sleep through lunch."

A pair of uniformed police constables walked up to the Chief Fire Officer. One of them spoke to him for several minutes.

"People aren't going to be happy," Ted warned Margaret in a whisper.

"Why? What's happening?" Margaret whispered back.

Ted nodded toward the constables.

"Ladies and gentlemen, thank you for your patience," one of the constables said loudly. "The building is just about ready to be cleared for re-entry. While we wait for that to happen, my colleague and I have just a few questions for each of you. We're going to work by flat number, so please bear with us while you wait your turn."

"I have nothing to say to the police," someone in the crowd said.

"You can tell us that when it's your turn to be interviewed," the constable said flatly. "We're going to start with flat 201. Are the residents of flat 201 here?"

As an older couple waved their hands and made their way toward the constables, Ted pulled Margaret a short distance away.

"I need to help with this or those two will be questioning people until Monday. I know there are more constables on the way. Mark should be here soon, too, but things will go more quickly with more people conducting interviews."

"Off you go, then."

"Are you certain you're okay?"

"Mostly, I'm tired. The faster you can get me back in the building, the better."

Ted nodded before kissing the top of her head. "Love you," he said quickly.

"Love you, too," she said to his back as he rushed away.

He spoke to the two constables before walking away with the

couple from apartment 201. Margaret watched as he spoke to them for several minutes. More constables arrived, and Mark Hammersmith, another Douglas police inspector, was right behind them. He gave Margaret a wave as he approached the crowd.

A few minutes later, Mark had taken charge. He spread the constables out on benches along the promenade. Then he started working his way through the crowd, asking everyone for their apartment numbers and then sending them to wait in a queue behind one of the benches where the constables were working. He left Margaret for last.

"I'll take your statement myself," he said, winking at her. "Let's go and sit on that bench over there."

They walked the short distance to the nearby bench. The Chief Fire Officer was now talking to Ted, who'd finished with the couple from apartment 201. As Margaret took a seat next to Mark, the Chief Fire Officer answered his cell phone. He said a few words and then pocketed his phone. After saying something to Ted, the pair walked together back toward Promenade View.

"Tell me what you know about the fire," Mark said to Margaret as he pulled out a notebook.

She shook her head. "I know nothing at all. I was fast asleep until the fire alarm went off. I got up and threw on some clothes. Then I grabbed Katie and went out into the hallway. A bunch of us stood there, staring at each other, until a fireman came and told us that we needed to evacuate the building. He started working his way down the corridor, knocking on doors as I started down the stairs with my neighbors. When we got to the ground floor, we were sent over here to wait."

Mark nodded. "And what did you hear from the crowd? Have you already started hearing rumors or speculation?"

"Someone told me that the fire started on the fourth floor. She said she knew the owners of that particular apartment, but she didn't tell me who they were. I don't know anyone who lives on the fourth floor, though, so it wouldn't have mattered if she had told me their names."

Mark made a note. "Anything else?"

"Nothing. The woman I was talking to, Marcia Baker, told me her whole life story, but I can't imagine any of that is relevant to the fire."

"It might be, if there was something in it that gave her a motive for starting the fire."

"It was arson?"

"I didn't say that."

"You implied it."

Mark chuckled. "I did, didn't I? As of right now, no official determination has been made. As in the case of an unexpected death, where we treat the death as suspicious until told otherwise, the fire will be treated as suspicious while a thorough investigation is taking place."

"But you think it was arson."

"I suspect it might have been from what I've been told so far. I haven't even been inside the building yet, though."

Margaret nodded. "Sorry. It's just a little scary to think that someone deliberately started a fire in the building that I call home."

"Meroowww," Katie said from Margaret's lap.

"Yeah, it's Katie's home, too," Margaret added.

"We're investigating. If it was arson, you know we'll do everything in our power to find out who started the fire."

"I know."

"I'm going to run a list of names past you. Tell me if you recognize any of these names."

"Sure."

"Harry Mackey?"

Margaret shook her head.

"Tara Mackey?"

"Nope."

"Neil Mackey?"

"Also no."

"Cassie Black?"

Margaret shook her head again.

"Boris Black?"

"No, but I don't think I would name my child Boris if my last name was Black."

Mark grinned. "I'm with you on that. But I'm not fond of the name Boris."

"This is getting dangerously close to a conversation about UK politics," Margaret said with a laugh.

"We'd better stop there, then. I don't have any more names to run past you, at least not now. I know where to find you if I have more questions."

Margaret nodded. "Do you know how much longer it will be before we're allowed back inside?"

"I suspect you're going to get your answer now," Mark said, looking over her shoulder.

She turned around and spotted Ted walking toward them.

"Everyone who has been interviewed can go back inside," Ted told her and Mark. "I'm going to go from constable to constable with that information. I'm expecting a mad rush of angry people, so maybe you should just wait here for a minute or two," he said to Margaret.

She nodded. "I'll wait for you to come back."

He grinned. "Thanks."

She watched as he approached the group of people standing next to the nearest bench where a constable was conducting interviews. The people on one side of the bench were waiting for their turn to be interviewed. The people on the other side were already finished. Ted said something to the constable and then spoke to the group. He was still talking as the first people began to walk away, hurrying toward the building. It took Ted several minutes to speak to each group. In every case, the people who were still waiting to be interviewed had a few angry words to say to him.

"That was rough," he said when he walked back over to Margaret and Mark.

"I'll go and help the constables get through the last of the interviews," Mark said. "You escort Margaret and Katie back up to their flat."

"Is that an official police order?" Ted joked as he put out a hand to help Margaret to her feet.

"It is indeed," Mark said.

"Do you need to stay and help Mark?" Margaret asked as Mark walked away.

"You heard him. I've been ordered to escort you home. This is Mark's investigation. I have to follow his orders."

"In that case, let's go."

They walked back across the street together. The initial rush of people seemed to have cleared. The lobby was almost empty. A pair of firemen were talking to a member of the building's management team, but otherwise the space was deserted. Ted led Margaret to the elevator and pushed the call button.

"The fire is out, then," Margaret said as they waited.

Ted nodded. "You wouldn't have been allowed back in if it wasn't."

"It smells of smoke in here," Margaret said as they boarded the elevator car.

"I suspect much of the building will smell of smoke for a day or two. No doubt the building management team will start working on that first thing in the morning."

The sixth floor wasn't nearly as bad as the elevator had been. Margaret and Ted walked to her door.

"I'd come in for a chat, but you look exhausted," Ted said after Margaret opened the door.

"I am exhausted," she admitted as she put Katie down. Katie immediately disappeared into Fenella's room.

"We were supposed to have lunch together tomorrow, or rather, today. Why don't you ring me when you get up. If that's not until late, then we'll have dinner together instead."

"I'm too tired to process all of that. I'll call you when I'm awake."

Ted pulled her into a kiss that went a long way toward waking Margaret up.

"Love you," he said when he released her.

"Love you, too," she replied. She shut the door behind the man and then leaned against it.

"Bed is only a few steps away," she told herself. After checking that the door was locked, she went into the kitchen and poured out Katie's breakfast cat food. The tiny animal woke her every morning at exactly seven for her first meal of the day. Hopefully, she'd sleep late after all of the middle of the night excitement, but if she didn't, at least she wouldn't have to wake Margaret.

In her bedroom, Margaret stripped off the clothes she'd pulled on a few hours earlier. She wrinkled her nose as she realized that they smelled faintly of smoke. "Laundry tomorrow," she muttered as she pulled her nightgown back over her head. She crawled into bed and was asleep within seconds.

***

"I hope you and Katie are okay."

The voice made Margaret jump. She sat up in bed, feeling completely discombobulated.

"I know you needed some extra sleep, but it is nearly midday," Mona said. She was standing at the foot of the bed, looking luminous as always.

When Margaret and Megan had come to visit their aunt, Fenella hadn't said a word about Mona. It wasn't until Margaret had moved to the island that Mona suddenly became visible to her. While Mona had passed away some years earlier, Margaret quickly learned that the woman hadn't gone far. Her ghost still occupied the luxury apartment that she'd left to Fenella.

Sharing the apartment with Mona was proving interesting. She often made spectacular entrances and exits, sometimes leaving behind clouds that wouldn't disappear or piles of glitter that seemed to stick to everything. But she was also a useful source of information about the island and its residents and, for the most part, Margaret enjoyed her company.

"I can't believe I slept so long," Margaret said. "Katie probably needs water. She'll want lunch soon."

"She's still fast asleep in Fenella's bed," Mona told her. "She hasn't touched the breakfast you put out for her before you went to bed."

Margaret took a deep breath. "I'm still tired, but I need to get up and get moving."

"We'll talk when you're ready for the day." Mona snapped her fingers and disappeared in a bright flash of light.

"Maybe no entrances or exits that are too fire-like for a few days," Margaret muttered as she headed for the shower.

Half an hour later, she took her first sip of coffee and immediately felt better. Katie wandered in and started to nibble on breakfast as Margaret reached for the phone. She frowned when she got Ted's answering machine.

"It's Margaret. I just got up. I'm starving, so if you don't call me back in the next five minutes, I'm going to eat something. I know we were going to have lunch together, but I need to eat."

She put the phone down and then began to pace back and forth. After a minute, she walked out of the kitchen and into the living room. When pacing just seemed to make her stomach growl even more loudly, she decided to start a load of laundry while she waited to hear from Ted. She'd just started the machine when the phone rang.

"Eat," Ted said with a laugh. "I ended up staying at the scene until just a short while ago. I came home smelling of smoke, so I was in the shower when you rang. I'll grab some lunch here. We didn't have any definite plans for the day. Should I come over after I eat?"

"I'd love to spend what's left of the day with you, if that's what you mean."

"I don't know what I mean. I've been up since three."

"Why don't you take a nap, then?"

"I'm too hungry to sleep right now."

"So have some lunch and then take a nap. Come here when you wake up. I'll be here."

"I want to say no because I really want to see you, but I think it might be best if I sleep for an hour, at least."

"Sleep all afternoon if you need to. Set an alarm so we can have dinner together."

"I love you even more when you're understanding."

"I love you, too. Get some sleep."

Margaret put the phone down and then nearly ran into the kitchen. It took her only a minute to put together a sandwich. She took a big bite out of it before she got down a plate to put it on. As she added a handful of potato chips to the plate, she frowned.

"I never buy potato chips. Where did these come from?" she asked Katie.

Katie looked up from her bowl and shrugged.

"I never buy them, but they sound really good right now," Margaret said as she put her plate on the table. She refilled her coffee mug and then sat down and ate her lunch.

"Delicious," she said as she put her plate and mug into the dishwasher. She'd only just shut the machine when someone knocked on her door.

The building had strict security, which meant that no one who didn't live there was supposed to be able to get into the building. Guests were an exception, and Margaret had added Ted to her guest list not long after she'd arrived on the island. But he was supposed to be at home, sleeping. That suggested that her visitor was someone who also lived in the building.

Margaret crossed to the door and then opened it slowly. She smiled with relief when she recognized Elaine Coleman. Elaine was currently staying in the apartment next door to Margaret. It was owned by Elaine's niece, Shelly Blake, but Shelly had recently remarried and typically spent her time at her husband's house nearby. Elaine had grown up on the island but had moved across to the UK as a young adult. When she'd come back to the island for Shelly's wedding, she'd decided that she wanted to move back for good, but as her house in Bolsover had yet to sell, she hadn't been able to buy herself a new property. Shelly was happy to let her aunt stay in her apartment for the time being, anyway.

"Hello," Margaret said, smiling at the seventy-something woman who was leaning heavily on her walker.

"Hello," Elaine replied. "That was quite a lot of excitement last night."

"The fire? I'm not sure I'd call it excitement, exactly."

"It was exciting from where I was standing, or rather, from where I was sitting."

"Oh?"

Elaine looked up and down the corridor. "Invite me in," she suggested.

"Sorry, please come in," Margaret said. "I just woke up a short while ago, and I'm still not thinking clearly."

Elaine pushed her walker into the apartment and then took a few steps away from it. "I wouldn't want people to get the wrong idea," she said, winking at Margaret. "I simply couldn't imagine trying to walk down all of those stairs last night, not when there were other alternatives."

"Oh?"

Elaine shrugged. "I simply told the handsome young fireman that I couldn't manage the stairs. He was kind enough to escort me down to the lobby in one of the emergency lifts. Then he found me a quiet place to sit, out of the way of the confusion."

"In the building?"

"Oh, no, of course not. The entire building was evacuated. But they set up a command center in the building next door. They found me a chair in the corner, which gave me a front row seat for all of the action."

"Really? How nice," Margaret said. "Come into the kitchen. I just finished lunch. I need a cookie or two."

"Perfect," Elaine said. "I hope you have coffee or tea to go with the biscuits."

"I have both or either. Which do you prefer?"

"Coffee today. I didn't get much sleep last night. After they found me a quiet corner, I'm afraid the fireman forgot all about me. I sat there until nearly seven when someone finally noticed me and told me that I could go home."

"My goodness. You must be exhausted."

"I don't need all that much sleep anymore," Elaine said. "Besides, I nodded off once or twice when nothing interesting was happening."

Margaret walked into the kitchen with Elaine on her heels. As Elaine sat down at the table, Margaret poured two cups of coffee from the pot she'd made earlier. When she turned around, she nearly dropped them both when she noticed that Mona had joined Elaine.

"Boo," Mona said, smiling at Margaret's surprise.

Margaret put the coffee cups on the table before dumping half a box of chocolate-covered cookies onto a plate. She put that in the middle of the table and handed Elaine a smaller plate. As she sat down, Margaret grabbed a few cookies and put them on a small plate of her own.

"So what happened next door?" Margaret asked after Elaine finished her third cookie.

"I got to hear what was happening," Elaine said. "The fire started in a flat on the fourth floor. Luckily, they had smoke detectors, so the residents woke up and rang 999 even as they rushed to get out of the flat."

Margaret shuddered. "How terrifying for them."

Elaine nodded. "But they all got out safely. I learned all of that and then, a few minutes later, they brought the entire family into the command center. They came and sat near me."

"I'm sure they were badly shaken," Margaret said.

"I'm certain Elaine asked them rude questions anyway," Mona said.

Margaret nearly choked on her cookie as she struggled not to laugh.

"Are you okay?" Elaine asked.

"Sorry. That cookie went down the wrong way," Margaret explained, sipping coffee while glaring at Mona.

"I couldn't help but overhear some of their conversation," Elaine said, her face a picture of innocence.

"So what did you learn?" Margaret had to ask.

"The flat is owned by Harry and Tara Mackey. They sold their family home and bought the flat four years ago after their children both left home."

"How old are Harry and Tara?" Margaret asked.

"Mid-fifties, I believe. Their son is twenty-five and their daughter is a year or two younger."

"And they were all staying in the apartment last night?"

Elaine grinned. "Apparently, the children had left home only temporarily."

"Oh dear."

"Neil went across for university and then took a job in Manchester. He'd been there for a year before his parents decided to sell the family home. From what was said last night, I was led to believe that he recently realized that he missed the island and decided to come back."

"I suppose I can understand that."

Elaine shook her head. "There was more to it than that, though.

Neil got really upset when he was told that he was going to have to speak to the police. He said something about having talked to them enough in the past year. Tara shook her head at him. I think he came back to the island because he'd done something that got him into trouble with the law in Manchester."

"It really isn't any of our business," Margaret said.

"It is if he decided to set his parents' flat on fire so that they could collect the insurance money and use it to buy a new house."

Margaret frowned at her. "Is that what you think happened?"

"It's one possibility. When I asked Neil about the flat, he said it was too small for all four of them, and that he was sorry that he hadn't argued more with his parents about keeping the family home."

"We don't know that the fire was started deliberately."

"Oh, we do know that," Elaine said. "Or rather, I know that, because I overheard the Chief Fire Officer talking to Mark Hammersmith and the Chief Constable."

"I'm surprised they talked about something so confidential in front of you," Margaret said.

"They didn't even notice me. This was before the Mackey family came into the room. I was sitting quietly on my own in the corner, surrounded by a few plants that may have made it difficult for anyone to see me."

"How long did it take her to rearrange the pots so that she was hidden?" Mona asked.

Margaret nodded. "So it was definitely arson?"

"Everyone seemed to think so last night. It wasn't an official conclusion, but the Chief Constable said something about the evidence being compelling."

"So what else did you learn?" Margaret asked. "You said there were four people in the apartment?"

Elaine nodded. "It wasn't just Neil who'd moved back in with his parents. Their daughter, Cassie, was living with them, too. Their flat only had two bedrooms. From what was said last night, Cassie got the guest room and poor Neil was sleeping on the couch."

"Where had Cassie been, and why did she move back in with Harry and Tara?" Margaret asked.

"She'd been living with a man called Boris Black since she'd left school. About a year ago, they got married. Apparently, they were only married for about five minutes before Cassie decided that she'd made a mistake. Boris owned the house that they shared, so she didn't really have anywhere else to go."

"And was she unhappy about the living arrangements, too?" Margaret asked.

Elaine nodded. "To be fair, it didn't sound as if anyone was happy about the living arrangements. The flat was too small for four people, especially since they'd previously lived in a house with four bedrooms."

"Harry and Tara could have just put the apartment on the market and started looking for another house," Margaret said. "Setting the place on fire seems a bit extreme."

"From what was said last night, that was what Neil and Cassie wanted to happen. Harry and Tara weren't interested in buying another house, though. It was obvious that Harry thought that both of the kids should find their own places and move out. Tara seemed more inclined to indulge them, but I got the feeling that her patience was running out, too."

"Do any of them have jobs?" Mona asked.

Margaret took a sip of coffee and then remembered that Elaine couldn't hear Mona.

"Do any of them have jobs?" she asked Elaine.

"Harry is a car salesman. Apparently, he sells high-end luxury vehicles, and he earns good money. Tara hasn't worked since the children came along, but she does a lot of charity work."

"I knew I recognized the name," Mona said. "Tara does a lot of very visible charity work, chairing committees and giving press interviews. When it comes to actual work, though, it isn't really her thing."

"Interesting," Margaret murmured.

"Neil worked for a bank in Manchester," Elaine continued. "His father said something about him throwing away a bright future, so maybe he stole some money from the bank."

"I can't imagine anyone thinking they could get away with stealing from a bank," Margaret said. "But what about Cassie?"

"Cassie works for her ex-husband, Boris. He owns a restaurant in Peel. She acts as hostess and waits tables there."

"I'm surprised she still works there, even after their marriage fell apart."

"Apparently, they're still friendly. Cassie said it wasn't her fault that she and Boris both changed once they made their relationship official."

"I gather all four of them claim they were asleep when the fire started," Margaret said.

"Oh, yes, of course. Harry and Tara were in their room. Cassie was in the guest room. Neil was on the couch. Apparently, the fire started in the kitchen. They all woke up when the smoke alarms went off."

Margaret looked around her kitchen. "Do all of the apartments have the same basic layout? If their kitchen is in the same place as mine, then anyone who wanted to start a fire would have had to walk past a sleeping Neil to do so."

"Unless it was Neil who started the fire," Mona said.

"The layouts aren't all the same," Elaine said. "They might have been when the building was originally converted into flats, but some owners have made significant changes in the years since. Tara said something about their kitchen being close to the front door."

"They were lucky they could get out, then," Margaret said.

Elaine shrugged. "I believe the fire was at the far end of the room, as far from the door as it could have been. And apparently, they had a fire extinguisher in one of the bedrooms. Neil did his best to put the fire out while the others escaped."

"Do the police think that someone who was inside the apartment started the fire, or do they think someone got into the apartment and started it while the others were sleeping?" Margaret asked.

"At this point, they aren't certain," Elaine said. "And apparently, there are other possibilities, too."

"Other possibilities? Like what?"

Elaine shrugged. "Ghosts maybe, or aliens."

"Ghosts don't start fires," Mona said sharply.

"Aliens?" Margaret echoed doubtfully.

"Ted's here. Hopefully he'll bring some sense to this conversation," Mona said.

3

The knock on the door a moment later didn't surprise Margaret.

"Are you expecting someone?" Elaine asked as Margaret got to her feet.

"It's probably Ted."

"Oh, good. He can answer some of my questions."

Margaret paused in the kitchen doorway. "He can't talk about active investigations."

Elaine waved a hand. "We'll persuade him to talk."

Margaret was still shaking her head as she opened the door. Ted greeted her with a kiss.

"Elaine is here," she whispered in his ear before shutting the door.

"I'm sorry about earlier. I really wanted to spend the entire day with you," he said as they walked toward the kitchen.

"You needed sleep. I understand."

"Good afternoon," Elaine said as Margaret and Ted walked into the kitchen. "We were just talking about the fire."

Ted nodded. "I suspect everyone in the building is talking about the fire."

"Have you discovered who set the fire yet?" Elaine asked.

31

"We're working on it."

"From what I heard, it seems as if everyone staying in the flat wanted to move out," Elaine said. "One of them must have decided that selling would take too long. This way, they can take the insurance payout and buy the house they needed."

"I'm not certain that's how it works," Ted said. "The insurance company is going to pay for repairs to the flat. I don't think they will be giving the homeowners a lump sum."

Elaine shrugged. "But the family will have to stay elsewhere while the repairs are being carried out. Perhaps whoever started the fire is expecting the insurance company to rent them a house for the next few months."

"We've no idea what the arsonist was expecting, but the family is now going to have to work with the insurance company on the details."

"Does it look as if the fire was started by one of the people who lived in the apartment?" Margaret asked.

"At the moment, we're investigating multiple possibilities," Ted said with a small smile.

Margaret nodded. "We should get some dinner."

"I'm not hungry yet. Let's talk for a bit longer about the fire," Elaine said. "What does the website for the paper have to say about it?"

Margaret grabbed her phone and pulled up the website for the *Isle of Man Times*.

"The headline suggests that the police think one of the people living in the apartment started the fire," Margaret said. "But Heather also gives several other suggestions for ways that the fire might have been set."

"Such as?" Elaine asked.

"According to Heather, the fire started in the kitchen, but only a short distance into the room. She says that someone could have started it from right inside the apartment's front door, and she reckons that anyone could have broken into the apartment and done it."

"Right inside the front door?" Elaine echoed, looking at Ted.

He shrugged and then nodded. "The layout of that particular flat is completely different to this one. And if you keep scrolling, you'll find that Heather kindly included the flat's floor plan in her article."

"Where did she get the floor plan?" Margaret asked.

"It was included in the sales listing for the flat when the flat was last sold," Ted explained.

Margaret scrolled down. "The foyer looks very small," she said.

She put the phone on the table so that Elaine could take a look.

"Anyone could have stood in the foyer and thrown something into the kitchen to start a fire," Elaine said. "Or maybe someone just poured out some petrol or some other flammable agent and then dropped a match."

She and Margaret both looked at Ted.

He chuckled. "It was something along those lines, anyway. The items used to start the fire were not anything difficult to obtain."

"Heather also suggests that someone could have actually started the fire from the corridor," Margaret said as she read more of the article. "She reckons someone could have stuck a thin tube under the door and into the kitchen and then used that to make a puddle of something flammable on the kitchen floor."

"Just making a puddle of something flammable doesn't start a fire," Mona said.

"What about the match?" Elaine asked.

"Heather suggests that the arsonist could have left a small trail of flammable liquid all the way to the door and into the corridor and then simply lit that on fire," Margaret said.

"From what I heard, the fire started in the kitchen," Elaine said.

They all looked at Ted.

"We're considering all possibilities," he said.

"So the fire might have started in the hallway?" Margaret asked.

"You know I can't comment on an active investigation," Ted replied. "But in theory, if there had been a small trail of accelerant leading from the kitchen to the front door of the flat, it would be almost impossible for us to tell whether that trail ignited first and led to the larger blaze or if the fire started in the kitchen and simply burned out along that trail as it spread."

"So either the arsonist kept pouring out accelerant as he or she left the flat or the arsonist started the fire from the corridor," Elaine said.

"There are other possibilities. Perhaps the arsonist poured the accelerant out in the kitchen and started the fire, and then his or her container dripped accelerant as the person left the flat," Ted said.

"How would anyone fit a tube under the door?" Margaret asked. "There shouldn't be any gap there, should there?"

"From what I've been told, most of the flats have small gaps between the bottom of their doors and the floor," Ted said. "If the doors opened directly outside, there would be a strip of weatherproofing material along the bottom of the door. Because the flat doors all open into interior corridors, such weatherproofing is unnecessary."

Elaine frowned. "So you really don't know if the arsonist got into the flat or not."

Ted shook his head.

"Then anyone on the island could have been behind the fire," Elaine said.

"We're fairly certain it wasn't a random attack," Ted said. "The building has security at the door. No one simply wandered in and started a fire."

"What about cameras?" Margaret asked. "Aren't there cameras in the corridors?"

"There are," Ted said. "But several security cameras in the building were disabled around one o'clock this morning, about an hour before the fire was detected. The Chief Constable is going to include that fact in his press conference later today, so please don't tell anyone that little detail until after the press conference."

"When is that?" Elaine asked.

Ted glanced at his watch and chuckled. "It's happening right now. Heather will probably update the website in the next few minutes."

"So whoever did it knows enough about security cameras to find them and disable them," Margaret said.

Ted shrugged. "The corridor cameras are quite obvious if you look for them. The ones in the lifts are less so, but they still aren't completely hidden."

"I know exactly where they are," Elaine said. "I saw similar ones in a movie once, so I knew where to look. When I get on the lift, I always try to hold my hand up to cover the camera so that no one can watch me ride up and down."

Margaret laughed. "I've no idea where the cameras in the elevators or the corridor are."

"But you'd find them if you'd decided to start setting fires around the building," Elaine said.

"So if the cameras were interfered with, does that suggest that the arsonist was someone outside the family?" Margaret asked.

"Yes, although it's also possible that our arsonist left the flat to tamper with the cameras to make us think that."

"Surely the camera footage shows who was in the corridor just before it was shut down?" Margaret asked.

"I can't give you all the details, but I can tell you that we don't have any footage to review."

"So the arsonist stole the memory cards," Elaine said. "I saw that in a movie, too."

Ted laughed. "I never said that."

"Maybe we need to look for a suspect that has seen the same movies as Elaine," Margaret suggested.

Elaine named a recent highly successful film. "I think everyone on the island probably saw it," she said.

"I didn't," Margaret said.

Ted grinned. "I did. I went with some of the guys from work."

"So the arsonist could have been someone who was living in the apartment, or it could have been someone outside the apartment," Margaret said. "Who would want to set someone's apartment on fire? Do you think the arsonist was trying to kill someone?"

"We don't think so, but anything is possible. If the person behind the fire was trying to kill someone, I would have expected them to set a much larger fire, though."

"Are you saying it wasn't a large fire?" Elaine asked. "It seemed to take the firefighters a long time to put it out."

"I believe they put it out fairly quickly. That didn't mean it was safe for people to come back into the building immediately, though. Fires can smolder and then reignite. Everything has to be done according to necessary procedures."

"So if the arsonist wasn't trying to kill anyone, why did he or she start a fire? I said earlier that everyone in the family wants to move back into a house. Maybe someone else wants them out of the flat for some reason," Elaine said.

"Perhaps someone wants to buy their flat," Mona said.

Margaret stared at her for a moment. "No one would set an apartment on fire just because they wanted to buy it," she said.

Ted looked surprised. "I'd tend to agree with that."

"He can't hear me," Mona said with a small chuckle. "Do try to remember that."

"I think it was one of the children, Neil or Cassie, or maybe Cassie's ex-husband," Elaine said.

Ted frowned. "Where did you get their names from? We haven't released any information about the flat's occupants to the paper."

"I sat next door with the entire family last night for hours," Elaine told him. "I probably know more about them than you do."

"That's entirely possible. This is Mark's investigation, not mine. What can you tell me about the people who were living in the flat?"

Elaine smiled coyly. "Perhaps we could exchange information," she said. "I'll tell you everything I know about Harry, Tara, and their children and then you can tell us what happened to the security cameras before the fire."

"I can't tell you what I don't know. I was simply told that the ones that might have had helpful footage stopped being useful about an hour before the fire was reported. The person who shared that information was being deliberately vague."

"That's annoying," Elaine said.

Ted laughed. "It's information that I don't need to have. I offered to help watch the footage from the various cameras because that's a job no one enjoys. The person I spoke to told me that there was nothing to watch but didn't explain any further than that."

"Hurmph," Elaine said. "I'll still tell you everything I learned last night, but I won't be happy about it."

"I can simply read their interviews later," Ted replied.

Elaine shook her head. "Whoever interviewed them probably didn't learn as much as I did."

As she launched into a repeat of the things she'd told Margaret, Mona yawned.

"You need to go for dinner somewhere," Mona said. "Ideally somewhere nearby where you might cross paths with some of the suspects in the investigation."

Margaret started to shake her head before remembering that only she could see Mona. *I don't want to cross paths with anyone. I want to have a nice dinner with Ted,* she thought.

"You're stuck with Elaine now," Mona said. "At least if you get a chance to talk to a few suspects the evening won't be a total loss."

Margaret swallowed a sigh. Ted had taken out a notebook and was taking notes as Elaine talked about each of the four people she'd met the previous evening. When she finished, Margaret jumped up from her chair.

"I'm starving. Let's get dinner," she said.

Ted nodded. "I was hungry when I got here."

Elaine slowly got to her feet. "Where are we going?" she asked.

Margaret and Ted exchanged glances.

"The Chinese restaurant next door would be good," Mona said.

"Let's go to Laxey," Margaret suggested, wanting more than anything to get out of Douglas before Mona could start throwing arson suspects in their path.

"To the Italian restaurant there?" Elaine asked. "They have wonderful food."

"Maybe we could just drive to Laxey and then see what we find," Margaret suggested. "Maybe there's somewhere new to try."

"We could see what's across from the police station there," Ted said with a chuckle.

"Why is that funny?" Elaine asked.

"Because there has been a restaurant there for decades, but it seems to change hands almost monthly," Ted explained. "I used to go up there for meetings every other month, and they used to get us lunch from whatever restaurant was currently occupying the space. I don't think it was ever the same place twice."

"Let's just drive up and see what we find," Margaret said. "Give me a few minutes to get ready to go."

"I'm ready," Elaine said as she followed Margaret out of the kitchen.

Margaret brushed her hair and touched up her makeup before grabbing her purse and rushing back into the living room. Mona was sitting on one of the couches looking amused.

"Have a lovely time," she said.

We will, Margaret thought.

The trio walked to the elevators together. While they waited for the car to arrive, Ted pointed out the camera in the corner of the corridor.

"It is rather obvious," Margaret said, frowning. "But it's also out of reach up there."

"Not if you had a ladder," Elaine said.

"Surely a person carrying a ladder around the building at one o'clock in the morning would have been noticed," Margaret protested.

"There are easier ways to disable cameras," Ted said.

Elaine grinned. "I saw a different movie where someone smashed one with a cricket bat. I probably couldn't reach that camera with a cricket bat, but I'm fairly certain Ted could."

Ted nodded. "Not that I'm saying a cricket bat was used, but anyone of average height could easily reach that camera with one."

The elevator pinged before the doors opened. They walked inside and Elaine pushed the button for the ground floor. Then she put her hand over the mirrored surface above the row of buttons.

"Now they can't see me," she said.

Ted chuckled. "There's a second camera in the ceiling," he said.

Elaine frowned. "I can't reach the ceiling."

"You need an umbrella," Margaret said. "If you kept it up inside the elevator, it would block the camera above you."

"That's very clever," Ted said, winking at Margaret.

"Is that what the arsonist did?" Elaine asked. "It *is* very clever. He or she could have used the umbrella to hide behind when getting off, too. And I'd bet if you swing hard enough, you can take out one of those cameras with an umbrella, too."

"No comment," Ted said.

They walked out of the building. Ted was parked right outside. He helped Elaine into the passenger seat while Margaret climbed into the back. Then he got behind the steering wheel.

"Laxey?" he asked.

"What about Peel?" Elaine said. "There's a lovely little café near the castle. I found it by accident a few weeks ago when I was visiting the castle. I stopped for a cuppa and had a slice of cake with my tea. While I was there, I read through the menu and promised myself that I'd go back for dinner one day soon."

"We can go to Peel," Margaret said. *Mona won't be expecting that*, she thought, feeling satisfied.

She knew it was a small island, but she also knew that Aunt Fenella had frequently found herself involved in murder investigations and that during those investigations Fenella nearly always managed to bump into the various suspects in the case. It had taken a while for Fenella to start to suspect that Mona was somehow working to make the meetings happen, but it had seemed immediately obvious to Margaret.

She had no idea how Mona was doing it, but Margaret was convinced that Mona was capable of getting just about anyone on the island just about anywhere. Tonight though, Mona didn't know where Margaret was going to be having dinner, which meant Margaret, Ted, and Elaine should be able to eat a nice meal without seeing anyone involved in the fire.

The drive to Peel didn't take long. Elaine gave Ted directions to the café, which was a bit off the beaten path. He parked outside and then opened Margaret's door before walking around to help Elaine out of the car. When they walked into the small café, it was mostly empty. One couple was sitting in a booth in the back corner, and there were two people sitting at separate tables on the opposite side of the room.

"Sit anywhere," the waitress said as she crossed the room carrying a plate full of food.

"I don't want to walk any farther," Elaine said, taking a seat at the first table by the door.

It was a table for six.

"Maybe we should take a table for four," Margaret suggested.

"You're fine," the waitress said as she walked back toward the door at the back of the room. "We won't get much busier than this. Actually, this is pretty busy for us." She disappeared through the door.

Margaret looked at Ted, who shrugged. Elaine had already picked up a menu and was reading through it.

Ted sat down across from Elaine. Margaret took the seat next to her. As she reached for a menu, the door behind her opened. Elaine looked up and grinned.

"I forget how small the island is," she said, waving at the new arrivals.

Margaret looked up and smiled tentatively at the strangers. They appeared to be in their fifties and then didn't look terribly happy to see Elaine.

"Why don't you join us?" Elaine suggested.

The couple in the doorway exchanged glances. The female half of the couple shrugged and then the pair walked the short distance toward them.

"Join us," Elaine said again.

"We don't want to intrude," the man said.

"You aren't intruding," Elaine replied. "We were just talking about you."

They both frowned.

"Maybe it would be better if we..." the woman said.

"Margaret, this is the couple I met last night," Elaine said. "Margaret Woods, meet Harry and Tara Mackey. Harry, Tara, Margaret is my next-door neighbor. This is her boyfriend, Ted Hart."

"We've met," Harry said, nodding at Ted.

Ted smiled broadly. "You're more than welcome to join us," he said. "I'm not working tonight, just spending time with friends."

"It's just that we'd rather not talk about the fire," Tara said in a low voice. "We came all the way out to Peel to get away from everyone and everything."

"That's fine," Ted assured her. "I'm certain we can find plenty of interesting things to discuss over dinner."

Harry looked at Tara, who sighed and then pulled out the chair next to Margaret. Harry walked around and sat down opposite her.

"Ah, it's a good thing you took the big table," the waitress said as she rushed past again. "I promise I'll be right there to get your order."

"I haven't even looked at the menu yet," Harry said sharply.

The waitress had kept walking, so it didn't appear that she heard him. Tara reached across the table and patted his hand.

"Take all the time you need," she said. "We aren't in a rush."

Harry shook his head. "I want to get home before dark. You know I don't want to drive after dark."

"I can drive us home."

"I'd rather drive myself in the dark than ride with you," Harry said.

Tara shook her head. "You're a bear tonight," she said, picking up her menu.

A minute later, Harry used a finger to pull Tara's menu down. When she looked up at him, he gave her a small smile.

"I am a bear tonight," he admitted. "I'm sorry."

"You have reasons to be upset, but so do I. So does everyone in the world. We'd all do better if we tried to be kind to one another," she replied.

He flushed. "I know. I'm sorry."

She nodded. "You should have taken a nap."

"I did try. It's difficult to sleep when you're homeless."

"The hotel is lovely."

"And ridiculously expensive. We can't stay there while they rebuild our flat."

"We can stay there for a few nights, which will give us time to decide what we want to do next. We've done everything we can for today. It's time to have a nice meal and then head back to the hotel and relax."

Harry sighed. "You're being much too nice to me. I don't deserve you."

Tara laughed. "You never did. My mother told me that every day for our entire married life, right up until she passed away."

Harry stared at her for a moment and then laughed heartily. "I knew she didn't care for me, but I did think she'd grown more fond of me over the years."

"Oh, she did, but she didn't think you were good enough for me. Mind you, she'd decided when I was a baby that I was going to marry a minor royal or maybe an ambassador or something. She was quite disappointed when I fell in love with a fairly ordinary man."

Harry shrugged. "I do my best."

"And you've always been more than good enough for me," Tara told him. "I never wanted to be minor royalty or the wife of an ambassador anyway."

"Have you had enough time with the menus? Would you prefer to order drinks first? What can I do for you?" the waitress asked as she approached the table.

Margaret saw her give Harry a wary look. Clearly she'd heard his comment even if she hadn't replied.

"I'd love some coffee," Tara said. "Not decaf, either. I know it's late, but I'm exhausted. I need the caffeine."

The waitress made a note. "Anyone else?"

"I'll have decaf," Margaret said. "Otherwise I won't sleep tonight."

Elaine nodded. "Same for me. I slept until midday after our interrupted night last night. I probably won't sleep anyway, but if I drink caffeine I definitely won't."

Ted and Harry both ordered regular coffee. As the waitress walked away, Tara looked around the table.

"It's nice to meet you," she said to Margaret. "I always wanted to meet your aunt, but I never had the opportunity."

"You're the second person who lives at Promenade View to say that to me," Margaret said. "Maybe we need to have some sort of building social hour or something once in a while."

"That would be nice," Tara said. "When we had our house, we lived on a small cul-de-sac, and we knew all our neighbors. I don't really miss the house, but I do miss feeling as if we belonged to a small community. We don't really know anyone in Promenade View."

"Except now everyone in the building knows us," Harry said. "And they hate us for keeping them up all night last night."

"No one hates you," Margaret said quickly. "If the fire was set deliberately, then the arsonist has a lot to answer for, but no one could possibly blame the victims."

"A few people have been less kind," Tara said.

"A dozen angry people have rung me," Harry said. "Everyone knows where I work. The phone there has been ringing off the hook with angry people who've rung just to complain about how little sleep they got last night."

"That's terrible," Margaret said.

"They've been pretty vocal with their accusations, too," Harry said. "It's quite unpleasant to have someone accuse you of setting your own property on fire to defraud your insurance company."

"You need to ignore them," Tara said as the waitress started passing out drinks.

"Ready to order?" she asked when she was done.

Harry shrugged. "You start. I'll find something while the rest of you are ordering."

Margaret changed her mind twice as the others ordered. Everything sounded good to her overtired brain. When it was her turn, she ordered quickly before she could change her mind again. After Harry was finished, the waitress walked away.

"They aren't going to be my problem for a few days, anyway," Harry said.

After a moment's silence, Tara shook her head.

"Who aren't going to be your problem for a few days?" she asked. "I'm afraid I lost track of the conversation."

"The people who are ringing my office and accusing me of setting the flat on fire," Harry told her. "The owners got so frustrated by the situation that they told me to take a few days off."

Tara nodded. "We have a lot of things to work through. That's probably for the best."

"Do you have any idea who did start the fire?" Elaine asked.

Harry stared at her for a minute and then slowly shook his head. "I don't know, and I don't want to talk about it."

"It wasn't one of us," Tara said. "No one who was staying in the flat would have started a fire, at least not deliberately. Cassie has been known to burn toast, but it's never her fault."

"How can she be such a terrible cook?" Harry asked. "You're brilliant, and she used to help you all the time."

"She did help, but she was never really interested," Tara replied. "Neil enjoyed cooking with me. He learned a lot, too. Cassie just enjoyed spending time with me. We used to talk about everything that was happening in her life while we were kneading bread dough or making dinner. She never paid much attention to the cooking part, though."

"Why would anyone else want to set your flat on fire?" Elaine asked.

Harry frowned at her. "We've been asking ourselves that question since last night. It doesn't make any sense. No one had any reason to set our flat on fire, least of all the people who live there."

"I'd hate to think that it was a random stranger, but that seems to be the only possible answer," Tara said.

"Unless it was someone who bought a car from me and didn't think he or she got a good enough deal," Harry said with a small chuckle.

"Maybe it was someone you work with," Elaine said. "Maybe someone thought you took a sale away from them or something."

Harry shook his head. "I've worked with the same team for the past ten years. We all work together, and no one has ever accused anyone else of taking away a sale."

"Maybe one of your children has unsavory friends," Elaine said.

Harry and Tara exchanged glances.

"If you're going to keep asking rude questions, maybe we should sit elsewhere," Harry said.

That's struck a nerve, Margaret thought.

"I grew up supporting Liverpool," Ted said. "What about you?"

"Man City," Harry replied.

The two men talked about football until the waitress returned with their dinners. They all ate silently for several minutes.

"This is very good," Margaret said, breaking the silence.

"It is good," Tara agreed. "We've never been here for dinner, but we wanted to get away from Douglas tonight."

"Maybe we should try to find a flat to rent out here," Harry said. "Just until ours is habitable again."

"You'd have to drive back and forth to Douglas for work every day," Tara pointed out.

Harry sighed. "Maybe I could find a new job in Peel."

Tara laughed. "You love your job. And you're good at it. What would you do out here?"

He shrugged. "Not have to be in Douglas."

"It's all going to be fine," Tara told him. "We've been through difficult times before. It's always worked out in the end."

"Your mother was right. I don't deserve you," Harry said.

Tara just laughed again.

They all ordered Eve's Pudding for dessert. The warm apple pieces under sponge cake, served with a generous amount of custard, made for a delicious end to the meal. After the plates were cleared and the checks were paid, they all walked outside together.

"If people keep ringing and harassing you, please let me know," Ted told Harry. "We can investigate and put a stop to it."

"Thank you. As I said over dinner, I'm going to take a few days off. I'm sure people will have moved on by the time I go back."

"Let's hope so," Tara said.

"I think Harry suspects one of Neil's friends," Elaine said as Ted drove them back across the island. "He was in some sort of trouble across. He probably had all sorts of unsavory friends."

"They seemed like very nice people," Margaret said. "I feel sorry for them. I can't imagine how awful it would be to have a fire."

When they got back to Promenade View, Ted parked as close to the building as he could.

"Let me walk you home," he said to Elaine. "I want to be certain you're safely tucked up in your flat before I go home myself."

Elaine blushed and then took Ted's arm. The pair chatted together all the way to the door and then onto the elevator. Margaret let herself into her apartment as Ted walked Elaine home. He knocked on Margaret's door a few minutes later.

4

"That was very smoothly done," Margaret said after she'd let Ted into the apartment. "Elaine probably didn't even realize you were just trying to get rid of her."

Ted laughed. "I was hoping no one realized that."

"I was flattered."

He grinned and then pulled her close. "I didn't mind taking her with us to dinner, but I wasn't about to sit and chat about the fire all night," he said before he kissed her.

"I can't believe we went all the way to Peel and ended up having dinner with the victims," Margaret said when he released her. "I know it's a small island, but that's just crazy."

Ted nodded. "Daniel always said that everywhere Fenella went she was bound to bump into someone who was involved in whatever investigation he was currently conducting. It seems that luck has rubbed off on you."

"I'm not sure I'd call it luck."

"It was an interesting dinner, though. I got the same impression as Elaine. We need to do more digging into Neil's past."

"Elaine said that she thought he might have tried to steal from the bank where he was working."

Ted shook his head. "That isn't what he did, but he did find himself in some trouble with the police – enough trouble that he decided to move back to the island. I can't say any more than that."

"Did you have a nice dinner?" Mona asked.

Margaret jumped. She hadn't noticed the woman who'd appeared behind her.

"Are you okay?" Ted asked as Margaret glared at her great-aunt.

"Sorry, I heard a weird noise," Margaret said. "It was probably Katie."

The small cat looked up from where she'd been dozing by the window and frowned at Margaret. Mona chuckled.

"It's getting late, and we both had interrupted nights last night," Ted said. "I should go."

"Are you working tomorrow?"

Ted shook his head. "Mark is in charge of the investigation into the fire. I'll ring him tonight before I go to bed and tell him about our dinner conversation. Crime rates are still down a bit below average, which means I get the day off tomorrow, and I'm not even on call."

"So let's spend the day together."

"Where do you want to go?"

Margaret thought for a minute. "What about Rushen Abbey? I've only been there once, and I don't really remember much of what I saw."

"We can do that. If we're there when they open, we'll be finished in time to get lunch at the restaurant there."

"Perfect."

"And if we're very lucky, we won't see anyone connected to the fire."

"Fingers crossed," Margaret said, shooting Mona a dark look.

"And over lunch, we can talk about murder," Ted said dramatically.

"Murder?"

"I've been asked to look into another cold case," he explained. "And this one has a Manx connection, which makes it all the more fascinating."

Margaret yawned. "Tell me tomorrow. Right now, the only thing that I think I'll find fascinating is the inside of my eyelids."

Ted laughed. "I'm too tired to remember anything about the case anyway. I'm going to go and ring Mark and then get some sleep. I'll collect you around half nine tomorrow."

"Perfect."

Margaret walked with him to the door. They kissed again before she let him out. He waved as the elevator doors slid shut. Margaret waved back and then shut her door. She checked it was locked and then headed into her room.

"I don't really have to wash my face," she muttered as she headed for the bathroom.

"Yes, you do," Mona said. "It's important to take good care of your skin. I always looked years younger than my age because I took time to take care of my skin."

Margaret made a face at her as she turned on the tap.

"How did you get Harry and Tara to Peel tonight?" she asked as she waited for the water to get hot.

"I want to hear about this cold case," Mona said, ignoring the question. "Ted said there was a Manx connection."

"He did, didn't he?" Margaret replied. "I wonder what that means."

Mona frowned. "There aren't many cold cases on the island that involve murder. Murders always get solved here."

"You're going to have to wait until tomorrow to find out what he meant," Margaret said after she'd brushed her teeth. "For now, I need sleep."

"I don't miss being tired," Mona said. "If I did, I'd probably miss coffee."

Margaret crawled into bed and switched off the light. A moment later, she heard Katie running through the apartment. She felt the animal jump onto the bed a few seconds later.

"Good night, Katie," she said.

"Mewoowww," Katie replied sleepily.

"Good night, Mona," Margaret said.

"I wonder if he's looking into what happened to Joel Ward," Mona said. "Now that would be interesting."

Margaret sighed. "Good night."

"Yes, of course. Good night."

Margaret waited for the flash of light or the cloud or the confetti. Nothing happened. She sat up in bed.

"Mona?"

"Yes?"

"Are you still here?"

"Yes."

"I can't see you."

"You turned off the light."

"I'm going to sleep."

"Yes, you said that already."

"So you can leave."

Mona chuckled. "I'll be in the living room if you need me."

Margaret sat there for a minute, wondering if she should turn on the light so that she could be certain that Mona had truly left the room.

"It doesn't really matter," she muttered eventually before flopping back on the bed. As soon as she rolled over into a comfortable position, she fell fast asleep.

"Is it already seven?" she muttered when Katie began tapping on her nose the next morning.

A quick look at the clock revealed that it was indeed seven. Margaret dragged herself out of bed and into the kitchen. After getting Katie her breakfast, she started a pot of coffee brewing.

"I feel jet-lagged," she muttered as she watched the coffee maker. "I feel as if I could sleep for another three or four hours, but that would just further confuse my body clock."

Once she'd had her first cup of coffee, she headed for the shower. After a healthy breakfast, she went out and took a long walk along the promenade. She got back to the apartment just minutes before Ted was due to pick her up for their trip to Rushen Abbey. She was pacing back and forth in the living room when Ted knocked on her door.

"Good morning," she said as he pulled her close.

"It is a good morning," he said when he released her. "I slept until half eight, which was a huge indulgence. It felt wonderful, though."

"Katie woke me at seven, but I'm glad she did. After sleeping late yesterday, I need to get back into my routine."

"My life never has any proper routine. Work keeps me busy at all sorts of odd hours."

"But you love your job."

"I do, but that doesn't mean I'm not prepared to think about doing something else. But that's a conversation for another day. Let's get going."

"You said something about murder," Margaret said when they were in the car heading south.

Ted nodded. "It's an odd case. I can't imagine we've any chance of solving it, not after thirty-five years, but I was fascinated when I heard about it."

"Thirty-five years?"

"Yeah, I know. You probably hadn't even been born when Joel Ward was murdered."

Margaret frowned. *So Mona was right,* she thought.

"What happened to poor Joel?"

"Let's talk about him over lunch, assuming we can get a quiet table in a corner. For now, let's enjoy the abbey," Ted said as he pulled into Rushen Abbey's small parking lot.

They went inside and had a brief chat with the man behind the ticket desk before they began their tour. Margaret stopped to read each of the signs that told the history of the abbey before following Ted outside, where the excavated ruins of the original abbey building could be found. They wandered around the site and strolled through the gardens before having a brief conversation with one of the men who was part of the team of archeologists digging in a corner of the site.

"We're always looking for volunteers," he told them after they'd spoken for several minutes. "If you ever want to climb into a pit and scrape at soil for a few hours, let us know."

Margaret laughed. "You make it sound so tempting."

"I might be interested in having a go," Ted said. "I'm fascinated by what you're finding."

"You know where to find us," the man said.

As they walked away, Margaret looked at Ted.

"Do you really want to volunteer with the dig?"

He shrugged. "Haven't you ever wanted to be Indiana Jones, if only for a short while?"

"No?" Margaret replied questioningly. "I suppose I never really thought about it. History was never a particular interest of mine, although that might be partly because American history isn't as rich and extensive as European history."

"A proper nine-to-five job would give me time to volunteer here," Ted said thoughtfully. "But it wouldn't let me investigate Joel Ward's death."

"I can't wait to hear all about him."

"That's good, because I'm starving."

Margaret laughed. "I'm ready for lunch, too. Breakfast seems to have been a long time ago."

"I didn't bother with breakfast, which was a bad decision on my part."

"You need someone to look after you."

"Are you volunteering?"

Margaret gave him a quick kiss. "Maybe," she said with a smile.

They walked the short distance from the abbey to the nearby restaurant. There, Ted requested a table in a quiet corner. They were shown to a small nook that overlooked the abbey gardens.

"This is lovely," Margaret said as she slid into her seat.

"It's very nice," Ted agreed. "And it's a table for two, so even if Elaine does wander in, she can't join us."

Margaret laughed. "What would Elaine be doing here this afternoon?"

"You never know, but I probably should have said even if some of the suspects from the fire investigation wander in, shouldn't I?"

"It doesn't matter who wanders in. Lunch today is just us," Margaret said, taking Ted's hand.

He gave her hand a squeeze and then interlaced his fingers through hers.

She picked up the menu and then realized that she couldn't open it with only one hand. Ted gave her a slightly bemused smile.

"We can hold hands after we order," she said, pulling her hand away.

"Everything sounds good," Ted said a moment later.

"In that case, let me help," the waiter said as he began to fill the water glasses on the table. "We have a few specials today. I'll tell you about those first, and then I can help you decide what sounds best."

Margaret's mouth was watering by the time he'd finished telling them about the specials.

"Now, what questions do you have about the menu? I've actually eaten every single dish on it, so I can give you honest opinions on everything," he said.

"I want the chicken special," Margaret said.

Ted laughed. "I'll have the beef thing. It sounded wonderful when you were describing it."

"It is wonderful. You've both made excellent choices. Can I get you something else to drink beside water?"

They both ordered soft drinks. The waiter nodded and took their menus from them. "I'll have your drinks and some bread rolls out in just a minute or two," he promised before he walked away.

Ted reached over and took Margaret's hand. "Just until the bread arrives," he said with a laugh.

"Do you want to talk about Joel, then?" she asked.

He grinned at her. "Not many women want to talk about murder over lunch."

"But it's a subject that interests you."

"I don't know that murder in itself interests me. I don't read true crime novels or murder mysteries when I'm not working. What interests me is working through an investigation and finding the guilty party."

"I can understand that."

"Joel was fifty-five when he died."

"That's very young."

Ted nodded. "It feels younger every day."

"So what happened to him, and what's his island connection?"

"Joel was a wealthy man with business interests around the world. He also owned property around the world, including a home on the Isle of Man. For tax purposes, he was an island resident, and he spent at least half the year here."

"But he wasn't murdered here?"

"He was not. I was only vaguely aware of the case before one of my colleagues from my time in Liverpool mentioned it. I vaguely remembered reading articles in the local paper about the case over the years, but they were all 'why hasn't this case been solved' sort of articles. Because the murder took place in Canada, the island paper didn't have much information about the investigation. Our local reporter did what he could, of course, but he couldn't fly to Canada and report from there."

"Joel was murdered in Canada?"

Ted nodded. "And one of the guys I met in Liverpool while I was there knows the lead detective who investigated the case. Actually, that's not right. He knows the lead detective who is currently investigating the case. The original lead detective passed away more than a decade ago."

"So Joel died thirty-five years ago in Canada and now you're investigating?"

Ted shrugged. "I wouldn't say 'investigating.' Howard Reed is the detective in Canada who is currently in charge of the investigation. He was excited to make a connection with someone on the island. The murder took place in Canada, but nearly all of the suspects lived on the island."

"Do you mean that they lived on the island thirty-five years ago?"

"Yes, although most of them are still here."

Margaret frowned. "If Joel was fifty-five, then he would be ninety now if he were still alive. If the suspects are of a similar age, I hope Detective Reed isn't expecting you to interview them."

"Howard isn't certain what he wants me to do. For right now, we're simply discussing the case. He's shared a lot with me. He was hoping I might be able to tell him more about the suspects, especially what they're doing now."

"I'd be surprised if many of them are still alive."

"Some of them are, anyway. But let me start at the beginning. Everything I'm going to tell you is a matter of public record. There are a few things that the police in Canada never released, but I don't think any of them are going to help us solve the case. One or two of the small details might help confirm that we have the right killer, though."

"Oh?"

Ted nodded. "They've never released any information about the gun that was used to shoot Joel, for example. That's the sort of information that's useful to keep quiet in case someone confesses and we doubt their guilt."

"Okay, so don't tell me anything about the gun. I know nothing about guns, so it wouldn't mean anything to me anyway."

"Sorry about the wait," the waiter said as he put a basket full of golden-brown rolls on the table. The drinks were next, followed by a small bowl filled with wrapped pats of butter. "Anything else right now?" he asked as Margaret let go of Ted's hand to reach for a roll.

"We're good," Ted told him.

As he walked away, Ted took a roll and some butter. Margaret ate a bite and sighed happily.

"These are wonderful," she said as she buttered her next bite.

"Let me start at the beginning," Ted said after he'd finished one roll and taken a second from the basket. "As I said, Joel was a wealthy businessman. He'd been born in Canada. His father was English, and his mother was American. I'm not certain why they were living in Canada, but maybe they were simply visiting the country when his mother went into labor. Regardless, by virtue of his birth there, he was granted Canadian citizenship. His parents were able to give him both US and UK citizenship, which gave him many options for places to live as he got older."

"But that doesn't include the Isle of Man, does it? Or can UK citizens come and live here if they want to?"

"They can, but they need work permits if they want to work over here," Ted told her. "But Joel came to the island to establish it as the base for his business. There were tax advantages for him for doing so."

"Okay, so when did Joel move to the island?"

"When he was in his forties, not long after he'd inherited a fortune following the death of his father."

"You said he lived on the island for half the year?"

"He came and went a great deal, but he did make the island his home. When he first arrived, he brought his wife Donna with him. She was quite a bit younger, but after a few years, he divorced her and married Lynda."

Margaret held up a hand. "Tell me everything about the wives."

Ted chuckled. "I don't know much about the wives, really. Howard didn't have much in his files about them, and they both refused to speak to the press on the island."

"Was Donna his first wife? Was she American or Canadian or English or something else altogether? What happened that ended the marriage? And did she stay on the island after they split up?"

"Here we are," the waiter said. He put steaming plates in front of each of them. "What else can I get you?" he asked.

"I think we're good," Ted told him.

"Let me know if you need anything." The man walked away as Margaret picked up her fork.

"Everything looks delicious," she said as she speared a baby carrot.

Ted nodded. "It really does." After a few bites, he took a drink and then smiled at her. "It's very good."

"It is," Margaret agreed.

"Now, let's see if I can answer any of your questions. Yes, Donna was Joel's first wife. They got married on his fortieth birthday. She was twenty-five."

Margaret made a face.

"She's American, or she was when they got married. She's probably taken British citizenship now, since she's been on the island for decades."

"She's still here?"

Ted nodded. "She'll be seventy-five now. Howard has been hinting that he might put in a formal request that I reinterview everyone involved in the case. It would be interesting to meet her."

"Do you know what went wrong with the marriage?"

"I have no idea. She was thirty-five when they got divorced. Joel's new wife was only thirty when he married her less than a year later."

"That isn't that much of a gap. I was expecting you to say that he'd married another woman in her twenties."

Ted shrugged. "Lynda was thirty when they got married. She was also American. I should add that I've no idea when he met either of them. She's also still on the island; in fact, she still lives in the house that she shared with Joel."

"Oh?"

"House is the wrong word, though. It's a mansion by the sea. Donna lives in one of the outbuildings."

Margaret winced. "That's awkward."

Ted chuckled. "She was given the house on the grounds of Joel's estate as part of the divorce settlement. Prenuptial agreements weren't really a thing in those days. Donna got a large lump sum, a house, two cars, and she got to keep everything that Joel had bought for her during their years together, including some very expensive jewelry."

"Good for her."

"Where was I? I've told you about Donna and Lynda. They were both suspects, of course."

"They were? They were both in Canada with Joel?"

"They were both on that side of the Atlantic, anyway. Joel and Lynda flew to New York a few days before the murder. Joel had an apartment in the city. Donna was already there. She had her own apartment in the city that she'd purchased with some of her divorce settlement."

"But New York City isn't Canada."

Ted nodded. "Joel had his own private plane and a private pilot's license. He kept the plane at a small airfield just outside of New York City. He and Lynda flew to a small airfield in Canada the day before the murder. They had booked a week at a luxury resort there. It was off the beaten path, so arriving by plane was the easiest way to get there. Most of the guests had their own planes or were happy to hire a chartered flight."

"How the other half live," Margaret murmured.

"Exactly."

"So Joel was murdered at a luxury resort?"

Ted shook his head. "He was murdered at Collins Airfield. That's the airfield that everyone used for the resort. According to Lynda, Joel's business partner, Trent Walsh, rang Joel the night they arrived. He told Joel that there was a problem that Joel needed to handle himself, so Joel packed an overnight bag and headed back to the airfield. His body was found in the cockpit of his plane the next morning."

"What happened to him?"

"He'd been shot once in the head."

Margaret winced. "He'd left Lynda at the resort?"

"Yes, but there was no way she could prove that she didn't follow him to the airfield."

"Was it within walking distance of the resort?"

"Arguably, yes, but everyone got around the resort by golf cart. Each individual cabin came with a pair of carts, and there were extras available at the main office if people needed more. Joel drove himself to the airstrip in one of the carts from their cabin, but there was a second cart that Lynda could have used."

"And where was Donna while all of this was happening?"

"She claims she was in New York City, but she can't prove it."

"Surely someone would know if she'd flown to the airfield."

"If she'd flown, probably, but she could have driven. She had a car in the city. The drive would have taken her seven or eight hours, probably, but it could have been done."

"Surely it would have been noted if she'd crossed the border?"

"Apparently, in those days, the border was a good deal more open than it is now. Americans didn't even need to use a passport to enter Canada; they could just show a US driver's license and be admitted. No records were kept of their comings and goings, either."

"Now that you've said that, I do remember going to visit Aunt Fenella in Buffalo when Megan and I were children. We used to drive up to Niagara Falls and sometimes over to the Canadian side, and we definitely didn't have passports in those days."

Ted nodded. "So Donna is on the short list of suspects."

"There must be other suspects besides Donna and Lynda, though; otherwise, the case should have been solved years ago."

Ted started to reply but stopped as the waiter approached.

"How was everything?" he asked as he began to clear away their empty plates.

"Excellent," Margaret said.

"Very good," Ted said.

The waiter smiled. "What about pudding? We have a lovely sweets menu. I highly recommend everything on it."

"I'm not sure I have room for pudding, but I'd love to look at the menu," Margaret said, happy to have remembered to use the English word for dessert.

The man pulled two small cards out of his pocket and handed one to each of them. "I'll be back in a few minutes to see if you want anything."

Margaret read down the list and sighed. "I want everything," she said.

Ted chuckled. "I feel much the same way. Let's get two different things and share."

"That sounds great, but which two?"

They finally settled on the flourless chocolate cake and the lemon tart. When the waiter came back, he smiled brightly as he wrote down their order. "Two of my favorites. You'll love them both," he told them.

"We were talking about other suspects," Margaret said when the waiter walked away.

Ted nodded. "There were several. One was a business associate of Joel's. Victor King was also at the resort that week with a woman he'd been seeing for a few months. She provided him with an alibi but recanted when their relationship ended a few months later."

Margaret frowned. "She recanted? That seems very suspicious."

"It might be suspicious, or it might be that she was angry with the man and wanted to get him into trouble. She'd originally said that she and Victor had been together and awake, watching television together, until three or four in the morning. The autopsy suggested that Joel had been shot around one or two, so that seemed to suggest that Victor couldn't have killed him. After the relationship ended, she went to the police and told them that she'd actually fallen asleep in front of the television and that Victor could have sneaked out and murdered Joel without her realizing."

"Interesting. Did she say that Victor had asked her to lie on his behalf?"

"Not at all. She just said that she'd been crazy in love with him and didn't want to think that he could have killed anyone. Once he'd broken her heart, she decided that she needed to tell the truth."

"Or maybe she was lying the second time, because she wanted to get Victor into trouble."

"Exactly. It's complicated."

"The best part of the meal has arrived," the waiter announced as he delivered their desserts.

"Wonderful," Margaret said as she looked at the small round chocolate cake that had been dusted with cocoa powder. The lemon tart had a layer of caramelized sugar over it, like a crème brulee. Margaret reached for her fork, uncertain where she wanted to start.

"I think we should cut them both in half and separate them before we start eating," Ted said. "And I'm saying that before I eat the entire chocolate cake before you've had a chance to take a bite."

Margaret laughed and then watched as Ted sliced each dessert in half. Then he carefully moved half of the tart onto the cake plate. As he picked up half of the cake, Margaret moved the tart plate closer so he could more easily add the cake half to it.

"Which plate do you want?" he asked when he was done.

"I'll just take the one closest to me." Margaret pulled it closer and then started with the tart. "It's amazing," she said after her first bite.

"The cake is better."

"You haven't tried the tart yet."

"I know, but there isn't another pudding in the world as good as this cake."

The desserts were gone before Margaret spoke again. "You were telling me about Victor King."

Ted nodded. "He was at the resort, and he doesn't have an alibi. As I said, they were business associates who'd worked together on a number of projects over the years. He was ten years younger than Joel, and equally successful."

"Did he have a reason for wanting Joel dead?"

"That's a very good question. At the time, the police struggled to come up with a motive for the man, but it is interesting that less than a year after the murder, he and Lynda Ward got married."

"He married Joel's widow?"

"He did."

"Less than a year after the murder? Interesting."

Ted chuckled. "It is interesting, but is it criminal?"

"How was pudding?" the waiter asked.

"Wonderful," Margaret said.

"Very good. Is there anything else this afternoon?"

"Just the bill when you have time," Ted said.

He nodded. "It won't be a minute," he said as he carried away their empty dessert plates.

"What about other suspects?" Margaret asked.

"Aaron Crawford was also staying at the resort at the time. He owned another small plane that was parked at the airfield. It was reported that he and Joel had exchanged angry words when Joel arrived because of where Joel parked his plane."

"Did the two men know one another?"

"Not as far as the police could determine. Aaron was living in Boston at the time. When Lynda was questioned, she said she didn't think Joel had ever met Aaron before their altercation at the airfield."

"Did Joel end up moving his plane to accommodate Aaron?"

"No. Apparently, the manager of the airfield was called in to settle the dispute and he sided with Joel."

"What were they fighting about exactly?"

"Howard was told that the issue was that Joel had left his plane closer to Aaron's than Aaron thought was appropriate. One of Joel's wings crossed over a line by a few inches, which Aaron thought was a serious violation of airfield safety, but which the field manager decided was not a hazard. Apparently, Aaron told everyone around that he would never be coming back to Collins Airfield ever again."

"Lynda, Donna, Aaron, and Victor. Is that the entire list?"

"There are two others on Howard's short list. Trent Walsh, who was Joel's business partner, and Jeremy Olson, who was the manager of the resort."

"It was Trent who'd called to say that Joel needed to fly back to New York City, right?"

Ted nodded. "He was supposedly in the city, but, like Donna, he could have driven up to the airfield, killed Joel, and then driven back to the city again."

"What about Jeremy? What sort of motive would have caused him to murder a guest?"

"According to Lynda, Joel did nothing but complain from the time they arrived at the resort until he drove away to get back to the airfield. While it isn't much of a motive, it is possible that Jeremy was tired of listening to the man complain."

"It was a luxury resort filled with people who could afford to fly on private planes," Margaret said. "I suspect everyone there complained a great deal."

"That's probably very true."

The waiter returned with their check. Ted paid it and then they made their way back to his car.

"I wish that restaurant was closer to Douglas," Margaret said as Ted began the drive north. "I'd love to eat there more often."

"That makes two of us."

5

"How about a walk on the promenade?" Ted asked as he parked outside Promenade View.

"We could. It's a lovely day."

They'd only walked a few steps when Ted's phone rang. He glanced at the screen and frowned. As he took a few steps away from Margaret, he said "Hello?"

Margaret walked to the railing and watched the waves lapping the sand while she waited for Ted's conversation to finish. When he joined her, the look on his face told her everything she needed to know.

"I thought you weren't on call," she said.

He nodded. "I'm not, but there's been a development in a case that I was working on last month. A man was caught breaking into a house in the same neighborhood as the break-in that I was investigating. When his flat was searched, some of the stolen property from the earlier break-in was discovered in the flat. I can just leave the questioning to the detective working the case from last night, but I'd prefer to ask a few of my own questions."

"You go and do your job," Margaret said. "I'm just glad we had as much of the day together as we did."

"I shouldn't be long. Maybe we'll be able to manage dinner together."

"I'd like that."

He pulled her close and kissed her. "I love you," he said when he let her go.

"And I love you."

"Thank you for understanding."

She watched as he walked back to his car. As the car drove away, she turned around and walked for several minutes along the promenade. It was a lovely day, but the walk was less enjoyable on her own. After a short while, she decided to go home.

Mona was sitting on one of the couches in the living room when Margaret walked back into the apartment. Katie was on her lap, but she jumped down as soon as Margaret entered. She ran into the kitchen and began to shout loudly.

"I left lunch for you before I went out," Margaret told her. "It isn't my fault if you ate it early."

"Merroow," Katie said crossly.

"She ate it at exactly midday," Mona said.

"Then she shouldn't be the least bit hungry."

Mona nodded. "How was your day?"

"It was nice, right up until Ted had to go to work."

"Did Ted have anything to say about the fire?"

Margaret shook her head. "It's Mark's case to investigate, not his. How was your day?"

"I'm feeling a bit melancholy today. Our conversation last night left me thinking about poor Joel. I realized that he's been dead for thirty-five years. It feels as if no time has passed at all, but of course it has. And that reminded me that I've been gone for over two years. Time seems to move more quickly now than it did when I was alive."

"Except now you don't need to sleep."

"You would think that would make the days feel longer, but it doesn't seem to work that way." Mona waved a hand. "Never mind all of that. Did Ted have time to discuss his cold case with you? Is someone finally hoping to find the person who killed Joel Ward?"

"Yes, Ted did find time to talk about the case with me. And yes, a colleague of his in Canada is taking another look at Joel Ward's murder."

Mona smiled. "It's long overdue. It was complicated, of course, because nearly everyone involved was wealthy. Most of the suspects had high-powered attorneys on speed dial. At the time, I was told that guests had trouble getting to the resort in the days after the murder because there were so many lawyers flying in, ready to protect their wealthy clients."

"Ted and I talked very briefly about the various suspects. The short list wasn't all that long."

"No, but the police would have struggled to keep the suspects at the resort for any length of time. If I'm remembering correctly, Lynda was back on the island within a week and Donna was back before her. They couldn't stop her from going. She wasn't even in Canada when the body was found. Neither was Trent. He didn't come back to the island immediately, but he flew out to California a day or two after the murder."

Margaret walked to the desk and pulled out a notebook. "Okay, let's start at the beginning," she said. "You knew the dead man. Tell me all about him."

Mona grinned. "I knew this case would catch your interest."

As much as Margaret hated to admit it, Mona was right. There was something about Joel Ward's murder that had captured her interest. That Mona knew the dead man and probably many of the suspects was a bonus, but Margaret knew she'd have to be careful not to talk with Ted about the things that Mona told her. The other option was to tell Ted about Mona, but Margaret wasn't ready to go down that path, at least not yet.

"Tell me about Joel."

"Joel was loud and very American," Mona said as Margaret sat down next to her on the couch. "He was also a very attractive man who enjoyed female company. We had a brief flirtation. I was older, but that didn't stop him from flirting outrageously with me. Max didn't mind, of course, so I flirted back. I'm certain there was a great deal of gossip on the island about us."

"Of course there was," Margaret said with a wry smile.

Mona chuckled. "We met when Joel came to the island to look at properties. He came by himself and didn't bother to mention that he had a wife. I didn't ask, because I didn't really care. I had no intention of becoming involved with the man, whatever the gossips thought."

"So you had a brief flirtation. What then?"

"Before he left the island, he made an offer on a house. He went back to London while the sale was going through. When he returned, he brought his wife, Donna, with him."

"I want to hear all about her, too."

Mona shrugged. "She was considerably younger than Joel. She'd been a model before her marriage, and it was obvious to everyone that she'd only married him for his money. Of course, Joel knew that, too, but he didn't mind. He just enjoyed having a beautiful woman on his arm."

"Surely he didn't have to get married in order to accomplish that."

Mona shrugged. "Things were different then. People were still scandalized that Max and I had never married. Men like Joel were expected to get married, have a few children, have a few affairs, and then divorce the first wife for someone much younger as soon as the first wife got her first grey hair."

"That's awful."

"Joel didn't do things quite that way. For a start, he and Donna didn't have any children."

"But he had affairs?"

"I assume so, but I'm not certain. As I said earlier, we had a brief flirtation, but, of course, nothing came of it. Once he was living here with Donna, I never heard any rumors or stories about him, but perhaps he was a good deal more discreet when actually cheating rather than simply flirting."

"Or maybe he flirted with you because he knew you weren't really interested."

"Also a possibility. He made all sorts of outrageous suggestions when we were in public together, but he never made any attempt to see me behind Max's back. Our relationship was entirely for show, much like my relationship with Max, really."

"So he wanted everyone on the island to think that he was a player, even though it seems as if he wasn't."

Mona nodded. "I'd never really thought about it, but that might be right."

"Is it possible that he was gay?"

Mona looked shocked. She thought for a minute and then slowly shook her head. "I'm fairly certain I would have realized if he had been. It didn't take me long to realize with Max. Perhaps he simply wasn't interested in cheating on his wife."

"Tell me about Donna."

"She hated me," Mona said. "I suppose she felt she had good reason to hate me. No doubt as soon as she arrived on the island, someone told her that I'd had an affair with her husband. In her place, I'd have been furious."

"Did you try to explain?"

"When I met her, I expressed surprise and told her that Joel had never mentioned being married when I'd met him. She replied with 'Did you ask?' and I'd been forced to admit that I had not."

"But he should have told you."

"And I should have asked. I didn't tell Donna, but Joel did say several things that made me think that he was single, including talking about not being certain why he was looking at such large houses when he was going to be living alone. That isn't something you'd expect to hear from a married man."

"Maybe he was thinking of divorcing Donna before he moved to the island."

"Perhaps. They stayed married for at least a few years after they moved here, though."

"So Joel changed his mind for some reason."

"I suppose that's possible."

"So Joel and Donna moved to the island. Ted said he bought a huge mansion."

Mona nodded. "It was unnecessarily large for two people. Max and I often used to talk about it. I could never imagine why they felt they needed so much space."

"So what went wrong with the marriage?"

"I don't know anything for certain. At the time of the divorce, there were three different rumors. Any of them might have been true, or they all might have been wrong. The first was that Joel had found himself a younger woman."

"He did marry a younger woman."

"Yes, but not until nearly a year after the divorce. And he met Lynda in America. The rumor during the divorce was that Joel had met someone on the island, someone he was so desperate to be with that he was prepared to divorce Donna for her."

"If that was the case, they didn't stay together for long."

"There was a lot of speculation about who the other woman was. Many of the names put forward were for married women. Just because Joel was prepared to get a divorce for the woman doesn't mean that she was prepared to do the same."

"So he divorced Donna only to discover that the woman he loved wasn't prepared to divorce her husband for him?"

"That was one possibility. There were two different women most often named as the most likely candidates for that scenario. One was a dear friend of mine who found the entire thing embarrassing. She was quite used to people assuming she was cheating on her husband, even though she never did, but she found being linked to Joel's divorce more difficult. Even though Joel and Donna didn't have children, my friend hated that people thought she might have been a factor in ending a marriage."

"Even an unhappy marriage?"

"Remember, this was years ago in a very particular social class. Marriages weren't about happiness. Oh, it was a bonus if you could convince yourself that you were in love in the early days of the marriage, at least, but once the children had arrived, that polite fiction was usually dropped."

"So Joel didn't leave Donna for your friend. What about the other woman he was linked with?"

"I can see her having an affair with him, given the opportunity, but I can't see him leaving Donna for her. There was no way she was ever going to leave her husband for anyone else."

"Are they still together?"

"They were until he passed away about a decade ago. He was nearly twenty years older than she was. He'd been married and divorced once before, and after that first marriage ended, he only went out with younger women."

"Surprise, surprise."

"His second wife gave him three children in quick succession, which was why he'd married her in the first place. He'd had a son from his first marriage, but that son had tragically been killed in a car crash, leaving his father without an heir."

"So he married a much younger woman and had three more kids."

Mona nodded. "And once the children were a bit older, they both had relationships with other people, but neither of them would have ever considered divorce."

Margaret shook her head. "I can't imagine staying with someone if I wanted to get involved with other people."

"They were happy enough in their own way. When he passed away, he left most of his estate to the children. She took her share and moved to the Bahamas. The last I heard, she was living with a much younger man and doing nothing but sunning herself on the beach all day, every day."

"I'd get bored."

"She won't."

"What were the other possible explanations for the divorce?" Margaret asked, after taking a moment to rewind the conversation in her head.

"Ah, yes, the other two reasons were much the same reason -- children."

"Children?"

Mona nodded. "There were a few people who insisted that Joel had decided that he wanted children and that Donna refused to have them. Others thought that Donna was the one who wanted children, but Joel refused to have them. Another possibility is that one of them wanted children but the other couldn't have them, rather than simply refusing. There was endless speculation about every combination of possibilities."

"Joel and Lynda never had children, did they?"

"They did not. And Lynda never had children with her second husband, either. Donna never remarried and has remained childless."

"So if one of them wanted children, he or she ended up disappointed."

Mona nodded. "I was never happy with any of the rumors about why the marriage failed."

"Maybe Donna was the one who wanted the divorce."

Mona chuckled. "No. Donna was furious when Joel filed for divorce and only a tiny bit less angry by the time he died. I suspect even now, thirty-five years after his death, that she's still angry with him for ending their marriage."

"So what do you think happened?"

"I think Joel got tired of being married to Donna. I told you that when I met him, he never mentioned having a wife. I don't think he was happy, and I think one day he just decided that he'd had enough."

"People do that all the time."

"They do today. Forty years ago, they were less likely to do so, especially in marriages with money. Prenups were not yet commonplace, although they were starting to become more so in the US by the early eighties. Regardless, Joel and Donna didn't have one. The divorce cost him a great deal of money."

"But you still think he ended the marriage because he was tired of being married to Donna?"

Mona nodded. "There weren't any children involved. If there had been, the cost to Joel would have been considerably higher. Even so, though, I think Joel wanted to be single again and that he was willing to pay whatever it took to accomplish that. He was worth a fortune. Donna didn't get half of his net worth, but even if she had, he still would have been incredibly wealthy."

"Okay, so he divorced Donna. Ted said she was given a small house on the grounds of his estate, a few cars, and a lump sum."

Mona chuckled. "That 'small' house has six bedrooms and seven bathrooms," she said. "And its own carriage house, a three-car garage, and a tennis court."

"So, not small at all."

"Not unless you're comparing it to Joel's house, which, of course,

Donna always has. To her, having to move out of the mansion was a huge blow. She spent a fortune on her new home, redecorating and redoing bathrooms and the kitchen, but even after all of that, she was still bitterly unhappy with it."

"She should have sold it and bought something else."

"If I'm remembering correctly, she can't sell it. It's tied to the entire estate in some way. The property is hers for her lifetime, but I believe it reverts to Joel's heirs after her death."

"That doesn't seem fair."

Mona shrugged. "I'm certain she'd agree with you."

"So what happened next? Where did Joel meet Lynda?"

"In America. I believe they met in New York City, but I might be mistaken about that. No one on the island knew anything about her until Joel returned from a trip to the US with her about a year after his divorce had been finalized."

"Is it possible that they'd met while he was still married to Donna?"

"Anything is possible, but I think it's unlikely. When I met Lynda, I asked her when she'd met Joel and she laughed and said something about how he'd swept her off her feet and rushed her into marriage before she'd had time to think. She said he'd filled her head with tales of luxurious island life and that she'd been picturing something more like the Caribbean than what she actually got."

"Oh dear. Was she very disappointed?"

"She said she was happy wherever Joel was, which is what you would expect her to say, of course. She was quite a bit younger than Joel, but that was also to be expected."

"And were they happy together?"

Mona shrugged. "There were never any rumors of infidelity on either side, which suggests that they were at least reasonably happy. Of course, Joel traveled a great deal. He could have had other women in cities around the world. It would have been more difficult for Lynda to cheat. She rarely left the island, and when she did, she always went with Joel."

"So they were still happily married when they flew to New York City just before Joel's death."

"As far as anyone on the island knew, yes. They left here in the middle of August for a late summer holiday. I saw them both at a charity event a few days before their flight. They held hands all night. Lynda kept talking about how difficult it had been to talk Joel into a holiday, but how desperately they both needed one."

"How very sad."

"She told me all about the resort they were planning to visit as well," Mona said. "It was in the middle of nowhere in Canada. She said they'd have to fly in and out, which wasn't a problem for them because Joel kept a plane in the US, and he had his pilot's license."

"Ted said the resort was very exclusive."

"Yes, Joel told Max all about it. It was very costly, but the staff outnumbered the guests by two to one and they did everything they could to meet their guests' demands. They had three chefs, all of whom had earned Michelin stars during their careers. They had a spa that offered all of the newest and most luxurious treatments. They had three golf courses, a large swimming complex, a gym, and a full medical treatment facility."

"A full medical treatment facility?" Margaret echoed.

"I gather many of the guests left for home looking considerably younger or maybe thinner than they had when they arrived."

"Plastic surgery?"

Mona nodded. "That wasn't why Joel and Lynda were going, at least not on this trip, but it was an option there."

"Interesting."

"Anyway, we had a short chat about the resort and their plans and then we parted ways. Less than a week later, we heard that Joel had been murdered."

"That must have come as a huge shock to everyone on the island."

"It did. It's still shocking even after all these years."

"Ted said that Lynda and Donna were both suspects. I suppose I should say 'are' both suspects, though."

"Of course, Lynda was there, which makes her an obvious suspect. Donna was in New York City, which was some distance from the resort. I remember reading in the local paper that Donna could have driven to the resort, murdered Joel, and then driven back to the city.

According to the paper, it would have taken her eight hours or more to make the drive," Mona said.

"Ted said something similar."

"Then Donna didn't do it."

"Oh?"

"She hated driving around the island. When she and Joel were married, she had a car with a driver who took her everywhere. After the divorce, she was given two cars, but she couldn't afford to hire a driver. Having a housekeeper and a private chef were all she could manage with her budget."

"Only a housekeeper and a private chef? The poor woman," Margaret muttered.

Mona grinned. "Yes, well, it was difficult for Donna. As I said, she didn't enjoy driving. I can't imagine that she'd have driven that far, not even to kill Joel."

"Do you think she had a motive?"

"I'm not certain about that. She certainly hated him, but she'd had years to kill him. I don't know of anything that had changed in the time just before his death that would have made her decide to get rid of him then."

"What about Lynda? Can you think of a motive for her?"

"Perhaps. As I said, they seemed perfectly happy the last time I saw them. It's always possible that Joel was growing tired of her, though. Perhaps he'd already told her that he wanted a divorce. Or maybe she found out that he'd been cheating on her with someone in New York or elsewhere. There are possibilities."

"Ted had a list of other suspects."

"I'm certain Trent was on the list."

Margaret nodded. "He said that Trent Walsh was Joel's business partner."

"He was, after a fashion."

"What does that mean?"

"Trent was more of a junior partner. He was ten years younger than Joel. I believe they'd met in the US when Trent was just starting out. Of course, he started out with a few million dollars that his father gave him as seed money, but at that point, Joel was considerably more successful than Trent."

"What about when Joel died? Was he still much more successful than Trent?"

"By the time Joel died, I believe Trent was rapidly catching up to him. On paper they were partners, but I don't believe the partnership was strictly fifty-fifty. Of course, not long after Joel's death, Trent's father died and left him many millions – an inheritance that would have changed the dynamic between him and Joel, I would imagine."

"But that was after Joel's death. Did Trent have a motive for killing Joel?"

"After Joel's death, there was a lot of talk about the size of the life insurance policy that Trent had on him. Apparently, it's common in business for partners to carry large policies on one another, but it was still surprising how much Trent got when Joel died."

"And then his father died, and Trent got even more money."

Mona nodded. "I believe Trent more or less retired after Joel's death. He said something at the time about losing interest in making money following the loss of his close friend and mentor."

"Or maybe he was just so rich that he didn't have to worry about money any longer."

"After his father's death, he definitely didn't need to worry about money any longer," Mona said.

"And he lives on the island?"

"He has a house here. I'm not certain how often he stays there, though. Trent enjoys traveling, although I believe he's slowed down a bit now. He must be close to eighty."

"What about wives or children?"

"He never married. I don't believe he has ever had any children. He used to find a new girlfriend every time he traveled to the US. He'd bring her back to the island and then send her home a few months later. It was never the same woman twice."

"So if he killed Joel, it was probably for money."

Mona nodded. "He and Lynda profited the most financially from Joel's death. Victor did quite well, too."

"Ted mentioned Victor. He said they were business associates, and that Victor was at the resort with his girlfriend when Joel died."

Mona chuckled. "She was quick to give Victor an alibi after the murder. I believe she thought she could get herself a wedding ring in exchange for providing it. When Victor ended their relationship a few months later, she quickly took back the alibi."

"Which seems to have made little difference. It isn't as if Victor was then arrested."

"He won't get arrested unless the police are able to find hard evidence that he did it. The same goes for most of the suspects. Most of them are wealthy and well-connected."

Margaret sighed. "Money shouldn't be able to protect you from a murder charge."

"It won't, if the police can be completely certain of who did it."

"So did Victor have a motive? You said he did well out of Joel's death."

"He and Joel had some shared business dealings, so he also had a life insurance policy on the man. It didn't pay out nearly as much as the one that Trent had, but it wasn't a small sum, either."

"Ted didn't mention that."

"Did he tell you that Victor subsequently married Lynda, Joel's devastated widow?"

Margaret nodded. "But Victor had been at the resort with his girlfriend. Ted said there wasn't any evidence that he and Lynda were involved in any way before Joel's death."

"They might not have been involved, but that doesn't mean that Victor wasn't already interested. He certainly didn't waste any time in pursuing her once Joel was gone."

"Oh?"

"Victor sat next to Lynda at the memorial service that she had for Joel on the island. That was less than a month after Joel's death. While they didn't do anything else to suggest that they were already in a relationship, it was noticed and commented on. Within another month, they began to be seen out and about around the island together."

"So Lynda didn't waste a lot of time mourning."

"No, she did not."

"Which suggests that she and Victor might both have had a reason to want Joel gone."

Mona nodded. "I knew Lynda, Victor, Trent, and Donna. I'm not certain I can imagine any of them killing Joel."

"Ted named two other suspects."

"Did he? I don't recall anyone else."

"There was a man named Aaron Crawford who'd arrived at the resort not long after Joel and Lynda. Apparently, he and Joel fought over how Joel had parked his plane."

"It's difficult to imagine someone murdering someone else over parking."

"But it could happen. The other suspect that Ted named was Jeremy Olson. He was the manager of the resort."

Mona nodded slowly. "I remember reading something about him in the local paper at the time. There was all sorts of speculation that he was interested in Lynda or maybe that he was stealing from the guests and Joel caught him at it. If I'm remembering correctly, though, he'd been working at the resort for a number of years. He must have seemed trustworthy."

"Ted said that Lynda admitted that Joel had done nothing but complain at the resort."

"And is Ted suggesting that Jeremy murdered him to avoid having to listen to any further complaints? As I said, the man had been managing the resort for years. I'm fairly certain he'd learned to deal with complaints without resorting to murder by that time."

Margaret nodded. "He seems the least likely suspect to me, mostly because of lack of motive."

"Tell me your list in order, then."

"I don't really know enough about any of them to make a proper list, but I suppose I'd put Trent and Victor at the top. They both seem equally likely, really."

Mona nodded. "I always had Victor at the top of my list. But I knew both men. Victor was a cold, calculating businessman. Trent always seemed nicer, even though he was also very successful."

"So was Trent second on your list?"

"Yes, because of the sheer amount of money he inherited when Joel died."

"Who came next?"

Mona frowned. "One or the other of Joel's wives. I would have put Donna next with Lynda under her if Lynda hadn't remarried as quickly as she did. As it is, I consider them about equally likely."

"I agree. What about Aaron and Jeremy?"

"What do you think?" Mona countered.

"I suppose I'd put Aaron next. He was another wealthy man with his own private plane. I can just about imagine him getting so angry with Joel that he'd want to kill him."

"That leaves Jeremy for last, which seems right to me."

Margaret nodded. "Unless we discover that he had more of a motive than we originally thought."

"And now Ted is here. Remember, you didn't hear any of that from me," Mona said before she slowly faded away.

Margaret frowned. *How am I going to remember to keep quiet about what Mona has told me? Maybe I should tell Ted about her. Her information might be useful. Or he might think I've lost my mind.*

6

Margaret was still wondering what to do when Ted knocked on the door two minutes later.

He pulled her into a hug and then kissed her gently.

"I'm sorry about earlier."

"Was it worth your time, going in to question the man?"

Ted nodded. "It's a bit of a long story, but if you want to hear it, I can tell you. It's all going to be in the paper tomorrow, and it's probably already on the paper's website."

"Tell me, then. You know I'm fascinated by what you do."

Ted grinned. "It's actually a funny story, in a way. One of our fine young constables was doing a round of a neighborhood in Douglas. It isn't his usual patrol area, so he was looking around quite a bit, trying to take it all in. He happened to look into a window and spot a woman in a state of undress."

"Oh my. I'm not sure where this story is going, but I wasn't expecting it to start there."

Ted chuckled. "The constable was understandably flustered, so he quickly turned his head and got very interested in the house on the opposite side of the road. That was when he noticed that a window on the first floor was ajar."

Margaret frowned. "The first floor – so the one above the ground floor? What we would call the second floor in America?"

"Would you? I suppose I knew that. Yes, there was a partially opened window on the upper level. Because it was cloudy and looked as if it might rain, the constable thought about knocking to remind the homeowner that he or she had left a window open."

"But it's fairly warm. I'm surprised all the windows weren't open."

"That was what the constable thought next. He wondered why only that one window was open and why it was only open a small amount. So he watched the house for a minute. Then he saw someone walk past the open window. The person lifted the edge of the curtain and then dropped it again and disappeared. The constable decided that this was unusual behavior, so he walked over and knocked on the door. When no one answered, he rang the station."

"Just because no one answered his knock?"

Ted nodded. "We encourage our constables to go with their instincts. In this case, the constable felt as if something was off, so he rang the station and asked for more information about the property. That's when he discovered that the homeowners are in Spain. The constable who usually covers that neighborhood had made a note of their travel plans because, as I said earlier, there have been other break-ins there."

"So the constable on the scene knew there was a problem."

"He did. He knocked a second time and then started making plans to enter the property. When another pair of constables arrived, he walked around the house. He'd just walked around the back corner of the property when he spotted someone climbing out of one of the upper-level windows. He was sensible enough to stay where he was, using his phone's camera to capture what was happening."

"And once the person reached the ground, he arrested him?"

"Exactly. Not only had he been caught climbing out of the house, but he was carrying a bag full of jewelry and other things that he'd just stolen. He hadn't realized that it was the police at the door, or he'd have hidden himself somewhere in the house and hoped no one would find him."

"Why did he open a window at the front of the house? Surely he must have known that doing so would give him away."

"That's the funny part of the story, actually. He didn't open that window. The homeowners accidentally left that window ajar. The burglar's mistake was stopping to look out the window to see if the street was clear at the same time as our constable just happened to be looking up at the window."

"And that only happened because the constable just happened to see the neighbor changing clothes."

Ted nodded. "The burglar was absolutely furious that he'd been caught. So much so, that he started bragging about how long he'd been successfully breaking into houses on the island. We might have just cleared dozens of burglary cases out of the files."

"That's great."

"So what did you do while I was talking to our angry burglar?"

Talked to my dead great-aunt's ghost about your cold case. Margaret shook her head. *I can't tell him,* she thought. "I walked on the promenade for a short while and then came back here and did nothing much."

As she finished speaking, her stomach rumbled.

"I'm hungry, too," Ted said with a chuckle.

"We had a delicious and very substantial lunch. I shouldn't be hungry."

"Whether I should be or not, I am. Let's go and get dinner and then go to the pub."

Margaret grinned. "We can't stay out too late. I have to work in the morning."

"So do I, although I can go in a bit late, since I clocked a few hours today."

Margaret got ready to go out while Ted gave Katie her dinner. Then the pair rode the elevator to the ground floor.

"Where should we go?" Ted asked as they walked outside.

"Why don't we go to the Indian restaurant that's right next door to the pub?" Margaret suggested.

While there were many pubs on the island, Margaret knew that Ted could only have meant the Tale and Tail. It was one of her favorite places on the island, and she knew that Ted loved it as well. They had a quick meal at the Indian restaurant that was also a favorite before heading to the pub.

The Tale and Tail had originally been the private library in a large mansion on the promenade. When the original owners sold the huge home to developers, the new owners turned most of the property into a luxury hotel. The library, however, they left largely untouched. A small bar had been added to the center of the ground floor level. On the upper level, accessed by a winding staircase or a pair of elevators, a number of clusters of tables, chairs, and couches had been added. Then a dozen or more cat beds had been scattered around the place before the pub opened its doors to a number of rescued cats and kittens.

Margaret smiled broadly as she and Ted walked into the pub. She didn't know of anywhere else in the world where you could search for a good book, get a drink, and then sit and pet a kitten while you read. Not that she and Ted would be reading tonight, but if there was a lull in the conversation, she might take a minute to browse the shelves and find a book to borrow.

The bartender waved. "Your usuals?" he asked when they reached him.

"Yes, please," Margaret said.

Ted nodded.

They carried their drinks up the stairs and settled onto a couch together. A large orange and white striped cat jumped onto Margaret's lap and studied her carefully before stepping over to Ted's lap and curling up for a nap.

"I feel slighted," Margaret said with a laugh.

"He's heavy. You can have him back," Ted offered.

"He looks happy there. I don't want to disturb him."

They both sat back, and Margaret felt herself relaxing as she sipped her wine.

"Have you given any more thought to my cold case?" Ted asked as he scratched the cat's back.

"Yes, but I don't want to talk about it right now," Margaret said. "Let's talk about something pleasant."

"Tell me about your first kiss."

Margaret laughed. "I'm not certain I'd call that pleasant."

The pair shared dating and relationship stories while they sipped their drinks. Then Ted walked Margaret home.

"I'll ring you tomorrow night. If I get away early enough, I might just show up on your doorstep," Ted told her when they reached her door.

"I'd like that," she replied before she kissed him.

"Sleep well," he said some time later.

"You, too."

She let herself into her apartment and then watched him walk to the elevators. He waved as the doors slowly slid shut. There was no sign of Mona in the apartment. Katie was asleep in Fenella's room. Margaret made sure she had everything ready for work the next day before crawling into bed.

"Good night," she said to Katie, who'd jumped onto the bed as soon as Margaret was settled.

"Merrow," Katie replied.

"Mrs. Jacobson is back, so she'll be coming over to give you lunch tomorrow. I'm sure she'll spoil you, too."

"Mewwow."

"I know you missed her. I missed her, too."

Mrs. Jacobson lived with her daughter in the apartment across the hall. The daughter was allergic to animals, but Mrs. Jacobson loved them. When she'd first met Fenella, she'd offered to help out with Katie whenever Fenella needed a hand. Fenella hadn't often taken her up on the offer, but it worked well for Margaret, who worked full-time. Mrs. Jacobson was more than happy to come over and give Katie her lunch every afternoon, especially since it gave her hours of uninterrupted time with the animal.

The previous month, Mrs. Jacobson had gone away, leaving Margaret scrambling to find ways to make sure that Katie got fed on schedule. She'd tried an expensive automatic feeding machine, which had worked well for a short while, but one day Katie attacked the machine, completely destroying it. Ted tried taking over lunch responsibilities, but his job was too unpredictable. Eventually, Margaret had started driving home to feed Katie and then driving back to the office. It wasn't her favorite way to spend her lunch break, but she'd promised her aunt that she'd take good care of Katie for her. Now that Mrs. Jacobson was back, though, Margaret was looking forward to going out for lunch with her work colleagues again, at least a few times a week.

"Good night," Margaret added before she shut her eyes and drifted off to sleep.

Katie woke her right on time the next morning. Margaret gave Katie breakfast and then got ready for work.

"Be good for Mrs. Jacobson," Margaret said to Katie as she walked to the door.

Katie nodded and then began chasing some fluff across the floor.

"I should have vacuumed over the weekend," Margaret muttered as she let herself out.

The drive to work didn't take long. Margaret parked in her usual spot and walked into the building's small foyer. Joney Caine, the office manager, beamed at her.

"Good morning," Joney said.

"Good morning," Margaret replied.

Joney, who was in her sixties, had been working at Park's since Arthur Park started the company nearly forty years earlier.

"How are you today?" Joney asked.

"I'm fine, thanks. How are you?"

"I'm good. The weekend was too short, but it always is. Am I correct that your neighbor is back now? The one who helps look after Katie."

Margaret nodded. "She arrived back on the island on Friday evening. She rang me yesterday to let me know that she'd be over today to give Katie her lunch."

"In that case, do you want to get lunch somewhere today?"

"Yes, please."

Joney laughed. "When you first started, we went out for lunch nearly every day. Then we stopped going out at all. Maybe we can find a happy medium now, because eating in restaurants every day wasn't good for my budget or my diet, but I really missed it when we weren't going at all."

"Good morning," Rachel Bass said as she walked into the foyer. She was in her forties and worked as the company's business manager.

"Good morning," Joney replied. "We were just talking about going for lunch today."

"Oh, count me in," Rachel said. "I was running late, so I skipped breakfast. I'm already hungry."

"I have a granola bar in my office," Margaret offered.

Rachel shook her head. "I have a couple of boxes of cereal in my office for days when I don't have time for breakfast. I'll eat some as soon as I get in."

"Are you all recovered from the trauma of the fire?" Joney asked Margaret.

Both women and Arthur had rung to check that Margaret was okay after news of the fire had spread around the island.

"I'm fine. Aside from missing out on a few hours of sleep, it wasn't traumatic for me. Katie didn't seem bothered, either."

"We can talk about it over lunch," Rachel said. "You were there, so you probably know a lot more about what happened than Heather Bryant."

Margaret shook her head. "I don't know much of anything. The alarm woke me. I went outside. I chatted with a neighbor and then I went back inside."

"Well, we can talk about it anyway," Rachel said with a laugh. "It's the only interesting thing that's happened on the island recently."

Margaret opened her mouth to tell them about Ted's cold case and then stopped, unsure whether he'd said that she could talk about it or not.

"I'll see you around noon," she said.

"I'll let Arthur know we're going for lunch," Joney said. "He might want to come along."

Margaret nodded and then opened the door behind Joney. In her office, she put her purse in a desk drawer and then switched on her computer. A few minutes later, she headed to the production area at the back of the building. There she had a small laboratory. She waved at the production manager, Stan Mortimer, as she walked through the space.

The morning flew past as Margaret divided her time between her lab and her office. It was a few minutes past twelve when she joined Joney, Rachel, and Arthur in the lobby.

"Sorry I'm late," she said.

"No problem," Arthur told her. "We were just talking about the fire in your building. The newspaper's website had identified the owners of the flat that had the fire."

"Oh?" Margaret replied.

"It was Harry Mackey's flat," Arthur said. "I know Harry and his wife, Tara. I buy all of my cars from Harry."

"I wish I bought my cars from Harry," Joney said with a laugh. She looked at Margaret. "Harry sells very expensive luxury cars."

"Your great-aunt Mona probably bought her cars from him," Rachel said. "Except she probably didn't buy her cars. Max Martin probably bought them all for her."

"And he would have bought them from Harry," Arthur said. "Everyone on the island uses Harry when they need a new car."

"Does the newspaper article give any additional information?" Margaret asked.

"It just confirms that the fire was set deliberately," Arthur said. "Heather doesn't offer any speculation as to who might have started it."

"Because she doesn't want to upset anyone on Harry's client list," Joney said. "Every wealthy individual on the island is on that list."

"I can't imagine Harry starting a fire in his own home," Arthur said.

"I can't imagine anyone starting a fire in their own home," Joney said. "A fire can destroy everything, and what it doesn't destroy will get ruined by the water that's used to put the fire out."

Arthur nodded. "We owned a small summer home in the Lake District for a few years. It was really just a small cottage. Unfortunately, we allowed some friends to stay there for a weekend and they were incredibly careless when building a fire in the fireplace. They managed to set fire to the rug in front of the fireplace. The fire quickly spread to the furniture and then the curtains before starting up the walls. By the time the Fire Brigade put the fire out, the cottage was completely destroyed."

"How dreadful," Margaret said.

"We were fortunate that we had adequate insurance cover," Arthur said. "They rebuilt the cottage for us. We sold it a few years later, when the children were no longer interested in holidaying with their parents."

"Let's go and get lunch," Rachel suggested. "I have a meeting later."

They walked out of the building together. Joney locked the door and then they walked through the parking lot.

"Left or right?" Joney asked when they reached the sidewalk.

"Left," Rachel said. "Please. I woke up this morning craving their cottage pie. It's much nicer than the cottage pie at the other café."

"Does anyone else care?" Joney asked.

Margaret and Arthur shook their heads.

"Left it is," Joney said.

The walk to the café didn't take long. It was fairly busy, but they found a table for six in the back corner of the room.

"Is it okay if we sit here?" Joney asked a passing waiter. "There are only four of us."

He shrugged. "You can take it or you can separate into two tables for two. I think we have two available." He looked around and then shrugged as a couple grabbed one of the empty tables for two. "Or not. Go ahead and sit there."

They took seats around the table, leaving the empty seats together on the end.

"We welcome nice people to join us," Joney told the other waiter when he came to take their order.

He laughed. "We aren't usually this busy for lunch, but it is Monday. It's always our busiest day of the week."

They ordered drinks and heard about the specials before he walked away. A moment later, Margaret noticed as a couple claimed the last empty table.

"We're here because I wanted cottage pie," Rachel said as she studied the menu. "But now I want the chicken in garlic butter."

Everyone laughed.

"That does sound good," Margaret said. "I was planning to get fish and chips, but I can't stop thinking about that chicken."

"If a special sounds good, you should always get it," Joney said. "The other things will always be on the menu."

"That's true," Margaret said.

The door opened and another couple walked in. Rachel gasped. Joney looked up and raised an eyebrow.

"That's a surprise," she said.

"What's a surprise?" Arthur asked.

He looked around the room and then noticed the couple by the door. They appeared to be trying to find an empty table.

"Oh, it's Cassie," Arthur said, waving at them. "You're welcome to join us," he called across the room.

Margaret felt herself flush as everyone in the room seemed to stop what they were doing to stare at Arthur. He didn't seem to notice. The couple at the door had a quick conversation before they walked toward them.

"Hello," Arthur greeted them when they reached the table.

"Hi," the young woman said.

She appeared to be in her mid-twenties. Her hair was blonde, liberally streaked with bright pink highlights. The man with her looked about five years older. His brown hair had been cut short. They were both wearing jeans, T-shirts, and sneakers.

"We have two empty seats at our table," Arthur said. "It was more or less the only table available when we got here."

"Is it always this busy in here?" the man asked. "We came to lunch today because we were told their cook is doing great things, but we weren't expecting it to be this busy."

"Mondays are our busiest day," the waiter told him as he walked past. "If you don't mind joining your friends, I'll be back in a minute to get your order. I can bring drinks if you know what you want."

He paused just long enough for the couple to ask for soft drinks before continuing on his way to the kitchen. The pair sat down in the empty seats.

"Let me introduce everyone," Arthur said. "Cassie Mackey, er, is it still Black?"

The young woman smiled. "I didn't change it back after we ended the marriage. I'd only just finished changing it to Black everywhere. I didn't want to have to change it all back again."

Arthur nodded. "Cassie Black and Boris Black, meet Margaret Woods, my new chemical engineer."

They all nodded at one another as Arthur continued around the table, introducing the couple to Joney and Rachel in turn.

"I met Cassie many years ago when I bought my first car from her father," Arthur said. "I got to watch her grow up, and I feel fortunate that I was invited to be a guest at her wedding when she and Boris were married."

"It's nice to meet everyone," Cassie said. "We've been hearing a lot about this place, so we thought we'd give it a try."

"My restaurant isn't open on Mondays," Boris added. He looked around the room. "Maybe it should be."

Cassie laughed. "We work too hard on the weekends to be open on Mondays."

Boris shrugged. "Maybe."

"We were just talking about you," Arthur said after a short silence.

Cassie frowned. "Talking about me?"

"Not you specifically," Arthur clarified. "We were talking about the fire."

Cassie shook her head. "I don't want to talk about the fire. It was quite terrifying."

Boris took her hand. "Everyone got out safely. That's all that matters."

"Except now we're all homeless," Cassie said.

"You aren't homeless," Boris said.

Cassie sighed. "I know, and I'm hugely grateful to you for giving me a place to stay. Neil is struggling, though."

"It's very nice of your ex-husband to let you stay with him," Rachel said. "I don't think either of my ex-husbands would do the same. Having said that, I'd sleep in the street before I'd move back in with either of them."

Cassie laughed. "Boris and I get along better now than we did when we were married. I started working for him before we became romantically involved. I worked for him throughout our relationship, marriage, and divorce. And here we are now, post-divorce, still working together and still friends."

Boris nodded. "I love Cassie, and I always will. I wasn't about to let her be homeless."

"If only someone loved Neil," Cassie said with a small chuckle.

"Where is he staying, then?" Arthur asked.

"Mum and Dad moved into a hotel. Their insurance company is paying for them to stay there, at least temporarily. Neil is sleeping on the couch in the hotel room," Cassie said.

"And complaining about it constantly," Boris added.

"Boris has a spare bedroom," Cassie said. "I'm staying in the guest room, but he has another bedroom that he uses as an office. It does have a small bed in it, though, and Neil is desperate to move in there."

"And I'm certain I sound like a horrible person when I say that I'm not prepared to let him stay with me, but I'm simply not," Boris added.

"You're already being too kind letting me stay," Cassie said. "Neil can work something out himself."

"Are you all ready to order?" the waiter asked as he put drinks in front of Cassie and Boris.

"Are there specials today?" Boris asked.

The man nodded and then read through the list. When he was done, they all ordered.

"How are your parents?" Arthur asked Cassie as the waiter walked away.

"Badly shaken, which is to be expected, I suppose. We were all fast asleep when the fire started. When the alarm first went off, I think we all just assumed that something was malfunctioning or something. I know I didn't rush to get dressed and out of the flat. It wasn't until Neil started shouting that I realized there truly was a fire."

"I heard that your father isn't working at the moment," Arthur said.

Cassie nodded. "Lots of people were ringing into the office asking for him because they wanted to talk about the fire. He wasn't able to get any work done, anyway, so the owner told him to take a few days off. It's better for Mum to have him with her, anyway. She's finding it really difficult to sleep now. Dad doesn't want her driving until she's feeling better."

"That's very sensible," Joney said.

"Mum has been having a lot of nightmares about the fire," Cassie said. "When she wakes up from a nightmare, she doesn't want to go back to sleep."

"I can understand that," Rachel said.

"Maybe she'll sleep better when the police discover who started the fire," Arthur said.

Cassie shivered. "I can't get my head around the idea that someone deliberately set the flat on fire. It doesn't seem possible. Who would do such a thing?"

"Someone who dislikes your father," Boris said.

"Are there people who dislike Harry?" Arthur said. "I think he's a great guy."

Boris shrugged. "Perhaps he turned someone down for a car loan."

"That isn't part of Dad's job," Cassie said. "Dad just tries to talk people into buying cars. The business manager deals with financing."

"So maybe he talked someone into a car that the person then discovered he or she couldn't actually afford," Boris said.

"Sadly, that's possible," Cassie said. "But even if someone was angry with Dad, setting fire to his home seems awfully extreme. That fire might have killed all four people living in the flat. If it had spread unchecked, even more people would have been in danger."

"Maybe the person who started the fire was only trying to scare your father. Perhaps he or she was unaware of how quickly the fire would grow," Boris said.

Cassie shrugged. "Fire is such a dangerous thing. I can't imagine deliberately setting fire to someone's home for any reason."

Boris nodded. "The police are working on the case. I'm certain they'll find the person responsible soon."

"I hope so. The insurance company is giving Mum and Dad all sorts of grief over paying out a settlement. They want the final results of the investigation before they'll pay anything," Cassie said.

"Because they probably won't have to pay anything if it turns out that your father or mother started the fire," Rachel said. "They might even be off the hook if you or your brother started it."

Cassie frowned. "But none of us would have done any such thing. Why would we set our own home on fire?"

"Were you happy there?" Joney asked.

"Happy enough," Cassie said, looking down at the table. "The flat was really too small for all four of us, but we didn't complain, at least not much."

"Were your parents thinking of selling the flat and buying a house, then?" Joney asked.

"I don't think so," Cassie replied. "I think they were hoping that Neil and I would move out eventually. And, of course, we were both planning to move out. Housing is just very expensive on the island. I've been looking for a flat since Boris and I separated, but I can't find anything that I can actually afford."

Boris nodded. "I'm grateful I bought my restaurant and house when I did. House prices just seem to keep going up at an alarming rate."

"Except that's good for you, because you already have a house," Cassie said. "People like me will never get on the property ladder."

Margaret frowned. She'd never given much thought to buying a property on the island, but once her Aunt Fenella came home, she'd have to find somewhere to live. She couldn't keep living rent-free in Aunt Fenella's spare bedroom forever.

"Here we are," the waiter said. He delivered plates full of hot food to each of them. "Anything else right now?" he asked as he put the last plate in front of Boris.

"I think we're good," Arthur said. "It all looks wonderful."

For several minutes, everyone was focused on enjoying their lunch.

"I love this," Cassie said after a few bites. "We need to try this at your place," she told Boris.

He frowned. "Let me try a bite," he said.

"Just one little bite." Cassie cut him a piece of her chicken.

"It's very good," Boris said. "Mine is as well. You know I'd never directly steal a recipe, but I might try to create new dishes based on both of these."

A few minutes later, a man walked out of the kitchen. He looked around the room before heading straight for their table.

"Boris, what a surprise," he said, holding out a hand.

Boris took it. "Ned, stop making such good food," he said with a laugh.

Ned grinned. "I've been playing with different specials, and it seems to be working."

"No kidding. We got the last two seats in the room. I'm going to try some new things at my place, based on what I've had here today."

"Why don't you come in the kitchen? We can talk through the recipes so you have a place to start."

Boris quickly ate his last bite of lunch before getting to his feet. "Please pardon me," he said before he followed Ned into the kitchen.

"Is that normal?" Joney asked Cassie. "I would have thought that chefs would closely guard their recipes."

Cassie shrugged. "Boris is friendly with a lot of the other restaurant owners on the island. They share recipes and marketing ideas and all sorts. It's a small island. It's better if everyone gets along."

Boris was back a few minutes later. The waiter cleared the table and then, without asking, brought out a tray full of desserts.

"With Ned's compliments," he said as he put the tray in the center of the table.

"I'm not going to be polite any longer," Joney said after everyone had stared at the tray for a minute. "I want one of the slices of chocolate cake."

Everyone laughed. It only took them a moment to agree to the distribution of the desserts. Margaret was more than happy with her slice of apple pie with custard.

"It was good to see you," Arthur said to Cassie after the checks had all been paid. "Tell your parents that I'm thinking of them."

Cassie nodded. "Thanks. I'll let them know."

She and Boris left the restaurant a moment before the others followed them outside. The foursome from Park's talked about the delicious food they'd enjoyed as they walked back to the office.

7

Margaret texted Ted about her unexpected lunch companions as soon as she was back in her office. He replied quickly.

> If nothing you think was important was said, we can talk about it over dinner.

> That sounds good.

After a busy afternoon, she was happy to head for home. When she got there, she found Mrs. Jacobson napping on the couch with Katie on her lap.

"Oh, goodness," she exclaimed when Margaret shut the door behind herself. "I told Katie that we'd have a very short snuggle before I left. I must have fallen asleep. I'm terribly sorry." She looked down at the sleeping cat on her lap and shrugged.

"You've no need to be sorry," Margaret assured her. "I'm just happy that you're back and still willing to help with Katie."

"I love helping with Katie. She's very dear to me."

"I'm glad."

Margaret hesitated near the door, unsure of what to do next. She wanted to change out of her work clothes into something more comfortable, but having an unexpected guest made that awkward.

"Katie, wake up, darling. I need to go home. My daughter is going to get home from work any minute now. She'll be expecting me to have dinner ready. Clearly, I'm not going to manage that," Mrs. Jacobson said.

Katie opened one eye and then squeezed it shut again.

"Katie, treats," Margaret said, walking toward the kitchen.

That woke the small animal. She opened her eyes and then slowly lifted her head. Margaret walked into the kitchen and found a bag of Katie's favorite treats. As she opened the bag, Katie walked into the room.

Margaret dropped a few treats into Katie's food bowl before putting the bag away. Then she walked back into the living room. Mrs. Jacobson was slowly getting to her feet.

"Can I help?" Margaret asked as the woman rocked back and forth a few times.

"Oh, no. I just have to build up a bit of momentum and then I'll get there," Mrs. Jacobson replied with a smile.

She moved back and forth again before slowly beginning to rise to her feet. Once standing, she took a few deep breaths before she began to shuffle toward the door. Margaret rushed over to open it for her.

"I don't bring my walker when I come to see Katie," Mrs. Jacobson said when she reached the door. "Perhaps I should, though, especially if I'm going to sit down for a few hours. I can't believe I slept for as long as I did. I never take naps."

"You must have been very tired."

"I was, yes. Traveling is difficult for me. I still enjoy it, but I struggle to sleep in strange places, and I miss my routines. I'm ever so glad to be home."

"You know Katie and I are both happy that you're back."

Mrs. Jacobson nodded. "I wonder if I can persuade my daughter to go out for our evening meal tonight. It's rather late to start cooking now."

"Good luck. I hope you can talk her into going somewhere nice."

Margaret watched as the woman let herself into the apartment that she shared with her daughter. Mrs. Jacobson gave her a quick wave before she shut her door. Margaret turned around and nearly screamed when she spotted someone standing in the kitchen doorway.

"I floated in while you were saying goodbye to Mrs. Jacobson," Mona said.

Margaret nodded and took a few deep breaths to steady her heartrate. "Hello," she said.

"How was your day? Did you meet anyone interesting? Did you talk about the fire or the investigation into Joel's murder?"

"My day was fine. You probably already know who I met at lunch. We did talk about the fire, but not the murder investigation. I'm not sure I'm allowed to talk about that."

"You met someone at lunch? Who?"

Margaret stared at Mona, wondering if the woman's feigned ignorance was legitimate or not.

"Hello?" Mona said after a minute.

"Sorry, I'd just assumed that you'd set up my lunch meeting."

Mona shook her head. "While I will admit to doing what I can to help you when you're investigating murders or other crimes, today I thought it would be best if I minded my own business."

"Really? Interesting."

"So, who did you meet?"

Margaret frowned, still not certain she believed that her great-aunt was innocent. She briefly considered lying, just to test Mona, but she couldn't bring herself to do it.

"Boris and Cassie Black."

Mona looked surprised. "Did you have lunch at the restaurant that Boris owns?"

"No, they came to the café near our office. Apparently, his restaurant is closed on Mondays."

"Interesting. I suppose that makes some sense. He's probably busier on weekends than he would be on Mondays. I can't imagine he'd want to work seven days a week, so shutting on Mondays is probably smart."

Margaret shrugged. "He said he was reconsidering when he saw how busy it was at the café today."

"What did you think of him? And what about Cassie? Did either of them say anything about the fire?"

"Ted should be here soon. I have to tell him the whole story. I'd rather not have to tell the story twice."

Mona frowned. "I suppose if one of them had confessed, you'd have already spoken to Ted about it."

Margaret laughed. "Neither of them confessed to anything. Cassie really didn't want to talk about the fire, but it did come up."

"Of course it did. But I'm not even certain how you came to eat lunch with them."

Margaret told her about the busy restaurant while she got Katie her dinner. Then she went into her room and changed her clothes. As she walked back out of the bedroom, someone knocked.

"Hello," Margaret said after a lengthy kiss.

Ted grinned at her. "Hi," he said softly before kissing her again.

"Are you okay?" she asked when he released her.

"I didn't have a good day. Those kisses made it a lot better, though."

"I hope nothing is seriously wrong."

"Not really. There is a bit of a reshuffle going on at the station. People are being moved around and reassigned, and no one is happy about it."

"No one?"

Ted chuckled. "Okay, the people who are behind it all are happy, but they sit behind desks and look at numbers and maps and then decide to make changes. They've no idea what it's really like out on the streets."

"Oh dear. I am sorry."

He shrugged. "It happens. Let's talk about other things. Tell me about lunch today."

They sat together on one of the couches. It didn't take long for Margaret to tell Ted about her lunch with Cassie and Boris. When she was done, he sighed.

"I know it was too much to hope that one of them confessed, but it would have been nice."

"I would have called you instead of texting if that had happened."

Ted laughed. "Of course you would have. And then one of them would be behind bars, and the case would be solved."

"Maybe Mark is about to solve it any second now."

"Maybe. I didn't see him today, so maybe he was out chasing down a solid lead. We could check the newspaper's website, but the news probably hasn't broken yet."

"We could get dinner," Margaret suggested.

"We should have had that conversation over dinner. It isn't as if anything in that conversation was confidential."

But then Mona wouldn't have been able to listen in, Margaret thought as she got to her feet. "I'll put on some lipstick and my shoes," she said.

A few minutes later, they walked outside.

"Where do you want to go?" Ted asked.

Margaret shrugged. "We keep talking about trying that new place that just opened on the quayside. If you feel like a short walk, we could go there."

"That sounds perfect. I could do with a walk. You're hungry, though."

"I'm not so hungry that I can't wait while we walk to the quay. I wouldn't have suggested that restaurant otherwise."

They walked along the promenade and then turned and strolled up North Quay. Margaret had first noticed the new restaurant a few weeks earlier, and they'd been talking about trying it ever since. The sign outside said, "Good Food, Good Friends, Good Times."

"Is that the name of the place?" Margaret asked as they approached.

Ted shrugged. "I don't see any other signs, but it seems an odd name."

There was one other sign on the door. A very tiny one that said "Open." Ted held the door for Margaret. She walked into the building and then frowned. They'd walked right into the dining room, which was dark and smelled faintly musty. Dozens of tables had been crammed into the space, making the small room feel crowded.

"Two?" the man at the back of the room shouted.

Margaret and Ted exchanged glances. There was no one else in the room.

"Yes, please," Margaret said after a moment.

The man waved them toward a table at the back of the room. Ted sat facing the door with his back to the wall. Margaret sat down opposite him.

"If the menu doesn't appeal, we can go somewhere else," Ted said in a low voice.

"If we can read the menu," Margaret replied, looking up at the low wattage bulbs overhead.

"Good evening. Welcome," the man who'd seated them said a moment later. He sat down in a chair between Margaret and Ted. "We're really glad you're here," he said.

"Thanks," Margaret replied after an awkward pause.

"We've only been open for a few weeks, and we have something of a different concept here. Have you heard anything about our restaurant?" the man asked.

Both Margaret and Ted shook their heads.

The man grinned. "Word will get out eventually. We're counting on word of mouth to build the business. May I ask how you heard about us?"

"I just noticed the sign when I was in the area," Margaret said.

"Ah, very good. So the sign is working. Excellent."

Ted reached over and took Margaret's hand. "We don't have menus," he said politely.

The man nodded. "Sorry, I'm going about this all wrong. Let's start over. I'm Jack."

"Hi," Margaret said. "I'm Margaret."

"And I'm Ted. We're both quite hungry."

"Excellent. You've come to the right place. I'm so glad you're here."

"If we could just see menus," Ted said after another short silence.

"We don't have menus," Jack told him. "We prefer to prepare food for our guests based on what they truly want to eat."

"I thought that was the point of menus," Margaret said. "You give us a list of options, and we pick what we want to eat."

"Ah, but imagine there were no limits to your options," Jack replied. "You can have anything that you can imagine."

"Anything?" Ted asked.

Jack shrugged. "Obviously, we don't have absolutely every ingredient for every recipe in the entire world, but we do have a very gifted chef who will do his best to create a masterpiece based on your desires."

"I think I'd rather have a menu," Margaret said.

Jack chuckled. "That's just because the entire concept has blown your mind. Once you've tried our concept, though, you'll want to keep coming back again and again. We're certain of that."

Margaret looked at Ted. "What do you think?"

He shrugged. "I'm intrigued, but also confused."

Jack nodded. "We get that a lot. Let's talk about some of your favorite foods. I can help you find what you're craving."

"What about spaghetti and meatballs?" Margaret asked.

Jack frowned. "Let's not rush things. Let's start by talking about your favorite childhood meals."

Margaret looked toward the door, hoping that some additional customers would come in. Surely, if there were multiple tables full of guests, Jack wouldn't be able to stay and talk to them all evening.

"Shepherd's pie," Ted said.

"Ah, yes, didn't everyone love shepherd's pie when they were children?" Jack asked.

"I didn't," Margaret said. "I grew up in America. I never had shepherd's pie until I moved to the island."

"What a shame," Jack said. "What did you enjoy when you were a child, then?"

"My mother made delicious chicken casseroles with dumplings. I also loved my grandmother's spaghetti. She made the best sauce. I have her recipe, but it doesn't taste the same when I make it."

Jack nodded. "That's often the case with food from our childhoods. If you were home alone with every possible ingredient, what would you cook for yourself?"

Ted grinned. "A ready meal from M & S. I don't like to cook."

Margaret knew that ready meals were freshly prepared food items that were sold in packaging that was oven or microwave ready. She'd tried several from Marks and Spencer and had found them all delicious. In the US, such meals were usually fully cooked and then frozen.

Ready meals usually consisted of raw ingredients and were chilled, but not frozen.

"Okay," Jack said. "What if you had a cook to prepare whatever you wanted for you? What would you have?"

"That would really depend on my mood," Ted said. "Tonight I'm hungry for something like beef stew or steak and kidney pie."

"This isn't working," Jack said. "I want you to unleash your imaginations."

Before Margaret or Ted could reply, the door opened and a group of four men walked into the room. Jack jumped up.

"Think about your favorite flavors," he said. "I'll be right back to talk about them."

He rushed over to the group and showed them to a table on the other side of the room. After a short conversation, Jack nodded and walked away, disappearing through the door at the back of the room.

"Now's our chance," Margaret said, nodding toward the door. She was only half kidding.

Ted chuckled. "We can leave if you really want to, but I'd rather stay."

"Really? Because you want to discuss your favorite flavors with Jack?"

"No, because Neil Mackey is one of the men who just walked in, and I want to see if I can find out more about his companions."

Margaret frowned. Turning her head, she took a quick look at the group in the opposite corner. "I'm not sure how you'll find out more about them," she said.

"He's taking ages with the drinks," one of the men said loudly.

"He's always slow," another said. "But the food is okay."

"And it's cheap," a third said.

"Or maybe we'll hear every word of their conversation," Margaret whispered.

Ted nodded. "The one who hasn't spoken yet is Neil."

Margaret pushed her chair back and sideways so that she had a better view of the other table. Neil was sitting facing the back wall, so she could only see his profile.

"I need a menu to hide behind," she muttered.

"I need a menu to order from," Ted replied.

Margaret laughed. "That too."

When Jack walked back into the room, he was carrying a small tray full of glasses. He delivered drinks to the other table before walking back over to rejoin Margaret and Ted.

"Favorite flavors," he said as he sat down again. "What flavors make you happy?"

"Chocolate," Margaret said. "And fresh fruit."

Jack frowned. "We'll get to pudding later."

"I'd like beef stew, steak and kidney pie, or something similar," Ted said. "Anything at all similar would do. A steak, maybe. Or maybe some roast beef."

Jack sighed. "I'll ask the chef to prepare you something with beef," he said. "What about you?" he asked Margaret.

"Spaghetti?" she asked.

"I can ask the chef for something Italian."

"Sure, that will do."

Jack nodded. "I appreciate your willingness to try our concept. I'll go and talk to the chef now."

"What about drinks?" Ted asked.

"I'll bring you something appropriate."

"What does that mean?" Margaret asked as the man disappeared into the back again.

Ted shrugged. "I've no idea. You know, besides being incredibly annoying, not having a menu also means that Jack can charge us whatever he wants at the end of the meal."

"We should ask him for prices when he comes back with our drinks."

"Yeah, I think we should."

When Jack walked back out a moment later, he headed straight for the other table.

"Ready to order?" he asked them.

Margaret and Ted listened as the four men all ordered cottage pie.

"I'll have those out in a minute," Jack told them.

As he turned to walk away, Ted waved.

"Give me a minute," Jack said, holding up a finger.

Margaret sighed as Jack walked into the back again.

"We could just leave," Ted said.

"So have you recovered from your ordeal?" one of the men across the room said.

Margaret looked over and saw that Neil was blushing.

"It wasn't an ordeal, exactly, but it was pretty awful," Neil said.

"I read in the paper that you were a hero, bravely using a fire extinguisher to hold back the blaze while the rest of your family escaped," one of the other men said, his tone mocking.

"I did what I could," Neil said.

"If you'd been where you were supposed to be, you wouldn't have been able to fight the fire," the oldest of the men said quietly.

Neil stiffened. "I was where I was supposed to be – at home in bed. I told you that I'm not interested in working for you."

The man slowly shook his head. "I'm not offering you a job. I needed a small favor. Friends help each other, don't they?"

"Yes, sometimes," Neil said. "But helping you has already destroyed my life. I'm not interested in helping you again."

"You just have to be smart enough not to get caught," one of the other men said.

"It's a bit late for that," Neil told him.

The oldest man sighed. "I asked you to join us today for a reason. We're friends, and I know you're in a tough spot. I want to help you. That's what friends do."

"I'm fine," Neil said.

The door at the back swung open and Jack emerged. He was carrying two plates of food. He put one in front of the oldest man and the second in front of the man on his left. Then he went back into the kitchen. When he emerged a moment later, he had the last two plates for Neil's table.

"Anything else right now?" he asked the four men.

"No," the oldest man said flatly.

Jack nodded and then rushed back through the door before Ted could catch his eye. Across the room, the four men started to eat.

"It's good," one of them said, sounding surprised.

"It's better than what I had last time," another said.

"I understand you're staying with your parents," the oldest man said.

Neil shrugged and then nodded. "Their insurance company is paying for a hotel for them. I'm sleeping on a fold-out couch."

"How nice," one of the men said with a snort of laughter.

"It's fine," Neil said. "I don't have a lot of options."

"Which is why we're here." The oldest man put down his fork. "Come and stay at my place," he invited Neil. "I have a spare bedroom."

"And what will that cost me?" Neil asked.

The man shook his head as he reached for his glass. "I'm offering as a friend. I don't want your money."

"That's good, because you know I don't have any money."

"I can help with that, too."

"I'm not interested in working for you again."

"So just come and stay with me. If you can't pay, then maybe you can do a few favors for me now and again. If those go well, maybe you'd be interested in doing more."

Neil sighed. "You've already ruined my life."

"That was never my intention."

"I'm not interested in working for you or in doing you any favors. I'm trying to get my life back on track."

The oldest man nodded. "Good for you. I wish you luck."

Neil took a bite and chewed slowly. "Is that it?" he asked after he'd washed the food down with a sip of his drink. "You aren't going to try to change my mind or anything?"

The man laughed. "I felt sorry for you after what happened across. When you came back to the island, I offered to help. You refused. When I heard about the fire, I became worried about you again, so I invited you to dinner. I wanted to make another offer because I still feel bad about what happened before. But let's be clear on this. I don't need you. I was simply trying to help a friend."

Neil nodded. "Thanks," he said awkwardly.

"Besides, we all know you'll be back eventually," one of the other men said.

"I won't," Neil told him.

"You might not have a choice," someone else said. "You're already unemployed and basically homeless. If things get any worse, you'll come crawling back."

Neil shook his head. "I won't. I'm going to find a way to make things work. It just might take some time."

"If something unexpected happens, you know where to find us," the oldest man said.

Neil looked as if he wanted to reply, but after a minute, he took another bite of his pie instead. As the group fell silent, Margaret looked at Ted.

"Where is our food?" she asked.

He shrugged. "Maybe we aren't going to get any food. We still don't have drinks, either."

When the door at the back of the room opened a minute later, Margaret was happy to see that Jack was carrying plates of food again. He walked over to their table, a bright smile on his face.

"Penne pasta in a spicy tomato sauce," he said, putting a plate in front of Margaret. "And steak and kidney pie," he said, putting Ted's plate down. "I'll just get you some drinks."

As he walked away, Margaret stared at her plate. "This isn't exactly what I ordered."

"I think I mentioned steak and kidney pie on my list of things I'd eat," Ted said. "It wasn't at the top of the list, but it's close enough. I'm hungry enough to eat just about anything."

Margaret nodded. "I just hope this isn't too spicy. Jack never mentioned spice when he asked me what I wanted." She picked up her fork and took a tentative bite.

Jack came back a minute later with soft drinks for them. "How is everything?" he asked.

"It's good," Margaret said. "Even if it isn't exactly what I wanted."

Jack's smile faded. "It isn't? I was really hoping I'd selected wisely for you. I can get you something else?"

Margaret shook her head. "This is fine. It's tasty. I just don't usually like this much spice."

"I am sorry." Jack turned to Ted. "How is yours?"

"Fine," Ted said.

Jack waited a moment before shrugging. "If you need anything else, let me know."

He walked over to the other table and began to clear away their empty dishes.

"Pudding for anyone?" he asked.

Neil shook his head. "I really need to go," he said, getting to his feet. "I have a few appointments tomorrow."

"What sort of appointments?" one of the men asked.

"Job interviews."

"Good luck," the oldest man said. He sounded sincere.

"Thanks," Neil said. "How much do I owe you for dinner?"

"It's on me," the man said waving a hand. "It's the least I can do after all of the misfortune that's come your way recently."

Neil hesitated and then slowly turned and took a step away. "Thanks for dinner," he said over his shoulder.

The rest of the table was silent as Neil walked out of the restaurant.

"He wanted to accuse you of starting the fire," one of the men said as the door shut behind Neil.

"Yes, he doesn't understand how I work at all," the man replied. "I hope he finds some direction for his life now."

He handed Jack his credit card. It took a moment for Jack to run it through the register on the back wall. After the man signed the receipt, the three men got up together. They'd only taken a few steps when the oldest man stopped. He turned and walked over to the table where Margaret and Ted were sitting.

"Inspector Hart, good evening," he said. "I should have said something when we first arrived. I apologize for my rudeness."

"Good evening," Ted said. "No apology necessary. I didn't come over to say hello either."

The man nodded. "But you're having dinner with a beautiful woman. I don't blame you for not wanting to interrupt that."

"Margaret Woods, this is Kevin Mars. He's one of the island's most successful businessmen. Kevin, Margaret is Fenella's niece."

"Yes, of course. I've heard a lot about you," Kevin said to Margaret as he offered her his hand.

She took it as she smiled back at him. "It's nice to meet you."

Kevin nodded and then turned his attention back to Ted. "I'm sure you overheard everything that was said at our table. It's a small dining room, and my friends aren't quiet."

Ted shrugged. "We heard some of it."

Kevin smiled thinly. "I wanted to take a moment to reassure you that I had nothing to do with the fire at Promenade View. Arson has never been one of my vices."

"Good to know," Ted said.

"Neil is a smart guy who makes dumb decisions," Kevin said. "He worked for me for about a month, and in that time he managed to get himself into all manner of trouble. I gave him the job because we have many mutual friends. I brought him here today for the same reason. I feel sorry for the man."

"Losing your home to fire must be horrible," Margaret said after a short silence.

Kevin looked at her and nodded. "Indeed. Neil has my sympathies."

After another silence, Kevin shrugged. He turned around and walked out of the restaurant, his two companions on his heels. As they left, Margaret let out a sigh.

"He's terrifying," she said as the door slowly swung shut.

"It's mostly for show," Ted said. "He likes to think of himself as the head of a huge crime syndicate, but he really has a team of about half a dozen not very bright guys who work for him. They bend the law in every way they can, but they actually rarely break it. I'm curious now what he had Neil do that went so badly wrong."

"So you don't think Kevin started the fire in Neil's apartment?"

"It's possible. Prior to tonight, I'd been unaware that Neil even knew Kevin. I need to talk to Mark, but I can do that after pudding. Having said all of that, I do think it's unlikely that Kevin was behind the fire. It isn't the way he usually works."

"Maybe he has a new employee with his or her own bright ideas."

"It would be his. Kevin doesn't hire women. But he also doesn't let his people do their own things. I can't see Kevin agreeing to someone starting a fire, not in an occupied flat in a building full of people. Kevin is an expert at weighing up risks and odds. I can see him burning down an empty warehouse and then claiming it was full of expensive merchandise in his insurance claim, but that's a very different thing."

"He did say that arson wasn't one of his vices."

Ted nodded. "I'm going to have Mark check, but I don't actually believe Kevin has ever had his name associated with any arson investigations. He's definitely never been accused of arson."

"You say that as if he's been accused of just about everything else."

Ted chuckled. "He had a few brushes with the law when he was younger, but he's become a lot smarter over the years. I can't remember the last time he was accused of anything, actually."

"Surely it's better for you when criminals are stupid."

"It is indeed. But Kevin is a worry for another time. Right now, I'm thinking about pudding."

Margaret nodded. "My food was good, but there wasn't that much of it."

"Yeah, I was thinking the same thing about mine. It was good, but it wasn't a huge portion."

Jack emerged from the back a moment later. He was carrying two plates.

"Chocolate cake for you," he said to Margaret, putting the plate on the table. "And jam roly-poly with custard for you," he told Ted.

They waited while he cleared away their empty dinner dishes and then moved their dessert plates in front of themselves.

"I do love jam roly-poly," Ted said. "But it isn't what I would have ordered, given a choice."

He picked up his fork and took a bite.

"How is it?" Margaret asked after she'd tried her cake.

"It's good. It tastes exactly like the jam roly-poly you can buy from the shops."

Margaret nodded. "I was just thinking the same thing about this cake. I bought a slice at the store the other day that was very similar."

"Or maybe it was the same cake. Maybe Jack buys his puddings from the local shop."

Margaret frowned. "Maybe he buys everything from a local store. I'm certain I've seen that pasta dish somewhere before. I actually thought about getting it once, but I wasn't sure how spicy it would be."

"Clearly not too spicy."

"It was fine, but can they buy stuff from local stores and sell it as restaurant food?"

Ted shrugged. "I've no idea how that works, but I do know someone I can ask."

"I'd hate to think that Jack is doing anything illegal, but even if it isn't illegal, it feels unethical to sell people grocery store food in a restaurant."

When Jack came back, Margaret found herself staring at him. He cleared their empty dessert dishes.

"Anything else?" he asked.

"Just the bill," Ted said.

"Ah, Mr. Mars took care of your bill," Jack said. "Thank you for coming in. I hope we'll see you again soon."

Ted frowned. "I really can't let Mr. Mars pay for our meals."

"I'm afraid it's already gone through," Jack said. "Maybe you can take it up with Mr. Mars."

"Oh, I will," Ted said as he got to his feet.

Margaret quickly stood up. "Thank you," she said.

Jack nodded. "See you soon," he said brightly.

"No, you really won't," Margaret said as she and Ted stepped outside.

Ted laughed. "It was an interesting experience, anyway. Let's go back to your flat. I'll ring Mark from there."

8

The walk back to Promenade View didn't take long. When they got into Margaret's apartment, Ted gave her a kiss before he pulled out his phone.

"Do you want some tea or coffee?" Margaret offered.

"I'd love a cup of tea and a few biscuits. Dinner was okay, but not terribly filling."

Margaret nodded. "Even after the cake, I'm still a bit hungry."

Mona was sitting at the kitchen table when Margaret walked into the room. Margaret gasped and then made herself cough a few times to try to cover for the sound. Mona shook her head.

"He's busy with Mark. He didn't even notice," she said.

"We bumped into Neil Mackey at dinner," Margaret said.

Mona grinned. "How nice. I shall have to go and listen to Ted's conversation, then."

As she faded away, Margaret filled the kettle. While she was waiting for it to boil, she piled some custard creams and chocolate bourbons onto a plate. When Ted joined her a few minutes later, the tea was ready, and Margaret was nibbling on a custard cream.

"You usually have chocolate-covered biscuits," Ted said as he sat down and grabbed a custard cream.

"I know, because so many of them are so delicious, but I also enjoy custard creams and bourbons, so I thought I'd buy them this week."

"There is nothing better than a custard cream," Ted said taking a bite.

Margaret nodded. "I can't believe we don't have them in America."

Ted stared at her for a minute. "You don't have them in America?"

She shook her head. "I had them for the first time when I came to visit Aunt Fenella."

"But they're so good."

Margaret laughed. "I know, right? They're delicious. I don't know why an American cookie company hasn't tried to re-create them there. Or maybe the British company should try selling them in America. Either way, my countrymen are missing out on delicious custard-flavored cream sandwiched between light and crunchy vanilla cookies."

"You have bourbons, though, right?"

"Nope."

Ted stared at her for a moment. "Seriously?"

"We don't have them, either, although we have chocolate cookies with vanilla cream in the middle. The chocolate cream in the middle of a bourbon is different, and so are the chocolate cookies on the outside. And they're rectangles, not round. They're really completely different to anything we have in the US."

"I'd miss them both if I ever moved to the US."

"I'd miss them if I moved back, and I've only had access to them for a few months."

Ted grinned. "You'd better stay here, then."

"I think I might."

They chatted a bit more about biscuits and cookies and the differences between their countries for a few minutes. Mona wandered in and sat in one of the empty chairs while they were talking.

"What did Mark say about Neil?" she asked Margaret when the conversation lagged.

"What did Mark say about Neil?" Margaret asked Ted.

He shrugged. "Nothing much. He'd already found a connection between Neil and Kevin, so that wasn't a huge surprise to him. He has a constable looking into where Kevin's known associates were on the evening of the fire, but that's unlikely to turn up any useful results. It all adds to the picture, though."

Margaret nodded. "I've been thinking about your cold case, too. I wasn't sure I could talk to anyone about it, though."

"You can talk about everything I've told you. I haven't told you anything that isn't public knowledge. There's a very good chance that some of the people you know will know more about the case than I do, really."

"Oh?"

He shrugged. "I suspect Arthur knows all of the suspects. Let's call them witnesses, actually. Or maybe we should call them concerned parties. Whatever, Arthur probably knows some of them. He moves in that social circle."

"I didn't realize Park's was that successful."

"It's a thriving small business that makes a decent profit. Besides that, it supplies cleaning products to many other businesses on the island and to some wealthy households as well. Arthur has a reputation for offering discounts to people he considers friends, so he probably has more friends than most."

Margaret laughed. "He's also an incredibly nice person."

"He is, yes."

"So maybe I should ask Arthur about the murder. Except it would seem like an odd thing to bring up out of the blue."

"It won't be out of the blue after tomorrow."

"What's happening tomorrow?"

"The local paper is going to be running an article about the case being reopened. I told Heather her terminology was incorrect, because murder investigations are never closed until the killer is caught, but she didn't want to listen to me."

"So the case is officially being investigated again?"

Ted laughed. "Okay, reopened probably does sound better, but yes, my colleague's friend in Canada is taking another look at the case. As part of that, he's asked me to speak to each of the witnesses who still live on the island."

"But you won't be able to tell me what they say in their interviews."

"No, but you'd better believe that Heather is also going to be trying to speak to them. Knowing her, she'll manage to get at least something out of each of them."

"When do you start with the interviews?"

"Tomorrow. That's part of my frustration, actually. I've been formally asked to speak to everyone on behalf of the police in Canada, but some people at the station aren't fond of the idea."

"Why not?"

"At the end of the day, I don't work for the Canadian police. If Joel had been murdered yesterday, it would be different, but some people seem to feel that I'll be wasting my time digging into a thirty-five-year-old cold case."

"But the major suspects, er, witnesses are still alive. If you delay, you might not get another chance to speak to them."

Ted nodded. "That was part of my argument."

"I'm sorry that you're having to deal with all of this."

"It comes with the job. And mostly, I love my job. I think part of my dissatisfaction comes from the postcard we got today, really."

"Postcard?"

"From Daniel. I'm not certain when he sent it, but it was from Hawaii, and it was beautiful. He said they're having a wonderful time and not in any rush to get back to the Isle of Man."

"That reminds me, I haven't heard from Aunt Fenella lately. She's probably having too much fun to call me."

"I suppose I'm just a little bit jealous of Daniel and Fenella," Ted said. "I can't imagine taking a year off from work and traveling the world. It must be wonderful."

"Maybe you should start saving your pennies."

Ted laughed. "I'm pretty good about saving, but a year of traveling costs a lot of pennies."

"If you're unhappy at work, you could look for a different job."

"I think about it from time to time, but then something like this cold case comes along, and I remember why I love what I do. I can't wait to speak to the various men and women who knew Joel. I want to hear their stories. Ideally, I want to discover who killed the man."

"It's been thirty-five years. Do you really think you might be able to solve the case?"

"Anything is possible. I certainly plan to try my hardest. I'm hoping that after all these years, people might be more willing to talk than they were thirty-five years ago. I just need one person to say just a little bit too much to break the case wide open."

Margaret nodded. "Good luck. I'll look forward to hearing what you can tell me, even if it isn't much."

"I'll be able to tell you when I've spoken to people. I might even share what I thought of them."

Mona sighed. "He'll tell you more than that. He's just teasing."

"And you're starting tomorrow?"

"I am. I'm interviewing Donna Ward tomorrow afternoon."

"The angry ex-wife who still lives on the grounds of the mansion she once shared with the victim. She was in New York City when her ex-husband died. She would have had to drive up to Canada to kill him."

"Well remembered."

Margaret shrugged. "I'm fascinated by the case."

"Aren't we all?"

"Donna didn't like to drive," Mona said.

Margaret hesitated. "Didn't you say that Donna didn't like to drive?"

Ted shrugged. "Maybe. It was widely reported in the paper here that she only drove when she absolutely had to. Apparently, her friends all knew that when they suggested doing anything, Donna would ask them to collect her and take her home afterwards. Apparently, when she and Joel were married, she had a driver to take her everywhere, but after the divorce she couldn't afford one any longer."

"And maybe she got so angry about it that she decided to drive up to Canada and yell at Joel about it," Margaret said.

"Maybe. I'm going to ask her about that tomorrow."

"If she killed Joel, she's definitely going to say that she hated driving."

Ted chuckled. "Maybe she really loved to drive but told everyone that she hated it in case she ever wanted to murder someone who was a long drive away."

"That's an interesting idea. Hating to drive doesn't give her an alibi, but it does make her seem less likely to have done it."

"What else could you pretend to hate that might give you an alibi years later?" Ted asked.

"Flying? Before you tamper with the plane that's carrying your beloved husband to the resort, where you'll be joining him when your car finally arrives the next day."

"Perfect," Ted said with a laugh.

They chatted about motives and murder until Margaret began to yawn between sentences. Mona had faded away after the first half hour of the conversation. Now Ted got to his feet.

"I'm going to go so you can get some sleep. Watch for the article in tomorrow's paper. Then you can talk to everyone at the office about Joel."

"The paper doesn't come out until the afternoon, though. We do most of our talking over lunch."

"Then you'll have to wait to talk to them on Wednesday."

Margaret nodded. "I suppose I can wait. Actually, I was going to take a packed lunch tomorrow, so it's probably for the best that I can't talk about the case with anyone. I have some tests to run that need to be monitored for hours. Wednesday will be better."

She walked Ted to the door. He pulled her close.

"Maybe you could stay at my place one night," he suggested when he lifted his head.

"I could. Maybe after the investigations into the fire and Joel's murder are over and you aren't so distracted."

Ted flushed. "I will admit to being a bit distracted. Maybe we need to go away for a long weekend somewhere."

"Let's do that. Start thinking about where you want to go. I don't know if I have any vacation days yet, but maybe we can go away on a public holiday weekend."

"There's a bank holiday in late August."

"Maybe we could go somewhere that weekend."

"Us and everyone else in the UK."

Margaret laughed. "Okay, maybe not. Arthur will probably let me have a day off, even if I don't have any vacation days yet."

"You're entitled to four weeks of paid leave every year."

"I forget how generous the UK is with vacation time."

"It isn't the UK, it's all of Europe. I believe it's nearly all of the world, except for the US, actually."

Margaret nodded. "You're probably right. Okay, I'll talk to Arthur about taking a few days off. Maybe you'd better talk to your boss first, though. I suspect it will be harder for you to get time off than me."

"Yeah, probably." He kissed her again and then opened the door. She watched as he walked to the elevators. As the doors slid shut behind him, she pushed her door shut and checked that it was securely locked. Then she went back into the kitchen to tidy up. Katie was already asleep on Margaret's bed when she walked into her room.

"Good night," she told the kitten as she slid under the duvet a short while later.

Katie didn't reply.

Margaret checked the newspaper's website the next morning while she was eating breakfast. There was nothing on it about Joel's murder. After she'd eaten, she made herself a sandwich and put it into a bag with an apple, a banana, and a few custard creams. After a quick check on Katie, who was chasing her own shadow, Margaret headed to work.

"Good morning," Joney said when Margaret walked into the foyer. "I'm having lunch with my husband today, but if you wanted to go out, you're welcome to join us."

"Thank you, but I brought my lunch today. I have some tests to run that need close monitoring. If I eat lunch at my desk, I stand a chance of finishing them today."

"Have fun?" Joney made the words a question.

Margaret laughed. "I really do love what I do."

She wasn't so sure about loving her job when she left many hours later. Nothing had gone terribly wrong, but lots of little things had been problematic all day. She'd only just managed to complete the last of her tests before six. Joney had already left for the day as Margaret walked through the lobby. As she walked past the reception desk, she spotted an envelope with her name on it.

"I just saw in the local paper that Ted is reopening the investigation into Joel Ward's murder. We need to talk about that tomorrow," the note from Joney said.

Margaret grinned. "That sounds great," she said to the empty room before she walked out to her car and drove herself home. As soon as she got there, she fired up her laptop. A quick skim of the article on the paper's website didn't tell her anything she didn't already know, though.

"Maybe Ted will tell me more," she said to Katie as she stroked the animal.

"Meeooww," Katie replied.

They snuggled together for half an hour before someone knocked on the door. Margaret's smile faltered when she opened it to Elaine.

"I can't stay," Elaine announced. "I'm having dinner with Ernie, but I wanted to ask you about the murder that Ted's investigating."

"If you read the local paper, then you know as much as I do."

Elaine frowned. "That's disappointing. I was assuming that someone had uncovered new evidence that suggested that the killer was definitely on the Isle of Man. Why else would Ted be interviewing everyone involved?"

"According to the article, the detective in Canada has been wanting to reopen the case for years, but he never had the time. Now he's been moved onto light duty due to his age, he reckons it's the perfect time to start working through a few cold cases."

"I want to hear everything that Ted learns from the suspects."

Margaret laughed. "So do I, but Ted won't tell me anything. He can't talk about what he learns in police interviews."

"In that case, we'd both better hope that Ms. Nosy Bryant gets a chance to interview everyone. Heather will ask all the awkward questions, and if she doesn't get an answer to them, she'll have a lot to say about the silence."

Margaret nodded. "What time are you meeting Ernie?"

Elaine glanced at her watch. "I need to go now or else I'll be late.

I'll come and see you tomorrow morning. We can talk about the murder and the fire."

"I'll be at work in the morning," Margaret reminded her as Elaine began to walk away.

"Oh, darn, I forgot that you work all day. I'm supposed to go to a birthday party tomorrow night. I might not see you until Thursday. Take notes if you learn anything interesting."

"Sure," Margaret said.

She watched as the woman slowly made her way down the hall. A man getting off one of the elevators kindly held it for her. As the doors slid shut behind her, the doors to the other elevator opened. Margaret smiled as Ted walked out of the car.

"You just missed Elaine," she told him as he pulled her close.

"What a shame," he said before he kissed her.

"How was your day?" she asked after she'd shut the apartment door.

"It was good. I had a nice conversation with Donna Ward."

"Oh? And now you can't tell me anything about it, can you?"

"I can tell you that she did hate driving at one point, but over time she's come to only mildly dislike it."

"Which could mean that she was lying the entire time."

"Or it could mean that when she was married to a very rich man she was happy to have someone else drive her everywhere, but once she had to do it for herself she learned to tolerate it," Mona suggested as she appeared on the couch next to Ted.

Margaret nodded. Then she repeated what Mona had said.

Ted shrugged. "She knows exactly why I asked the question. She also knows that not enjoying driving isn't an alibi."

"Was she nice?"

"She was nicer than I'd been expecting. Everyone describes her as an angry ex-wife, but she seemed more sad than angry."

"Sad about the divorce? Even after all these years?"

"I think it's more sadness about how her life has turned out. I don't think she ever imagined that she'd grow old alone and bitter. I suspect she'd do things differently if she had a chance to do it all again."

"And not marry Joel?"

"Maybe. She did say he was the love of her life, though. And that's all I'm going to say on the subject. Let's go and get dinner. Here's a thought. Let's go somewhere that has menus."

Margaret laughed. "I love that idea."

They walked to one of their favorite Italian restaurants. It was only a short distance away, but they walked quickly under cloudy skies.

"It's going to be raining when we come out," Margaret predicted.

"It's raining now," Ted said, nodding toward the window just inside the restaurant's front door.

"It's pouring."

"Yup. Good thing we're going to be here for a while."

They walked the short distance to the stand where a man in a dark suit was taking names. Margaret could see several parties of people waiting for tables in the next room.

"Table for two," Ted said.

The man nodded. "It will probably be half an hour or more. We're very popular tonight."

Ted glanced at the window and then looked at Margaret. "Should we wait?"

"I don't want to go back out there."

Ted nodded. "We'll wait."

"Very good. You're welcome to wait in the lounge, but it's pretty full," the man told them, pointing toward the small room behind him.

Margaret and Ted walked into the lounge and looked around. The only empty seats were around a small table in the back corner of the room. An older woman was sitting in one of the chairs, reading a book. The chairs on either side of her were empty.

"We could sit there," Margaret said, gesturing.

Ted frowned. "It might be better if we don't."

"Why?"

As Ted opened his mouth to reply, the woman looked up from her book. She spotted Ted and waved.

"You know her," Margaret said as Ted waved back.

When the woman gestured at the empty chairs around her, Ted looked at Margaret. "Now we have to join her," he muttered, taking Margaret's arm and leading her through the crowd to the back corner of the room.

"I'm forever amazed by this island," the woman said when they reached her. "I never see any of the people I know, but when I meet someone new, they seem to wander through my life at every turn for months on end."

"Do you mind terribly if we join you?" Ted asked.

The woman laughed. "Please, please join me. I can move over so you can sit next to your beautiful wife."

"We're not married," Margaret told her. "And I think we can manage being separated for a few minutes."

"Ah, I do love how independent women are today," the woman said as Margaret sat down in the chair on her left.

Ted sat down on her right. "Donna Ward, my, er, girlfriend, Margaret Woods. Margaret, this is Donna Ward."

"It's nice to meet you, Mrs. Ward," Margaret said.

"Oh, call me Donna. Mrs. Ward is far too formal in this day and age. It's a pleasure to meet you. How long have you and Ted been together?"

"Just a couple of months," Margaret replied.

"Enjoy the early days of the romance. They're wonderful and fun and exciting in all sorts of ways. I always imagined that I'd fall in love again one day. Sadly, it never happened. At the time I didn't think I minded, but now I feel as if I missed out."

"It's never too late," Margaret said.

Donna looked surprised and then chuckled. "I suppose you're correct, but I find it difficult to imagine finding someone now. I rarely go anywhere where I might meet someone, for a start."

"Surely you could go out more," Margaret said.

"I could, of course, but I'm rather fond of my quiet life. I've learned to love living alone, which obviously contradicts everything I just said about finding someone else. I'm over seventy. I don't have to make sense."

Margaret smiled. "You make perfect sense to me."

"I only met your young man this afternoon," Donna said. "Does he tell you about his work?"

"Not nearly enough."

Donna laughed. "I suppose policemen have to be terribly discreet, don't they? But everyone on the island will know why I had a conversation with him today. He was kind enough to speak to me at my home. There was a small part of me that wished that he'd sent a marked police car to collect me so that he could interview me in one of the police station interrogation chambers. At my age, I long for new experiences."

"We don't have interrogation chambers," Ted said. "I would have been happy to speak with you in one of our interview rooms, though, if you'd asked."

"Perhaps there will be another occasion when you need to speak with me," Donna said.

"Anything is possible," Ted replied.

"Donna? Your table is ready." The man in the black suit had approached silently.

Donna looked at him and frowned. "Could you possibly give me a table for three so that my new friends can join me?"

The man hesitated and then nodded. "Of course. Give me a minute."

As he walked away, Donna looked at Margaret. "I hope that wasn't too presumptuous on my part. I should have invited you to join me before I asked Don about a larger table."

"We'd be delighted to join you," Margaret told her.

"I don't usually invite others to join me. I'm generally very happy to sit by myself and enjoy a good book. However, tonight I've found myself here without a good book," Donna said.

"You were reading when we came in," Margaret said.

Donna nodded. She pulled a book out of her purse. "This is most definitely not a good book," she said, holding it up.

Margaret read the cover. "I've read a few books by that author. In my opinion, none of them have been as good as other people seem to think."

Donna laughed. "This was a gift from a friend. She doesn't read, so she asked another friend for a suggestion. That second friend reads reviews more than she reads books. This one is, apparently, very highly rated everywhere."

"Donna, we have a table for you."

They all stood up and followed the man through the room and then down the stairs into the restaurant. He showed them to a table for four in a quiet corner.

"Two orders of garlic bread," Donna said as she sat down.

"Right away," the man promised.

"I can eat an entire loaf of garlic bread by myself," she told Margaret. "I'd rather get two plates of it and have too much than be polite and only take a slice or two."

"Their garlic bread is amazing," Margaret said.

Donna nodded. "I knew we'd get along."

They ordered drinks, which arrived with the garlic bread. After they'd ordered their meals, Donna sat back and sighed.

"Ted interviewed me about my former husband," she said. "He was murdered thirty-five years ago. It was one of the most awful things that has ever happened to me."

"I'm sorry," Margaret said.

Donna shook her head. "That's quite wrong, of course. Joel's murder didn't happen to me at all. It happened to Joel, and it was the most awful thing that ever happened to him. It devastated me, though, in all sorts of odd ways."

"Odd?" Margaret echoed.

"We were divorced. That was Joel's choice, not mine. When we got married, I thought that I was madly in love with him. That faded with time, of course, but I still cared about him. It was difficult to discover that he no longer cared about me."

"I'm sorry."

"Thank you, dear. Of course, divorce was less common in those days. In our social circle, people typically simply cheated rather than actually ending the marriage. Prenuptial agreements weren't common. Most men preferred to stay with wives they no longer loved and have mistresses on the side. That was considerably cheaper for them than divorce."

"I hope Joel didn't cheat on you," Margaret said.

Donna shrugged. "I don't think he did, but it's impossible to be certain. In a way, it's almost worse that he didn't, though. If he'd fallen in love with someone else, perhaps it would have been easier to accept that he'd fallen out of love with me."

"Fettucine Alfredo?" the waiter asked.

Ted raised his hand. The man put the plate in front of him and then put the other two plates in front of Margaret and Donna.

"Anything else right now?" he asked.

Everyone shook their heads.

"But where was I?" Donna asked after a few bites. "I was explaining why Joel's death was so difficult for me. Except it's impossible to explain, really. We were divorced. He had remarried. I hated his new wife, of course, but I couldn't bring myself to hate Joel. I wanted to hate him, but I couldn't manage it."

"She wasn't someone he'd met while you were still married, was she?"

"I don't believe so, but I don't know for certain. I hated her anyway, simply because Joel loved her. Our lives were far too entwined for anyone's good, really. I lived in a house on the grounds of Joel's estate. I used to see them coming and going all the time. Lynda, his new wife, used to wave awkwardly whenever she saw me. Joel simply ignored me, which was better."

"How uncomfortable for both of you."

Donna stared at her for a moment and then laughed. "Of course it was uncomfortable for both of us, but until you said that, I'd never once thought about what it might be like for poor Lynda. The problem was that the house had been given to me in the divorce, but I didn't own it. It's mine until I die, but then it goes back to Joel, or rather to Lynda and her heirs. So I was rather stuck where I was."

"I'd hate that."

"And I should have fought harder to get more money or maybe a house elsewhere on the island. I was too shocked and upset about the divorce to think things through, though. What I did do, after a while, was buy myself an apartment in New York City. There, no one knew me or Joel, and I could get away and live my own life."

"I'm surprised you didn't just move there for good."

"I considered it. I was seriously considering it, actually, before Joel died. I felt very different about living there, though, after his death."

"Oh?"

She shrugged. "I was a suspect in the investigation, which was shocking and fascinating and odd. Joel was killed in Canada, at a resort several hours away from the city where I was staying. It was a resort that Joel and I had visited when we'd been married, actually. The police speculated that I could have driven from the city up to the resort, killed Joel, and driven back to the city without anyone noticing."

"And did you?" Margaret asked.

Donna laughed loudly. "What a lovely direct question. No, I did not, but simply knowing that the police thought I might have done it was enough to make me want to leave New York City. I flew back to the island as soon as they gave me permission to go. I've only been back to my apartment in New York once since Joel's murder. It was part of a different life when I was a different person. I keep thinking that I should sell it, but there's a part of me that wants to believe that I'll go there again one day."

"Pudding?" the waiter asked as he began to clear away their empty plates.

"Profiteroles," Donna said.

"I'll have the same," Margaret said.

Ted ordered the strawberry trifle.

"I've been thinking about Joel all afternoon," Donna said as the waiter walked away. "I keep trying to work out who killed him. I've come up with several different scenarios, all of which seem equally likely."

"I'd love to hear them," Ted said.

Donna nodded. "I thought you might."

9

Donna took a sip of her drink. When the waiter returned with their puddings, she took a bite before she sighed and put her fork down.

"I read a lot of murder mysteries," she told them. "I used to read romance novels, but after Joel's murder, I found myself gravitating towards true crime. After a while, I began to find those too depressing. People can do unbelievably horrible things to other people. That's when I started reading murder mysteries. Horrible things happen, but everything gets wrapped up in a couple of hundred pages. The killer always gets caught. The good guys always win. I often wish life could be more like that."

Ted nodded. "It would be nice if we could catch every murderer, ideally within days. Unfortunately, murder investigations in real life are rarely as simple or straightforward as the ones in fiction."

Donna nodded. "I thought it would be interesting to try to look at Joel's murder as if it were in one of my books instead of in the real world. This was years ago now, maybe fifteen or more, after I'd been reading detective novels and mysteries for a while. I'd started to think that Joel's murder couldn't possibly be all that complicated, so I made a list of suspects and I tried to assign motives, means, and opportunity to each of them."

"And how did you do?" Ted asked.

Donna laughed. "Terribly. It turns out that real life murders are a good deal more complicated than fictional ones. I found that I was missing important clues or maybe just one vital clue. Whatever, after working on the puzzle for a week or so, I gave up and went back to my books. This afternoon, though, after we spoke, I dug out my old notes on the case."

"And did you have better luck this time?" Margaret asked.

Donna ate a bite of pastry before she replied. "No, but I've only just started, really. I feel as if I might get closer to the solution this time. I've read a lot more books since my first attempt."

Margaret used her knife to slice a profiterole in half. As she did so, Ted cleared his throat.

"Murders in real life are nearly always more complex than fictional ones," he said. "A team of trained investigators has been looking into Joel's murder for the past thirty-five years without finding the killer."

"Are you suggesting that reading a lot of fictional murder mysteries isn't as useful as actually training as a police inspector?" Donna asked. Before Ted could reply, she laughed. "I'm well aware of the limitations of my abilities. But I have the distinct advantage of being personally acquainted with nearly all of the suspects. You did ask me in my interview today who I thought killed Joel. At that point, I was feeling less chatty than I am now, so I simply shrugged."

"I'd love to hear your thoughts on any or all of the suspects," Ted said.

Donna smiled. "You should invite your girlfriend to join your interviews. I'm enjoying talking to her. She's the reason I want to talk about the suspects. She's never heard the story before."

"I did read the article in the local paper," Margaret said.

Donna waved a hand. "That article barely skimmed the surface of the situation. I've half a mind to ring up the paper and tell them how much they missed. I won't, though, because I prefer my privacy."

"Where do you want to start?" Ted asked after a moment.

"Let's start with Lynda," Donna said with a wicked grin. "Lynda was

Joel's second wife, and she inherited his considerable estate. I said earlier that I hated her, and that was definitely true when she and Joel first married. Over time, though, I softened slightly. When I'd been married to Joel, I'd thought he was wonderful, but from the outside looking in, I was able to see that he was misogynistic and narcissistic. He wasn't much different from other men of his generation, really, but he'd been spoiled by his parents, and he could be a very difficult person with whom to live."

"Difficult enough that his wife would want to murder him?" Margaret asked.

Donna shrugged. "We all have breaking points. As I said earlier, in our circle, it wouldn't have been unusual for them both to start seeing other people while maintaining the polite fiction of a happy marriage, but as far as I knew, neither of them was involved with anyone else at the time of Joel's death. Having paid for one expensive divorce, though, I can't see Joel being willing to go through a second one. I suspect he might have told Lynda that she was stuck with him forever, like it or not."

"So his death was the only way out of the marriage for her," Margaret said.

"Perhaps. If Lynda was unhappy, she certainly had a motive for killing Joel, even if he was willing to divorce her. She inherited a great deal more than she would have received in a divorce settlement. The central question is, was she unhappy?"

"What do you think?" Margaret asked.

"Living where I did, I saw a great deal of them. I saw them driving past, but I also saw them when they were out walking the dogs or when I was walking mine. I saw them in unguarded moments when they were simply being themselves. As much as I hate to admit it, I think they were still very happy together."

"I read in the paper that she remarried again fairly quickly," Margaret said.

Donna nodded. "Which actually suggests to me that she was still happy with Joel until his death. People who are happily married are more likely to try again, aren't they? It's bitter divorcées like me who decide never to go down that road again."

"Maybe," Margaret said.

"Ted, if you haven't interviewed Lynda yet, I suggest you ask her about children," Donna said.

"Children?" Ted repeated.

"Yes, children. That was the one issue about which Joel and I fought. I wanted children, but he always said that he was too selfish to have them. It took years to convince him to get a dog, actually, and we had staff who did most of the looking-after for him. Obviously, we could have done the same with children, but Joel knew me well enough to know that I'd want to be a part of raising my own children. I've often thought that, if I'd been less vocal about my desire to be a mother, we might have stayed together. I never threatened to leave him or even hinted that I might. Quite the opposite, actually. I always insisted that I didn't truly care, but I suspect that he was aware of my desire for children and that it was a factor in his decision to end our marriage."

"So if Lynda had decided that she wanted children, you think Joel would have said no?" Margaret asked.

"I know Joel would have said no. Would Lynda have killed him over the issue? Probably not, but it might have been a factor. Combine it with the amount of money she would inherit on his death, and it simply strengthens an already strong motive."

"But you said you thought they were still happy together," Margaret said.

"They appeared happy. It's possible that Lynda was nursing a deep desire to become a mother but hiding it from Joel. I speak from experience. I spent years pretending to be happy with him while desperately wanting a child. I discussed it only twice with Joel in all those years. I never discussed it with anyone else."

"If she wanted children so badly, then surely she would have had some with her second husband," Margaret said.

"It isn't that simple, though," Donna said. "Perhaps she and Victor tried for a baby but never managed to succeed. She was thirty-five when Joel died and thirty-six when she remarried. For some women, that's already too late. Modern medicine can do more now to help than it could thirty-five years ago, too."

"So how likely do you think it is that Lynda killed Joel?" Margaret asked, feeling as if Donna had been talking in circles about the woman.

"There's a part of me that still hates her for marrying Joel. That part wants to believe that she killed him. But if I'm honest, then I think I'd give her a four out of ten in terms of likeliness to have killed him. She had the means and the opportunity, but I question her motive."

"Who's next?" Ted asked. He'd slipped a notebook out of his pocket and was discreetly taking notes.

"Let's talk about Victor," Donna said. "He is just like Joel in many ways. Just as cold and calculating and ultimately successful at business. I never cared for him when Joel and I were together. I liked him even less after the divorce when he tried to convince me to sleep with him."

"He did?" Margaret asked.

Donna nodded. "We were at a party. Joel was there with some blonde woman he barely knew. I was in a corner, feeling all alone in the world. Victor came over and started telling me how beautiful I was and how he thought that Joel had made a huge mistake in divorcing me. For a moment, I was captivated. The man was charming and sweet and completely unlike the person I knew him to be. If he'd been a bit more patient, he might have persuaded me to do something foolish. As it was, he pushed too hard too quickly and broke the spell. Once I turned him down, he returned to type. I don't think we've said more than five words to each other since."

"Can you see him killing Joel?"

"Absolutely, if he felt he had a reason to do so. If he had decided to get rid of Joel, though, I think he'd have paid someone else to kill Joel while he was at least several hundred miles away. I can't imagine him pulling the trigger himself. That's what staff is for."

"Is it possible that someone was paid to kill Joel?" Margaret asked Ted.

He shrugged. "Anything is possible. The police in Canada spent some time working with the idea, but they were never able to find any evidence of a killer for hire."

"What motive did Victor have?" Margaret asked.

Donna sighed. "And that's where he falls apart as a suspect. I've spent years trying to work out a convincing motive for the man, but I've never managed it."

"Maybe he was interested in Lynda," Margaret said.

"He probably was, but I can't see him killing Joel for her. He and Joel worked together on a few projects, and they had life insurance policies on one another. The local paper made a big deal out of the fact that Victor received a big payout after Joel's death, but the amount involved wasn't much more than pocket change for Victor. Joel's death also ended what had been a very lucrative business arrangement. I know Victor lost money overall after Joel's untimely demise."

"Even after he married Joel's rich widow?" Margaret asked.

Donna grinned. "That was probably financially advantageous for him, but he couldn't have known that he'd be able to win Lynda's heart – not at the time that Joel died, anyway."

"So where does he fall on your list of suspects?" Ted asked.

"I'd give him a six out of ten," Donna replied. "He had the means and the opportunity. He was at the resort that night with his latest girlfriend. Still, I've given him a six more because I don't care for him than because I think he killed Joel. When you interview him, please do so in one of your interview rooms. Make it as uncomfortable as possible for the man."

Ted chuckled. "I'll see what I can do."

"Trent Walsh is another person who is ultimately probably worse off since Joel's death. Trent and Joel were business partners, but Joel was the smarter of the two. Trent has done fairly well in the years since the murder, but he would have done a great deal better if Joel had still been running the company."

"But did he know that thirty-five years ago?" Margaret asked.

"Maybe. But maybe not. Most men seem unaware of their own faults," Donna said. "He also inherited a great deal when his father died not long after Joel. Between that money and the insurance payout he got from Joel's death, he's been more or less retired for a long time. Perhaps, if he'd kept working, he'd have proven me wrong."

"Where would you put him on the list?" Ted asked.

"I'd give him a six or seven. He was in New York City before the murder. If that doesn't give me an alibi, then it doesn't give him one, either."

Ted grinned. "So he had means and opportunity."

"Exactly," Donna said.

"What about the gun?" Margaret asked. "Where had that come from?"

"It belonged to the man who managed the airfield," Ted told her. "He kept it in a drawer in his office there. The office was typically left unlocked during the day, and the desk didn't have a lock. When he was questioned after the murder, he was unable to remember the last time he'd seen the gun."

"How do you forget something like that?" Margaret asked.

"It was in the bottom drawer," Donna said. "It was old, almost an antique. Jake loved showing it to people, but otherwise, he never even opened the drawer. It was kept unloaded next to a box of ammunition."

Margaret frowned. "Did everyone who used the airfield know about the gun?"

"Probably," Donna said. "Jake showed it to Joel and me on our first visit to the resort."

"We're assuming that anyone who had access to the airfield had access to the gun," Ted said. "It could have been taken the night of the murder or as much as a month before Joel's death."

Margaret shook her head. "I don't understand how people can be so casual about deadly weapons."

"Who's next?" Ted asked Donna.

"Those were the main suspects. I know the police looked at Jeremy, too, but I never took him seriously as a suspect," she replied.

"Jeremy?" Margaret echoed. She knew she'd heard the name, but she couldn't remember how he was connected to the case.

"Jeremy Olson was the resort manager," Donna told her. "He's a lovely man who worked very hard to keep a lot of very wealthy and spoiled people happy. I'm fairly certain he'd have been quite pleased over the years if several of his guests had suddenly dropped dead, but I can't see him actually killing a guest, not even one as difficult as Joel."

"Maybe he had other reasons for wanting Joel dead," Margaret said.

"There was speculation at the time that he was interested in Lynda or that he was stealing from guests. Even if he was in love with Lynda, he had to know that he didn't stand a chance with her. She was never going to look twice at a man who worked as a resort manager for a living. As for stealing from guests, all I can say is that when Joel and I stayed there, we never had anything go missing. Jeremy has never been a serious suspect in my mind."

"Where would you rank him?" Ted asked.

"Oh, one or two, maybe. He had the means and opportunity, of course, but no discernible motive. I always thought he was very kind as well. It's difficult to imagine him as a killer."

"Is that everyone?" Margaret asked.

Donna shook her head. "I've always wondered about Aaron Crawford."

"Why?" Ted asked.

She shrugged. "I knew him, but apparently Joel did not." She looked at Margaret. "He was another wealthy businessman who was at the resort for a holiday. I'd met him on one of the trips that Joel and I took to the resort years before Joel's murder. We met in one of the bars. I was waiting for Joel and Aaron was waiting for his girlfriend of the week. We talked for several minutes before she turned up and they left together."

"Why was he a suspect in the murder?" Margaret asked.

"Because he and Joel had a fight over how Joel parked his plane," Donna said with a small smile. "Joel could be careless with his things. He had plenty of money, and plenty of insurance. He often left the keys in his cars or even in the plane. Aaron, on the other hand, had had to work a good deal harder to get where he was in the world. He'd dropped out of university and started his own business at nineteen. By the time I met him, he was in his mid-forties and worth a fortune. He was also very protective of his things. I can see him becoming enraged if he thought that Joel's plane was in danger of hitting his."

"Enraged enough to murder Joel?" Margaret asked.

"I truly don't know. I doubt it, but you never know. I only spoke to the man for a handful of minutes on one occasion years before the murder. At the time, I thought he was charming, but I didn't have a chance to truly get to know him."

"Did you see him around the resort after that?" Margaret asked.

Donna shook her head. "I never saw him again, but that wasn't unusual. The resort was designed to feel private and exclusive. Aside from meals, guests rarely saw one another, and even meals were often taken in private dining rooms or delivered to individual cottages."

"It all sounds lovely," Margaret said.

"It was lovely, but soulless," Donna told her. "After the divorce, I never once missed going there."

"What would you give Aaron in your rankings?" Ted asked.

"Either a two or an eight," Donna replied. "And that's entirely dependent on motive. He could have had one about which I know nothing."

Ted nodded. "That's everyone."

"Aside from me," Donna corrected him. "I might argue that I didn't truly have the means or the opportunity, but some poor policeman in Canada was tasked with the job of driving from the resort to New York City and back again in a single day. He managed it, but he didn't enjoy it. Still, that was enough to prove that I could have done it, no matter how much I hated driving."

"But what sort of motive could you have had?" Margaret asked. "You and Joel were divorced. He was married to someone else. Why kill him then?"

Donna grinned. "Maybe resentment had been building since the divorce was finalized. Or maybe I'd hated him for years but was waiting for the right time. To be fair to the police, there's no way I could have killed him here on the Isle of Man. I'd have been arrested immediately. But I might have thought that I'd be safe over there. I wasn't even in the same country, so how could I be a suspect?"

"I suppose that's possible," Margaret said.

"For what it's worth, there were times when I wanted him dead. I hated him so much for ending things. I hated him even more when he married Lynda. I really should have put more effort into finding someone else. I could have found happiness again if I hadn't wasted so much time being bitter."

"I'm sorry," Margaret said as the woman wiped her eyes with a tissue she'd pulled out of a pocket.

"Thank you. This has been a very interesting evening," Donna said. "Talking to you was definitely more entertaining than my book. If you'll excuse me, I'm going to go now."

They watched as the woman walked out of the room.

"She's left us with the check," Margaret murmured.

Ted shrugged. "I don't mind. That was an interesting conversation."

"Does it advance the investigation at all?"

"Maybe. I didn't realize that she'd met Aaron Crawford. I never thought to ask her about him today, and I don't remember reading anything about their meeting in the files I've been given, either. I'm going to have to talk to Howard about that."

"Right now?"

Ted grinned. "It can wait until we get back to your flat." He waved down the waiter. "We need the bill, please."

"Oh, Mrs. Ward told us to put it all on her tab. She eats here at least twice a week. The owners bill her once a month for all of her meals," the man replied.

"She shouldn't have done that," Ted said.

The waiter shrugged. "Do you want to speak to the manager?"

Ted looked at Margaret and then slowly shook his head. "It's fine. I'll send Mrs. Ward a check or something."

"Very good." He rushed away before Ted could speak again.

"Shall we?" Ted asked as he got to his feet.

They walked up the stairs and out of the restaurant together. It looked as if the rain had just stopped.

"We should walk quickly," Margaret said.

Ted nodded. "The skies could open again at any moment."

They were only a few paces away from the entrance to Promenade View when the rain started again. Margaret ran the last few steps and then held the door for Ted. As soon as they got to her apartment, he pulled out his phone.

"What time is it in Canada?" he asked.

"Which part? Near New York City they'll be five hours behind us."

Ted looked at the clock. "So Howard might still be at his desk."

Margaret went into the kitchen and made tea. She was too full of garlic bread, pasta, and dessert to put out any cookies. When the tea was ready, she sat at the table and sipped hers while she listened to the low murmur of Ted's voice coming from the living room.

He stuck his head in a few minutes later. "Babe, I love you, but I need to go," he said.

Margaret swallowed a sigh. "Sure," she said, getting to her feet.

She followed Ted to the door. Mona was sitting on one of the couches. She gave Margaret a small wave as Margaret walked past.

"Howard wants to go through a few things with me before I talk to more of the witnesses tomorrow. He's been going back through the files, and he found another pile of statements, including one where Donna talked about Aaron."

"I hope the new information is helpful."

"Every bit of information helps. Some bits help a lot more than others."

Margaret nodded and then pulled him into a kiss. When he lifted his head, he sighed.

"And now I want very badly to stay," he said.

"But you have to work."

"If it wasn't a murder investigation."

"From thirty-five years ago."

"But I'm interviewing the man's widow and her second husband tomorrow. I need all the help I can get."

"Go," Margaret said. "I still love you."

"I don't deserve you," Ted said as he opened the door. He rushed down the corridor toward the elevators.

"No, you don't," Margaret said sadly as she shut the door behind him.

"There are plenty of other fish in the sea," Mona said.

"Except I'm quite fond of that fish."

"He's very dedicated to his job."

"And he should be. He does important work."

"Indeed. It does seem as if you learn as much as he does, though, just going about your daily life."

Margaret shrugged. "I'd suggest that you had something to do with our dinner companion tonight, but apparently she eats at that restaurant regularly. It was just a coincidence that we happened to be there on the same evening."

"I'm going to assume that Ted told Howard everything that Donna said and I won't ask you to repeat the conversation."

"Thank you."

"I do want to know what you thought of her, though."

"She seemed very nice, but sad. I think she'd do things differently if she could live her life over again."

"Does that mean you don't think she killed Joel?"

"No, I don't think she killed Joel. She didn't really have any reason to want him dead."

Mona nodded. "You need to meet the other suspects."

Margaret shook her head. "I need to stay out of it. Besides, some of the suspects don't even live on the island. I'm not going to Canada to try to meet Jeremy, and I've no idea where Aaron is now."

"That's an interesting question. Where is Aaron now?"

"I can ask Ted, but it won't matter."

Mona nodded. "You ask Ted. I'll see what I can learn in the meantime."

As she slowly faded away, Margaret frowned. "What does that mean?" she asked.

"Meeoorww," Katie said.

"Yes, I know she's gone, but that doesn't mean I don't want an answer," Margaret muttered. "Maybe I should just go to bed."

She sat down on the couch and switched on the TV. An hour later, after watching a couple of programs about home improvements that didn't seem to improve anything as far as Margaret was concerned, she turned the set off and headed to bed.

"Maybe I can get through tomorrow without seeing anyone involved in Joel's murder or the fire in the building," she said as she slid under the duvet.

Katie made a noise.

"It isn't that small of an island," Margaret said, burying her head in her pillow.

"Did you bring your lunch today?" Joney asked when Margaret arrived at work the next morning.

"I forgot all about lunch this morning," Margaret admitted.

Joney laughed. "Arthur will be delighted. He has a lunch booking at his club, and he needs guests."

"How does that work?"

"It's a golf club. Besides having to golf there at least weekly, one of the membership requirements is that everyone has to dine there a certain number of times each month. Arthur has regular bookings for certain dates, some for dinner and some for lunch. He usually takes customers or potential customers when he goes, but this time the man he was planning to take had to cancel at the last minute. Even if Arthur doesn't go, he'll still have to pay for lunch."

"That's dumb."

Joney laughed again. "I keep telling him that, but he loves the club and the golf course. Besides, it's usually very useful for him. Our customers all love being taken there. If he'd had a bit more notice, I'm certain he could have found someone else who'd have been happy to join him. As it is, he can't start ringing people now to invite them. It would look as if they were a last-minute substitute for someone that Arthur would have preferred to spend time with."

"So I get to feel that way, instead," Margaret said with a laugh.

"Oh, Arthur would much rather spend time with you than with most of our customers. But some of them love nothing more than lunch at his club. Can I tell him that you'll join him?"

"Sure, why not? Are you coming, too?"

"I wish I could. The food is excellent, but I already have plans. Rachel is having lunch with some guy she met on a dating app or else she'd have happily gone. You were Arthur's last hope."

"Surely he could have just gone alone."

"He could have, but he would have had to pay for two meals. There's a two-person minimum in the dining room."

"How very odd."

"And before you ask, Mrs. Park is out of town. Not that she'd have wanted to join him. The last time I spoke to her about the club, she said that she'd rather have to pay the penalty than eat there again. I gather she and Arthur eat dinner there at least twice a month."

"I don't know if I'm looking forward to this or not."

"It will be fun. I promise," Joney told her.

"Fingers crossed."

Margaret spent the morning working hard. Knowing that she was going to be having lunch with the boss made her feel as if she needed to push herself even harder than normal. Just after noon, Arthur stuck his head into her office.

"Are you about ready?" he asked.

"Sure," Margaret said. She grabbed her purse and stood up.

"I really appreciate this," Arthur told her as they walked through the building together. "I wouldn't mind paying the penalty, but they also do their best to make you feel guilty about missing your assigned booking. I sometimes wonder why I bother staying a member."

"It doesn't sound like the club for me."

"Do you golf?"

Margaret shook her head.

"If you golfed, you'd understand," Arthur told her as he unlocked his car. "The island has nine golf courses, but the one at the club is the best."

"If you say so."

He drove them across the island, turning down a road that Margaret had never noticed before. They hadn't gone far before they were stopped by a gate. Arthur waved a card at a reader and the gate slowly opened. A minute later, they were driving past rolling golf course greens. Eventually, they reached a large building with parking outside. Arthur pulled into a numbered space.

"Welcome to the club," he said.

Margaret smiled. "Thanks."

Arthur used his keycard to open the door to the large clubhouse. Then they walked down a corridor. The restaurant was at the end of it. It was a large room with a wall of windows that overlooked the course.

The sea was visible in the distance. Arthur smiled at the man in the black tuxedo at the door.

"Good afternoon, James," he said.

"Good afternoon, Mr. Park," the man said. "Your table is ready."

He led them across the mostly empty room to a table for four near the windows. "Stuart will be taking care of you today. He will be right with you."

"Very good," Arthur said.

"Arthur, hello," a voice called from across the room. "Invite me to join you or I'll ring your wife and tell her that you're having lunch with a very beautiful young woman," the man continued as he walked toward them.

10

Arthur laughed. "She knows exactly where I am and who I'm with," he said. "Trent, meet Margaret Woods. Margaret is my excellent chemical engineer. Margaret, Trent Walsh is an old friend."

"It's nice to meet you," Margaret said.

"Likewise," the man said. "I'm old now, but I still love looking at beautiful women. I hope you don't mind if I join you. You can talk about chemistry. I'll just listen." He slid into a chair and winked at Margaret.

"I haven't seen you in ages," Arthur said. "How are you?"

Trent shrugged. "I was doing okay until someone decided to reopen the investigation into Joel's death. That's the last thing I need right now."

"Oh? What makes it such bad timing?" Arthur asked.

"Joel's murder was a horrible tragedy, but it happened a long time ago. I just don't see the point in bringing it back up now. The investigation is going to upset a lot of people, people who've worked hard to get on with their lives after the tragedy."

"The man was murdered," Margaret said. "The police should be doing everything they can to find his killer, and you should be doing everything you can to support their efforts."

Trent looked surprised. He stared at Margaret for a moment before chuckling. "Yes, of course. I didn't mean to upset you. Of course I want Joel's killer found and put behind bars. It's just difficult reliving the entire awful thing after so many years."

"My boyfriend is Ted Hart," Margaret said flatly.

Trent slowly shook his head. "What are the odds?" he asked Arthur. "I have an appointment tomorrow with Inspector Hart. I know it's a small island, but this is silly."

"You don't have to have lunch with us," Margaret said.

Trent laughed. "I'm more than happy to have lunch with you. I don't have any secrets. Besides, we aren't going to talk about Joel. I want to hear all about you."

Margaret gave him a two-sentence summary of her life. As she finished speaking, the waiter arrived.

"Mr. Walsh, will you be dining with Mr. Park and his guest today?" he asked.

Trent nodded. "They were kind enough to invite me to join them." He looked at Margaret. "My girlfriend had to cancel at the last minute. She's forty-seven."

"Congratulations," Margaret said, trying not to sound too sarcastic.

Trent just laughed. "I'm eighty, and I'd go out with a woman in her twenties if I could find one who was interested. I don't suppose you're interested?"

Margaret shook her head. "Ted and I are very happy together."

"I have a lot of money."

"Money doesn't buy happiness."

"It can rent it, though," Trent said with a laugh.

"Let me tell you about today's specials," the waiter said. He read down a list of delicious-sounding meals.

"First, we need wine," Trent said when the waiter was finished. "What do you prefer?" he asked Margaret.

"I'll just have a soft drink," Margaret said. "I'm going back to work after lunch."

Trent frowned. "Arthur, you'll have a glass of wine with me, right?"

"Sorry, but I drove," Arthur replied.

"But please, have wine if you want wine," Margaret told him.

Trent nodded and then he and the waiter got into a long conversation about the available wines. While they were talking, Margaret read through the menu. Whoever had written the descriptions was clearly an expert. Just about everything on the menu sounded wonderful.

Eventually, the waiter got drink orders from Margaret and Arthur. As he walked away, Trent spoke again.

"Joel and I were like brothers," he said. "I still miss him every day."

"I'm sorry for your loss," Margaret said.

"I blame myself in some ways," he continued. "I rang him that night and told him that he needed to fly back to New York. One of our clients was being difficult, and I was struggling. I should have found a way to deal with it myself, but I took the easy way out and called in the cavalry. At least, I thought I did. I was so angry the next morning when Joel didn't turn up at the meeting. The worst part, though, was that I did deal with the angry client myself. It wasn't until I called Joel to let him know that he was no longer needed that I found out that he was dead."

"Surely you don't think he was killed because he was flying back to New York?" Margaret asked.

Trent shrugged. "I've always wondered if maybe he was just in the wrong place at the wrong time. Maybe he got to the airfield just as a delivery was being made. The police have always denied that drugs were being flown in and out of that airfield, but I find it difficult to believe that they were making enough money off the resort guests to make the airfield viable."

"That's an interesting theory," Margaret said.

"I said as much to the police when they questioned me after Joel's death. They didn't seem interested in my theory," Trent said.

Margaret shrugged. "They're experts at seeming uninterested in things."

Trent laughed. "I hope that isn't true for your boyfriend when you're together. I can't imagine him not being terribly interested in you. He must hang on your every word."

Margaret was saved from having to reply by the arrival of the waiter. He delivered their drinks and then took their food orders. They all ordered different items from the list of specials.

"Very good. It shouldn't be long," the waiter said before he walked away.

"What shall we talk about?" Trent asked, looking from Arthur to Margaret and back again.

"Did I hear that you grew up in the US?" Margaret asked him.

"I did. I grew up in Virginia. My father was a developer who built houses in and around DC. After I graduated from Georgetown, I started my first business. Things took off from there."

"So how did you end up on the Isle of Man?"

Trent laughed. "I wish I had a more interesting story to tell you, but I don't want to lie, not if you're going to repeat what I tell you to your boyfriend."

"I will," Margaret said.

"Then I'll tell you the true but boring story. Not long after I started my first business, I met Joel. He was much more successful than I was, with business interests all over the world. He'd heard about the sort of investing that I'd started doing and offered me a piece of his latest project. I was tempted, but I hesitated, and he withdrew his offer."

"Joel always appreciated quick decisions," Arthur said.

Trent nodded. "When he came back to see me again three months later with a different proposal, I signed on the dotted line that afternoon. It was a decision I never regretted. I made millions on that deal, and before long, Joel and I were more or less partners."

"More or less?" Margaret echoed.

"He still did business with a handful of others, including Victor King, who is now married to Joel's widow. I did a few little things on my own as well, but the bulk of both of our businesses was held in our partnership. When Joel told me he was moving to the Isle of Man, I was intrigued."

"What made him choose the island?" Margaret asked as Trent paused to take a drink.

"I believe he'd been looking for a more favorable location from a tax perspective and someone had told him about the Isle of Man. He'd grown up dividing his time between the US, the UK, and Canada. He told me that he never wanted to stay in one place for too long, so he bought properties in all three of those countries. The house on the Isle of Man was his base, though, once he purchased it. And once he was settled here, he invited me to come and visit. I fell in love with the island within twenty-four hours."

"Why?" Margaret asked bluntly.

Trent laughed. "I wish I knew. Joel picked me up at the airport and drove me around the entire island. By the time we arrived at his home, I was already thinking about buying a house here. Over dinner that evening, Joel explained some of the tax advantages to being here, but by that time I was already ready to start looking for a home here."

"Trent bought a mansion that overlooks Ramsey Harbour," Arthur said.

"The views are amazing and houses on the island were far less expensive back then. The property has increased in value enormously."

"How nice for you," Margaret said.

"Madam," the waiter said, putting Margaret's lunch in front of her. He put plates in front of Arthur and Trent and then looked at them expectantly. "What else can I get for you?" he asked.

"We're good," Trent said, waving a hand.

"Thank you," Margaret said.

The man nodded before he walked away.

"I thought seriously about selling my house and moving off the island after Joel's untimely death," Trent said after everyone had started eating. "But after Joel's death, I thought about doing a lot of crazy things. Life felt as if it had been turned on its head somehow."

"It was a shock for the entire island," Arthur said.

Trent nodded. "If he'd died in a plane crash or a car accident or something else equally unexpected, it would have been difficult to handle, but the idea that he'd been deliberately murdered was almost impossible to process."

"Had you ever been to that resort?" Margaret asked. "You said earlier that you thought they might have been using the airfield for more than just resort guests. That suggests that you'd been there."

"I had been there. Joel recommended it, and I took his suggestions seriously. It was a wonderful place to get away from it all. I used to go at least once a year, but I haven't been back since Joel's death."

"How big was the airfield?" Margaret asked.

Trent shrugged. "I never paid that much attention to the airfield. While Joel was a pilot, I was never anything more than a passenger. I paid someone to fly me back and forth to the resort when I went. My flights were always met by the resort manager, who would drive me to my accommodation for the week. After my stay, the manager would drive me back to the airfield, where my plane would be waiting for me."

"That sounds wonderful," Arthur said.

"They probably still do things the exact same way," Trent said. "You could go and stay there anytime."

Arthur shook his head. "My wife would never agree. She prefers to holiday in big cities so she can shop and tour art museums. She'd go crazy stuck in the middle of nowhere for a week."

"There are pools, restaurants, shops, and a spa – or rather, there used to be all of those things. I've no idea what's there now. The entire resort might have gone out of business for all I know. I doubt it, though. It was always very popular when I was going. I don't think that will have changed, not even after one of their guests was murdered at their airfield."

"Can I share our sweets menu with you?" the waiter asked.

Margaret nodded. Trent shrugged as Arthur grinned. The waiter read out a long list of tempting desserts. When he was finished, Margaret was happy to order the chocolate and raspberry cake. Arthur ordered Eton mess.

"I don't want anything else," Trent said, waving the waiter away.

"So you think that Joel was simply in the wrong place at the wrong time?" Arthur asked.

"I think that's the most likely explanation. I also prefer to believe that over thinking that someone I know murdered my close friend. I know I'm being naïve, but I want to believe that if someone I knew was planning to murder someone, I'd pick up on some hint in their behavior. Barring that, I saw and spoke to everyone who knew Joel in the days, weeks, and months after the murder. None of them behaved in any way other than what I would have expected. I know it's foolish of me, but I can't help but think that I would have been able to spot someone who was feeling guilty or secretly happy that Joel was gone."

"But it doesn't work that way," Arthur said. "Just a few months ago, I discovered that someone I'd always thought of as boring and uninteresting actually murdered two people."

Trent shrugged. "If I were investigating the case, I'd look hard at Victor King."

"Oh?" Margaret said.

"Yeah. He never went out with the same woman for more than a few weeks, maybe a month, tops. Then, a year after Joel's death, he married Joel's widow. Thirty-five years later, they're still together. That seems odd to me."

"Maybe he just finally met the right woman," Arthur said.

"Or maybe they were seeing each other behind Joel's back," Trent said. "And maybe they worked together to kill him and then got married so that they can't be forced to testify against each other."

"Is that even really true, though?" Margaret asked.

Trent shrugged. "I believe it's the law in the US. I've no idea if UK law is different."

"Remember that the Isle of Man has its own laws," Arthur said. "Although if Joel's killer ever goes to trial, the trial will probably take place in Canada."

Trent chuckled. "And who knows what their law says about spouses testifying against one another."

"Is Victor at the top of your list of suspects, then?" Arthur asked.

After a short hesitation, Trent nodded. "I hate to say that, because we're friends, but if Joel was killed by someone who knew him, then Victor is at the top of my list, with or without the help of his now-wife, Lynda."

"Does that mean she comes second on your list?" Arthur asked.

Trent shook his head. "Not on her own, if that's what you mean. I can see her helping Victor, but if he wasn't involved, then I can't see her playing a part in the killing. I'd put Aaron Crawford next, actually. We'd met a few times, and I always found him thoroughly disagreeable."

"But Lynda didn't think he and Joel had ever met," Margaret said.

"They met the day before Joel's murder," Trent replied. "And Aaron had upset Joel so much that Joel asked me about him. As I said, I'd met him a few times."

"What was wrong with him?" Margaret asked.

"Everyone who stayed at that resort was wealthy and well-connected. Aaron still seemed to feel as if he was superior to everyone else there. He was a stickler for the rules, unless he was the one who wanted to break them. We had a bit of a run-in over the proper use of the golf carts. I will admit that I was driving carelessly on the night in question. I'll even admit that I'd had a few drinks before I'd decided to drive back to my cottage. I should have known better, but it was a short drive, and the carts didn't go much faster than a fast walk, anyway."

Arthur chuckled. "Please don't tell me that you crashed a golf cart."

"Chocolate-raspberry cake," the waiter said, putting a plate in front of Margaret.

She smiled at the chocolate dome. Several raspberries were dotted around the plate. She ate one of them before she started on the cake. When she cut into it, a warm, rich, red, raspberry sauce ran out from the cake's center.

"I did not crash a golf cart," Trent said. "I didn't even scratch one. I might have only missed Aaron's cart by a few inches, but I did miss it. Aaron was furious and threatened to have me thrown out of the resort. I let him shout at me for far longer than I should have before I simply drove away."

"It sounds as if he had trouble controlling his temper," Arthur said.

"He did, indeed. And he'd fought with Joel earlier in the day. Perhaps when Joel got back to the airfield, Aaron was already there. Aaron was inordinately fond of his plane. Maybe he and Joel had another fight. I can almost picture it. Joel climbs into his plane, ready to fly back to New York. Aaron runs into the office and grabs the gun that we all knew was there. In my imagination, Aaron doesn't mean to kill anyone. He's just angry enough to want to make a point, so he jumps onto the wing and waves the gun at Joel, trying to frighten him.

I suspect, if it happened that way, that he was as surprised as Joel when the gun went off."

"Surely there would have been other people at the airfield," Margaret said.

"During the day, when flights were expected, there was a small team there. After hours, there was a single security guard who was responsible for keeping the planes safe. He sat in a shed at the gate to the field, a considerable distance away from where the planes were kept."

"Why was Joel there then? Could he have just gotten into his plane and flown away?" Margaret asked.

"I believe he'd arranged to fly out around six the next morning," Trent said. "I'm sure it was Lynda who told me that he'd decided to sleep in the plane so that he wouldn't disturb her when he got up in the morning."

"I can't imagine trying to sleep in a small plane," Margaret said.

Trent chuckled. "It was small, but the pilot's chair was pretty luxurious. It reclined, and I know for a fact that Joel had spent nights in the plane before. He loved that plane almost as much as he loved Lynda. Okay, if I'm honest, he might have loved the plane more."

"What else can I get for you today?" the waiter asked.

"I think we're done," Arthur said.

The man nodded. "Very good."

As he walked away, Margaret picked up her purse. "We need the check," she said.

"You don't get a bill here," Trent said. "Everything is simply added to the member's account."

Margaret frowned. "But I should pay for what I ate."

Arthur shook his head. "I'd have to pay for your meal whether you were here or not. In fact, if you weren't here, I'd have to pay more, because the penalty for not using your booking is more than what you ate today."

"I don't understand that at all," Margaret said.

Trent laughed. "This place finds new and creative ways to take our money at every turn. If the golf course wasn't so bloody brilliant, I'd never come back again."

"It was good seeing you again," Arthur said as they all stood up.

Trent nodded. "Likewise. And if you and the inspector don't work out and you want to try getting involved with an older and much wealthier man, give me a call," he said to Margaret, holding out a card.

"Lovely to have met you," Margaret said, turning and walking away while hoping that she'd done it fast enough to give the impression that she hadn't noticed the man's outstretched arm.

Arthur caught up to her in the parking lot.

"Trent wanted me to give you his card," he said as he unlocked the car doors. "I told him that I was your employer, not your matchmaker, and that I didn't feel it was appropriate for me to get involved. Having said that, if you ever decide you are interested in the man, I can give you his number."

Margaret waited to reply until they were in the car and on their way back to the office. "I can't imagine ever wanting Trent's number, but thanks."

Arthur chuckled. "And I didn't mean what I said. If you ever did come to me and say you were interested in Trent, I'd try to talk you out of it before I'd give you his number."

Back at the office, Margaret sent a quick text to Ted before she started working again. He hadn't replied by the time she was ready to head home.

He's probably just busy, she told herself as she drove back to her apartment. *You don't need to worry about him. He can take care of himself.* No amount of positive thoughts could keep her from worrying, though. She was thinking about sending another text as the elevator let her off on the top floor. Ted was standing outside her apartment, leaning on the wall. She rushed toward him and pulled him into a tight hug.

"Hi," he said with a laugh when she released him.

"I wasn't worried," she said. "Okay, I was a little bit worried."

"Worried? Why?"

"You never replied to my text."

Ted frowned and pulled out his phone. He tapped through a few screens and then sighed. "It never sent my reply. I just assumed that it had gone through. I probably closed the phone too quickly." He tapped on the screen again. A moment later, Margaret's phone buzzed.

"'I'll see you at your flat before six,'" she read.

"And here I am."

Margaret kissed him again. "Here you are," she said softly, happy in his arms.

"And I'm starving," Ted said a few minutes later. "I had an early lunch because I had an appointment with Victor and Lynda King in the afternoon. Then I spent hours dealing with them. Let's get dinner now."

"Were they difficult?" Margaret asked.

"Let's just say they didn't make things easy for me. I'll tell you more over dinner if you can be ready to go in five minutes."

Margaret laughed. "I can be ready in two minutes, but you'll have to feed Katie."

They walked out of the apartment together just a few minutes later.

"You can't repeat any of this," Ted said on the way to the lobby. "But I need to complain to someone."

"Complain away."

"I arranged to meet Mr. and Mrs. King at their home. When I arrived, I was shown into a parlor or a formal sitting room or something. It was a big room with hard, uncomfortable furniture and a grand piano."

"This is the house that Lynda used to share with Joel, right?"

Ted nodded. The elevator doors slid open. They walked outside.

"Where to?"

"We could get fish and chips and eat on the promenade," Ted suggested.

"That sounds good."

"And it will be quick."

The nearest chippy was only a few doors away. They ordered and paid and then took their food to the nearest bench on the promenade.

"Where was I?"

"In a stuffy parlor waiting to talk to Victor and Lynda."

Ted made a face and ate a fry. After he swallowed, he nodded.

"They kept me waiting for nearly half an hour. I thought about leaving and then sending a car to bring them down to the station, but I decided it was better not to upset anyone at this stage."

"That was probably wise," Margaret said while Ted took a bite of fish.

"Eventually, Mr. and Mrs. King joined me. We exchanged polite hellos before Mr. King told me that we were just waiting for his solicitor and then we could get started."

"They brought in a lawyer?"

Ted nodded. "And not just any lawyer. They brought in a London solicitor who works in criminal defense."

"That seems very much like what a guilty person might do."

Ted laughed. "I said as much when the solicitor finally arrived. To be fair, Mr. King agreed with me, but he insisted that he was simply doing what he felt he needed to do in order to protect himself and his wife."

"Protect them from what?"

"I believe they thought that having a solicitor there would keep me from asking too many difficult questions."

"Did it?"

"Not at all. I might have phrased them a bit more carefully, but I still asked every question on my list. Of course, the solicitor stepped in several times to suggest that the questions were unnecessary, but I think he just wanted to be seen to be doing something. I'm certain he was charging them a fortune for his time."

"Did they answer the questions in spite of him?"

"Most of them. We really just went back over everything that happened thirty-five years ago. Most of their answers matched what they'd told the police at the time. The few discrepancies can easily be explained away when you consider how much time has passed."

"What did you think of them?"

Ted frowned. "That's a difficult question. They were both polite but distant. Of course, I'm just a lowly police inspector, and not at all the sort of person they typically associate with. I suspect they would have been much nicer to your Aunt Fenella than they were to me."

"Because she's also rich."

"Exactly."

Margaret sighed. "Wait until you meet Trent Walsh."

Ted raised an eyebrow. "Was he awful? You said in your text that you had lunch with him. How did that even happen?"

Margaret told him all about her unexpected lunch plans and how Trent had invited himself to join them. She did her best to repeat as much of the conversation as she could remember.

"He accused drug dealers and Victor and said that he could see Aaron being angry enough to grab the gun and wave it at Joel," she remembered. "And then we started talking about why Joel was at the airfield in the middle of the night. He said he thought Joel was probably planning to sleep in his plane so that he could leave early the next morning," she concluded.

Ted nodded. "That was what Lynda told the police at the time. She said as much again today, but I never told you that."

"Is it possible that Joel interrupted a drug deal?"

"Anything is possible, but traffic in and out of the airfield was monitored twenty-four hours a day. At least it was supposed to be monitored at all times. Howard went back through the notes and from what he read, it is very unlikely that anything illegal was being done at Collins Airfield at that time. Howard did say that he would be less confident in making that statement today."

"Oh? That's worrying."

"The resort is still there, but another property has been built nearby. It caters to a younger crowd. It's an all-inclusive sort of destination with an indoor pool complex and several bars. Howard said that it wouldn't surprise him to learn that recreational drugs are among the offerings available there, if you find the right person to ask."

"How awful."

Ted shrugged. "Howard said they've sent undercover cops to the resort on a couple of occasions, but none of them ever found anything. I suggested that they were simply saying they hadn't found anything in the hopes of being sent again."

They both laughed.

"Let's take a walk," Ted suggested. "I'm feeling far less cross with the world now. It's a beautiful night. Let's enjoy it for an hour or so and then go to the pub."

"Perfect," Margaret said.

"Do you want ice cream or something?"

Margaret shook her head. "I'm getting far too fond of desserts and cakes and ice cream. I never ate sweets when I lived in the US. I think the sea air makes me crave sweets."

"Everything in moderation."

"I know, but I had a lovely chocolate cake with raspberries at lunch today. I don't need a second dessert."

Ted nodded. They threw away their garbage and then started a slow stroll. Ted took her hand and squeezed it gently. Margaret took a deep breath and exhaled slowly.

"I do love it here," she said.

"I do, too, but this has always been home. I can't help but wonder if I'd be happy living anywhere else."

"You spent two years in Liverpool. Did you like it there?"

"I did enjoy my time there, but that was partly because I knew I was only going to be there for two years. Just about anything is bearable if you know exactly when it will end."

"I suppose that's true. Tell me about Liverpool. I've never been."

Ted talked about Liverpool and then Manchester, another city where he'd spent some time. "We should take some trips," he suggested as they reached the end of the promenade and turned around. "We could spend a long weekend in Liverpool or Chester, maybe."

"We should definitely start planning something," Margaret said. "I don't know that I'm going to stay on the island forever. I need to see as much of England and also Europe as I can while I'm living here."

They were still talking about all the places Margaret wanted to see when Margaret heard someone calling Ted's name.

"Inspector Hart?"

When they turned around, Margaret smiled at Harry and Tara Mackey, who were walking toward them, waving.

11

"Good evening," Ted said when the couple reached them.

"We saw you as we were driving past," Harry said. "I was certain we were going to have to chase you all the way down the promenade."

"And I told him to leave you be," Tara said. "It's obvious that you are out enjoying a lovely evening with your special friend. The last thing you want to do is talk about our problems."

"Our problems are his job," Harry said.

"But only during working hours," Tara replied.

"Police inspectors are always working," Margaret said.

Ted shrugged. "I wish I could disagree, but she's right. We are always working – or almost always, anyway."

"See?" Harry said to Tara.

"We were just hoping for an update," Tara said to Ted, sounding apologetic.

"I wish I had one for you. The fire is really Mark Hammersmith's investigation. I was out of the office for most of the day. I didn't see Mark."

"We'll let you get on with your evening," Tara said. "Sorry for interrupting."

"It's not a problem," Ted said.

"Is the Fire Inspector absolutely certain it was arson?" Harry asked.

Ted looked at Margaret.

"Why don't you walk with us for a bit?" she suggested. "Or we could sit on a bench."

"I'd love to walk," Tara said. "I miss walking on the promenade. I used to walk the entire thing at least once a day unless it was blowing a gale."

"It's a lovely place to walk," Margaret replied. "I love watching the water. It's a picture that changes constantly."

The two women fell into step together behind the men. Tara nodded toward them.

"Do you want to listen to Harry talk about the fire?" she asked.

"Not at all. How are you?" Margaret replied.

Tara frowned. "I'm mostly okay, except when I'm not, which isn't at all a proper answer."

"I can't imagine how it would feel to wake up to a fire. It must have been terrifying. I think I'd struggle to sleep for weeks or even months after."

"I'm doing better. I made Harry buy an extra smoke detector for the hotel room, which is silly, because they have an entire system throughout the entire hotel. It makes me feel better, though, having an extra one."

"I don't blame you. I think I'd want a fire extinguisher, too."

Tara flushed. "It's just a small one, but it would help us get out in an emergency."

"Which is very sensible of you."

"I hope so. It's difficult to know if I'm being sensible or paranoid."

"I don't think it matters. If the fire extinguisher helps you sleep at night, that's what matters."

"It's very kind of you to say that. I appreciate it."

"I hope the children are coping with the situation."

Tara sighed. "That's a rather more difficult question."

"It's a lovely night, isn't it?" Margaret asked. "I've been told you can walk to the Tower of Refuge once or twice a year."

Tara chuckled. "Thank you, but I don't mind talking about the children. I might even feel better if I do talk about them. Where should I start? Neil or Cassie? You've never met either of them, have you?"

"I have met Cassie. She and Boris joined me and some of my work colleagues for lunch on Monday. Arthur Park invited them because there weren't any empty tables at the café where we were dining."

"What did you think of Boris?"

"He seemed nice enough."

Tara nodded slowly. "It's probably just me, imagining things."

"What things?"

She looked at Ted and then back at Margaret. "You're going to repeat what I say to him, aren't you?"

Margaret nodded. "If I think it's relevant to the investigation into the fire, then yes."

Tara sighed. "Harry told me that I'm imagining things. He's always thought the world of Boris. He'll be angry if he finds out that I said anything."

"He doesn't have to know. I won't say anything to Ted in front of Harry."

"The thing is, Boris seems happy."

Margaret waited for Tara to continue, but the woman said nothing for several seconds.

"I'm not sure I understand," she said eventually.

"Because I don't know how to explain myself properly," Tara said with a sigh. "Cassie and Boris met years ago. They were together for a long time before they decided to get married. The marriage, though, was a disaster. I've no idea what happened, but I do know that Cassie moved out of Boris's house just a few weeks after the wedding."

"That seems odd."

"What was even more strange is that she kept working for him. She told us at the time that they'd realized that they couldn't be married to one another, but that didn't mean that they couldn't still be friends. Cassie filed for divorce, but she kept her job."

"They seemed quite happy together when I met them."

"That's just it. They are quite happy together. Too happy."

"Too happy?"

"I didn't see much of Boris after the marriage fell apart. Cassie moved into the flat with us. She went back and forth to work, so she was still seeing him every day, but he wasn't visiting her at our flat and we weren't eating at his restaurant. I did bump into him once or twice in different places and he was always polite, but he also seemed quite sad on both occasions."

"Maybe the divorce was Cassie's idea, and he didn't really want the marriage to end."

"I did wonder that, but when I asked Cassie, she insisted that the decision had been mutual. She said that she and Boris had both realized that it wasn't working for them. She also pointed out that she was still working for Boris, so clearly he didn't feel as if she'd dumped him."

"I suppose that makes sense."

Tara nodded. "But that doesn't change the fact that Boris seemed unhappy when I saw him. Now maybe he'd just had bad days on both occasions or maybe other things were happening that were making him sad, but he just seemed off to me."

"But now he doesn't?"

"No, he doesn't. I'm seeing a lot more of him, of course, because Cassie is staying with him. Harry and I have been eating lunch at his restaurant most days. We're still staying in a hotel, so we don't have a kitchen or any way to prepare meals. Boris's restaurant is nice, and we get to see Cassie when we eat there." She flushed. "And Boris won't let us pay for our meals there, either, so it's cost-effective. We're still working with the insurance company on everything, so we're being very frugal at the moment."

"That's kind of him."

"It is, which is another reason why I hate to say anything unkind about him."

"But he's happier now than he was after the divorce."

"He's definitely happier now that Cassie is living with him again. And that worries me. It worries me because I'm afraid that he started the fire with that as his goal."

"Surely he could have just asked her to move back in with him."

"He could have. He might have actually done so. But Cassie was happy on her own. She'd actually gone out a few times with a couple of different guys. She was getting on with her life. I kept telling her that she needed to find a new job if she was going to properly move on, but she loves that café."

"So you think Boris started the fire?"

"I think he had a strong motive. I definitely think he was the person who gained the most from the fire. Harry and I are homeless. No amount of insurance money is going to make up for the emotional distress that going through the fire has caused me. And Neil has been a mess since the fire. Arguably, he was a mess before the fire, though."

"Oh?"

She sighed again. "We did everything we could to raise our children correctly. We taught them right from wrong, and we thought that we'd given them a healthy respect for the law. And then Neil turned his back on everything he knew was right in pursuit of a bit of extra money."

"I'm sorry."

"He had such a brilliant future ahead of him. He was doing so very well, until he let himself get tempted by the idea of easy money. There's no such thing, of course. Oh, some people do get lucky and inherit a fortune, but for most of us, such things are the stuff of dreams, not our reality."

"Aunt Fenella was very fortunate."

Tara looked surprised. "Oh, of course. I'd forgotten who I am speaking to for a moment. I didn't mean any offense."

"None taken."

"Anyway, Neil made a stupid mistake and then, when things started to go wrong, he compounded his error until he ended up losing everything and having to come back to the island. It's impossible for him to find work if he's honest about his past. And someone just told me that he recently had dinner with the man who got him to break the law in the first place. I'm terrified that Neil is going to get desperate enough to go to work for him."

"Neil is an adult. You have to let him make his own choices."

"Now you sound like Harry. I know that he's an adult, and I'm trying to let him make his own choices, but it's incredibly difficult to sit back and watch your child make bad choices. When he was across, I thought everything was going well. I had no idea that there were problems until everything had already gone horribly wrong. Now he's here and I'm struggling with wanting to know where he is at every minute of every day. I want to protect him from himself."

"I can understand that, but you have to trust that he's learned from his mistakes."

"I truly thought he had until I found out he'd been socializing with the man who got him into trouble in the first place. I just wish someone on the island would give him a chance. If he could find a decent job and get his own flat, I think he'd be okay."

"I'll let you know if I hear of anyone who is hiring."

"I'd appreciate that." Tara sighed deeply. "After everything I said about Boris, you'll probably just laugh, but there's a little bit of me that wonders if Neil's former associate was the one who started the fire."

"Oh?"

"He and Neil had dinner together after the fire. What if the man started the fire in order to make Neil's life so awful that Neil would go back to work for him?"

"Starting a fire seems a bit extreme. If things are as bad as you say they are, surely he just has to wait until Neil feels he has no other choice?"

Tara nodded. "I want to believe that, mostly because the idea that a known criminal is targeting my son terrifies me."

"Is Neil still staying with you?"

"He is. He doesn't have anywhere else to go."

"Where are you staying?"

Tara named a nearby hotel.

"I'll call you there if I hear about any jobs."

"Thank you, dear. I just hope Neil stays away from that man until something materializes. Last night he was talking about going back across. He said maybe he could settle somewhere on the other side of the country where no one would know anything about him."

"But you'd prefer it if he stayed here."

"He's my son. I was happy that he was able to build a life across, but I missed him terribly. The only advantage to him leaving the island again is that the man I mentioned earlier is here. Leaving would get Neil away from his evil influence."

"But we're neglecting our better halves," Harry said loudly. He turned around and smiled at Tara and Margaret. "I suppose you're having a lovely chat about hats or your favorite movies or something."

Tara nodded. "Or something," she said. "Have you finished talking with Ted, then?"

Harry glanced at Ted and shrugged. "He can't tell me anything. I suspect that's because there hasn't been any progress."

They all stopped in front of Promenade View.

"I've been thinking that we should sell the flat," Harry said.

Tara nodded. "I've been thinking the same thing. We won't get much for it in its current state, though."

"But we'll get the insurance money on top of whatever we can get for the flat. I think I'd rather do that than get all of the necessary work done. We wouldn't be able to move back in until the work was finished, and that could take months. If we sell it 'as is' and take the insurance money, we could probably buy something else in a week or two."

"We could buy a little house," Tara said.

Harry sighed. "Or we could buy another flat. I'm not certain I want to go back to looking after a garden."

"A larger flat, with three bedrooms," Tara said.

"The children aren't going to be staying with us forever. Two bedrooms are plenty."

Tara shook her head. "I want three, and I'd quite like a small garden again. I miss being able to sit outside on our property to watch the world go past."

"Maybe we could move out of Douglas."

Tara looked surprised. "Out of Douglas?" she repeated. Then she shook her head. "Ted and Margaret don't need to listen to all of this. I'm certain they have better things to do. And we should get back to the hotel. Neil should be there by now."

"And he needs lots of looking after," Harry muttered as he turned and started to walk away.

"Thank you for a lovely chat," Tara said to Margaret before she turned and rushed after her husband.

"Did you and Harry have an interesting conversation?" Margaret asked Ted.

He shook his head. "He wanted me to tell him everything I know about the investigation into the fire. Once I'd done that, because I don't know much, he insisted that I was withholding information."

"Oh dear. Tara had some interesting things to say."

"Do you want to talk here or in the pub?"

Margaret thought for a moment. "Let's talk here. I'd rather talk about more pleasant things in the pub."

She told him everything she could remember from her conversation with Tara. When she was finished, Ted rang Mark and repeated some of what Tara had said about Boris to him.

"I think he needs a closer look," Ted concluded. "Maybe you should bring him in for questioning."

When Ted slipped his phone back into his pocket, Margaret smiled at him. "What did Mark say?"

"He's going to talk to a few people who know Boris. He's curious to see if anyone else thinks Boris is happier than he had been before the fire. He's probably also going to bring Boris in for questions later in the week."

"Very good. And now we can go and have a drink and forget all about the fire."

"And everything else. What should we talk about?"

"Harry suggested that Tara and I were probably talking about hats. I don't know that I've ever spent anytime talking about hats."

Ted laughed. "Do you ever wear hats?"

They were discussing the pros and cons of various types of hats and caps as they walked into the Tale and Tail. A single customer was sitting at the bar, sipping a drink. When they reached the bartender, he nodded at them.

"It's busy upstairs," he said. "A large group came in after a funeral to drown their sorrows. They've moved nearly all of the chairs and couches together on one side of the room. The last time I went up to clear away glasses, there were still a few chairs scattered around the rest of the space, though."

Margaret looked at Ted. "We could just go home."

"Or we could have one drink. If we can't find anywhere to sit upstairs, we could always sit at the bar."

"Good point."

The bartender poured their usual drinks. They thanked him before they headed for the winding stairs. When they reached the upper level, they steered clear of the small crowd that was clustered in one corner. On the opposite side of the room, they found two small couches that had been pushed together around a tiny table near the elevator. As Margaret sat down, Ted moved over to sit next to her.

"If anyone else comes, we'll have to let them join us," Ted said, nodding toward the other couch.

"That's fine. We can talk about hats with strangers."

They were debating the relative merits of berets when another couple walked out of the elevator. They looked around, with frowns on their faces, before having a quick conversation. When they looked around again, Ted waved.

"I don't believe it," he muttered as the couple walked toward them.

"Inspector Hart? This is a surprise," the man said.

Margaret thought he looked at least eighty. The woman with him appeared younger, but it seemed obvious that she'd had some cosmetic procedures over the years. Margaret smiled at them.

"Mr. and Mrs. King, hello," Ted said.

"Please, join us," Margaret suggested.

The couple exchanged glances before they, seemingly reluctantly, sat down together on the other couch.

"Is it always this busy?" the man asked as he put his drink on the table.

"You never know with the Tale and Tail," Margaret said. "It can be very popular."

"Margaret Woods, this is Victor King and his wife, Lynda," Ted said. "Mr. and Mrs. King, this is Margaret Woods."

"In social situations, you're welcome to call us by our Christian names," Victor said, sounding as if he thought he was granting them a huge favor.

"Thank you," Ted said, winking at Margaret.

"It's very nice to meet you both," Margaret said. "I had lunch today with a friend of yours."

"Oh? With whom did you dine?" Lynda asked, her tone suggesting that she didn't expect Margaret to actually know anyone she would consider a friend.

"Trent Walsh."

There was an awkward silence before Lynda gave her a small smile. "I'm not certain I'd consider him a friend, exactly," she said.

Margaret shrugged. "He told me that he and your former husband were like brothers."

Lynda chuckled. "Did he really? What a ridiculous notion. He and Joel did business together when it suited Joel to work with him. There was nothing more to the relationship than that."

"I had a similar relationship with Joel," Victor added. "And I would never presume to suggest that we were anything more than business associates."

Margaret took a sip of her drink while she tried to think of an appropriate reply or maybe a complete change of subject.

"Have you spoken to Trent yet?" Lynda asked Ted.

Ted shook his head. "I'm interviewing him tomorrow."

"Interesting," Lynda said.

Margaret reached for her drink again during another awkward silence.

"We should ring Norman," Victor said.

Lynda frowned. "I'd agree if he'd been even the slightest bit helpful earlier today."

"But now we're drinking. We might say the wrong thing," Victor said.

"I won't," Lynda snapped.

Victor frowned. "If you start asking questions, I'm going to ring my solicitor," he told Ted.

"I have no intention of asking you any questions," Ted said.

"And I'll keep mine to polite small talk," Margaret said. "Do you visit the Tale and Tail often?"

Lynda shrugged. "Define often."

"Once a month," Margaret said, already tired of being nice to difficult people.

"Then no," Lynda said.

Margaret was torn between trying again with another question and simply giving up and finishing her drink so that she and Ted could leave. While she was debating with herself, Victor downed half of the contents of his glass of amber liquid and then put the glass down.

"We come here a couple of times a year," he said. "We used to know the owners, when it was a private home. Lynda and I spent many hours in this library, discussing books and other things. We visit when we're feeling nostalgic for the island the way it was thirty years ago."

Margaret smiled at him. "Was it very different?"

"Yes and no, which doesn't seem like a proper answer, but it's the best I can do. Many things have changed on the island over the years. But many things have also remained the same. Some of the things that made me want to move here when I first visited the island are things that have changed, though. If I were to visit for the first time now, I don't think I would make the island my home."

"Oh? Why not?" Margaret asked.

Victor shrugged and reached for his glass.

"It isn't the island that's changed, or not so much," Lynda said. "The problem is that we've lost so many of our friends. The island feels very different when you feel quite alone in the world."

Victor nodded. "When I first arrived, Joel and Lynda were already living here. Joel managed to persuade me to buy a property here as well. He also convinced Trent to make the island his home. We all had extensive circles of friends, and they all used to come and visit the island for weeks on end, year after year."

"And then Joel died," Lynda interjected. "And nothing was ever the same again."

Victor nodded. He reached over and took her hand. "I love my wife dearly. We've been married for over thirty years. But I'd trade all of our years together to have Joel back."

Lynda frowned for a moment and then sighed. "I suppose I should say the same, but I'm not certain that I would give up everything that Victor and I have experienced in order to bring Joel back. I loved him dearly, but he could be difficult as well. And my second marriage has brought me a lot of joy."

Victor smiled at her. "Thank you, my dear. I've always believed that you still miss Joel."

"I do miss him. I'll always miss him. But I'm realistic enough to know that if he were still alive, we'd probably no longer be together. Joel had a short attention span when it came to women. If his first divorce hadn't cost him so much money, he might have been quicker to end things between us."

"He loved you very much," Victor said.

Lynda shrugged. "We were starting to have problems. I was getting tired of some of his annoying habits. No doubt he was getting tired of mine as well. I kept expecting him to start cheating, but I don't believe he ever did. The night he died, I truly believed that he'd gone to spend the night with another woman. When the resort manager came and told me that he was dead, my first thought was that he'd had a heart attack while sleeping with another woman."

"Would that have been easier to accept than what actually happened?" Victor asked her.

"Maybe. I don't know. I'd already steeled myself to accept him cheating on me. It was just what men in our social circle did."

"I never cheated," Victor told her.

Lynda gave him a small smile. "Which is surprising, considering your past."

"I told you thirty-four years ago that you were the first woman with whom I'd ever truly fallen in love. Once I'd found you, I never wanted to do anything that might make me lose you."

"And they lived happily ever after," Lynda said lightly.

Victor chuckled. "I certainly hope so."

Lynda looked at Margaret. "When I first came to the island, I hated it."

"Really? Why?" Margaret asked.

"It was already Joel's home. We met when he was in Chicago. My family owned several businesses there. Joel came to meet with my father and his partners to discuss buying into one of the businesses. I was working for my father as a sort of assistant. The meeting didn't take long. At the end of it, Joel made an offer, contingent on me having dinner with him that evening. I knew my father was eager to make the deal, so I said yes."

"I would have said no on principle," Margaret said.

Lynda chuckled. "Things were done differently forty years ago. My father would have been furious if I'd said no. Joel was an attractive and wealthy man. My father would have expected me to say yes to just about any man, though. It was just dinner. He didn't expect me to sleep with anyone or anything."

"You've never told me this story," Victor said.

"It never came up," Lynda said. "We don't talk about Joel."

Victor nodded. "It's a difficult subject."

"But you were telling me why you didn't like the island," Margaret said.

"Oh, yes, I was, wasn't I? Joel and I had dinner together that night. I suppose it's fair to say that he swept me off my feet. I'd led a fairly sheltered life, really. I hadn't really dated much, in part because my father rarely approved of anyone. He liked Joel, though. Joel was wealthy, and he owned properties all over the world. We got married only a few weeks after that first dinner together."

"You made me wait a lot longer," Victor said with a small chuckle.

"I was in mourning for a while."

He nodded. "And even after a year, many of the island's gossips said it was too soon."

"Did you get married in the US?" Margaret asked Lynda.

"To Joel, yes. To Victor, no. Victor and I got married on the island, but Joel and I got married in Chicago. Then we started traveling. My parents didn't enjoy traveling and my father's business interests, although considerable, were all in one place. Traveling with Joel felt almost like magic. We got on a plane and when we got off, we were in a place where everyone spoke a different language, had different customs, ate different foods. I loved it."

"We should have traveled more when we were young," Victor said.

"After what happened to Joel, I didn't want to travel any longer," Lynda said. "But for the first months of our marriage, Joel and I went many places."

"That sounds lovely," Margaret said.

"It was lovely. We got to know each other better, and I got to see the world. Then we arrived on the Isle of Man. Joel had told me many things about the island, but I wasn't prepared for what I found here."

"No? What hadn't he told you?" Ted asked.

Lynda shrugged. "For a start, he'd neglected to mention that his ex-wife was living in a house on the grounds of his estate. That came as something of a shock. If you've met Donna, you might not be surprised to hear that she hated me without even knowing me."

"That must have been difficult for you," Margaret said.

"It was difficult because we were neighbors. The estate has beautiful gardens. I used to want to walk for hours through them, but every path seemed to wind its way past Donna's house. And, inevitably, whenever Joel and I strolled anywhere near it, she'd either be coming in or going out. Joel would always look the other way, but I always felt as if I should wave or nod and smile or something. It was unbelievably awkward."

"What else didn't you like about the island?"

"The weather, the limited number of shops, the way everyone knew everyone else and their business, the palm trees that don't seem as if they really belong here. I could go on, but I won't. Suffice to say that I didn't like much of anything, really, but I loved Joel, so I stayed. Over time, of course, I came to love the island, but that took years. If Joel and I had split up, I'm fairly certain I would have gone back to Chicago."

"But you stayed after his death," Margaret said.

"Because I fell in love again," Lynda said, giving Victor an affectionate look. "Victor was one of our first visitors when Joel and I arrived on the island after our marriage. We became friends. Joel and I used to laugh about the number of women who went in and out of Victor's life. I think his longest relationship lasted no more than six weeks."

"I was with Helene for seven weeks," Victor said. He shook his head. "I had a lot of fun, but I never fell in love. I never expected to fall in love, either. After Joel's death, I went to see Lynda to offer my support. I knew she had to be devastated. I wanted to be a good friend."

"And he was, for many months. Oh, I know people started talking about us within days, but for a very long time we were simply friends," Lynda said.

"It took every bit of courage I had and a gin and tonic before I worked up the nerve to tell her that I'd fallen in love with her," Victor said. "And I only did so because she was thinking of leaving the island."

"Up until that evening, I'd never thought about Victor in that way," Lynda said. "But as soon as he confessed his feelings, I suddenly realized that I'd been falling in love with him, too. Still, we took it very slowly. It was another six months before we finally got married."

"And then we lived happily ever after," Victor said before finishing his drink.

Lynda nodded. "We have been very happy together. That doesn't mean that I've forgotten Joel, though. I want more than anything for you to find the person who killed him," she said to Ted.

"We're working on it," Ted replied.

Lynda looked as if she had more to say, but Victor slowly got to his feet. "Our car will be here," he said.

"Oh, of course," Lynda said. She finished her drink and then slowly stood up. "Thank you for an interesting conversation," she said.

Margaret nodded. "It was nice meeting you."

She and Ted watched as the pair walked back to the elevator. As the car doors slid shut behind them, Ted sat back in his seat.

"That was interesting," he said.

"Indeed."

"That they came here tonight was either a strange coincidence or part of a careful plan."

"What do you mean?"

"I mean, everyone on the island knows that your aunt used to frequent the Tale and Tail. Many people probably know that you enjoy coming here as well. It isn't a stretch to imagine that Victor and Lynda came here tonight hoping to find us with the intention of sharing their love story with us."

"They didn't tell you all of that when you spoke earlier?"

"I was informed by their solicitor that they would only answer questions about the murder investigation, so I limited my questions to events over that weekend. Perhaps Victor and Lynda thought it would be useful to give me some additional perspective on their relationship."

Margaret frowned. "I hate the idea that they engineered all of that."

"I'm not saying that they did. I'm just saying it's possible."

12

They finished their drinks before Ted walked Margaret back to her apartment.

"Good luck with Trent tomorrow," Margaret said at her door.

"Thanks. I'm looking forward to meeting him now."

"If he says anything inappropriate about me, punch him."

"I might want to, but I also want to keep my job."

They kissed and then Margaret watched as he walked to the elevators.

Mona was sitting on one of the couches. "Tell me everything," she said.

Margaret sighed. "Everything? That will take ages."

"You've had a busy day, then."

"So busy that I'm convinced you're manipulating people."

"We've been through all of that. I'm not going to waste my limited energy denying anything. Who did you see today, then?"

"I had lunch with Trent Walsh, a stroll with Harry and Tara Mackey, and then drinks with Victor and Lynda King."

"My goodness, you have been busy. Start with Trent. I'm sure he was charming, or at least that he tried to be charming."

"Maybe he thought he was being charming. I thought he was being creepy."

Mona grinned. "I always thought the same about him. I don't suppose you talked about the murder?"

"We did, a bit."

Mona followed Margaret into the kitchen, where Margaret made herself a cup of tea. Then they sat together at the table while Margaret told her all about the various conversations she'd had with people throughout the day.

"So Boris started the fire," Mona said when Margaret was finished. "That much seems obvious."

"Unless it was one of Neil's unsavory friends."

Mona shook her head. "I know Kevin Mars well enough to be fairly confident that he didn't start the fire. He's a criminal, but a criminal with his own code of honor. He'd never do anything to coerce or force anyone to work with him. Regardless, if he had an issue with Neil, he'd confront Neil directly. I can't imagine him doing something that put innocent people's lives at stake."

"And you think Boris would?"

"I think Boris wanted Cassie back. It certainly sounds as if he's quite happy with the current situation, anyway. If I were in charge of the investigation, I'd put my focus on Boris."

"Great, so you've solved that case. What about Joel's murder?"

Mona sat back in her chair. "That's a very different matter. I used to visit the Tale and Tail regularly, and I don't ever recall seeing Victor and Lynda there. I suppose it's possible that we simply missed one another on our visits, but that seems unlikely."

"So you think they went there tonight to try to find Ted?"

"Perhaps. Or maybe they were looking for you. Maybe they were hoping that you'd provide a sympathetic ear and then take what you were told back to Ted."

"I think that's worse than thinking they were looking for Ted."

Mona laughed. "Regardless, I don't think it was a random coincidence."

"Does that mean you think that they killed Joel?"

"I'm not certain what I think. Trent seems a strong possibility, but their behavior tonight makes me suspect that Lynda and Victor were in on it together."

"Which is exactly what Trent suggested."

"And I hate the idea of agreeing with Trent about anything," Mona said with a small laugh.

Margaret yawned. "And now it's late, and I have to get up in the morning."

"You go to bed. I'm going to sit here and think for a few minutes."

"I'll see you tomorrow."

"We really need to talk to Jeremy and Aaron," Mona said. "I wonder if either of them has ever been to the island."

"I doubt it. And I can't imagine why either of them would decide to visit now. It's possible that neither of them is even aware that the island exists."

Mona grinned. "Maybe I should do something about that."

Before Margaret could reply, Mona slowly faded away.

***

On Thursday morning, when Margaret got to work, Joney was on the telephone. She waved at Margaret, gesturing for her to wait.

"I'll let Mr. Park know. Thank you for ringing," she said after a minute. She put the phone down and shook her head. "We don't get many complaints, but the ones we do get are incredible."

"Oh?"

"It doesn't matter. I forgot to ask you about the murder investigation yesterday. Tell me everything."

Margaret laughed. "Are you free for lunch?"

"Yes, let's go somewhere for lunch."

The morning seemed to fly past. When she went back to the lobby to meet Joney for lunch, Rachel was there as well.

"Joney says we're going to be talking about murder," Rachel said.

Margaret shrugged. "We don't have to, but we can."

"I read the article in the local paper," Rachel replied. "It's fascinating. I'm amazed the police are reopening the case, really. It's been such a long time."

"They never actually close murder investigations until they find the killer," Margaret told her.

"Let's hope they find the killer now, then," she replied.

"Let's go right today," Rachel said as the three women walked outside. "Maybe it will be less busy there."

The small café was mostly empty. They took a table at the back and ordered drinks while they looked over the menu.

"If it isn't busy, we won't get to have lunch with random strangers," Rachel said as she put her menu down.

"I don't think that's a bad thing," Margaret said.

They ordered lunch before Joney started talking about Joel's murder. Margaret let Joney and Rachel do most of the talking. She felt oddly reluctant to admit that she'd met most of the suspects over the past few days, although she did mention meeting Trent in case Arthur had already said something to Joney about it.

"I wish the police luck," Rachel said as they walked back to the office. "It seems an impossible task after so many years."

Back at the office, Margaret focused on her work for the rest of the day. It wasn't until she was driving home that she remembered that Elaine had mentioned seeing her again on Thursday.

"Maybe she's busy doing other things," Margaret muttered as she parked her car in the garage.

When she got to her floor, she found Ted waiting outside of her apartment again.

"What a lovely surprise," she said as she leaned in for a kiss.

"Things are fairly quiet right now. If I wasn't working on the cold case, I wouldn't have much of anything to do," he replied. "Okay, that isn't true. The island has plenty of its own cold cases for me to go through, but those are a lower priority than cases where we've been asked to assist by another jurisdiction."

"Really? That seems odd."

Ted shrugged. "We want to be seen to be as cooperative as possible, just in case we ever need help from Canada. Their cold case isn't as important as any current cases I might have, but at the moment, Mark is dealing with the fire, and my case file is pretty empty."

"That's good news, of course," Margaret said.

"Since it's early, what if we went to the shops and bought the ingredients and cooked dinner?" Ted asked. "I'm getting tired of eating in restaurants every night."

"I was thinking that same thing earlier. You're usually working so much that I get to cook several nights each week. I haven't cooked this week at all. But we don't need to go to the store. I have plenty in the kitchen. What sounds good?"

Ted frowned. "This would be easier if you had a menu."

"Ah, but what fun would that be? Tell me about your favorite childhood foods and then I'll just make you something random that you might not like and charge you whatever I feel like charging."

They both laughed and then decided together on a stir fry. Margaret chopped up the chicken while Ted sliced various vegetables. Once Margaret got the rice started, she heated up the wok. Twenty minutes later, the pair sat down to eat.

"This is wonderful," Ted said.

"You did the hard part."

"I forgot how much I enjoy cooking. I never bother when I'm home alone. We should do this more often, though."

"We really should. It's much healthier for us. It costs a lot less. And we don't have to worry about running into the suspects in your latest murder investigation."

Ted shook his head. "It's decidedly odd how often that happens."

"I think I've met everyone now, aside from the two men who don't live on the island."

"Yes, well, I can't imagine any reason why either of them would be here. You've met everyone involved in the fire investigation, too, haven't you?"

Margaret nodded. "I think Mark needs to take a good look at Boris."

"Oh, he is."

Ted loaded their plates into the dishwasher while Margaret looked through the cupboards and refrigerator for something sweet to finish the meal.

"What about vanilla ice cream with frozen berries on top?" she asked after a minute.

"I'd rather have hot fudge, but I suppose berries will do."

They'd just started on their ice cream when someone knocked on the door.

"It might be Elaine," Margaret told Ted as she got to her feet. "She said she'd come and see me tonight."

"Hello, hello," Elaine said brightly when Margaret opened the door. "I can't stay for long. Ernie and I are going somewhere fancy for dinner."

"How nice."

"It is, yes, but is there any news on the fire?"

Margaret hesitated before she shook her head. She wasn't about to repeat what Tara had said to her.

"What about the murder investigation? I read everything in the local paper, but that wasn't much. What else do you know about that?"

"Again, nothing, really," Margaret said.

Elaine sighed. "I'd love to go through all of the suspects with you, but I don't want to be late for dinner. Tell Ted that he needs to take a good look at the wife, though. She got married again with undue haste."

"I'll tell him."

Elaine nodded. "Ring me if you hear anything interesting. If I wasn't so busy with Ernie, I'd stay so we could talk through all of the suspects in both cases. Maybe another time."

As she walked away, Margaret shut the door. When she got back to the kitchen, her ice cream bowl was gone.

"I put it in the freezer so it wouldn't just be a puddle when you got back," Ted said.

After their treat, they watched an old movie on the TV until they were both yawning.

"It's Friday tomorrow," Margaret said as she walked Ted to the door. "Do you have to work this weekend?"

"I hope not. Not if it stays quiet."

She let him out and then got ready for bed. It wasn't until she was crawling under the duvet that she realized that she hadn't seen Mona all day.

"She was probably just busy," Margaret muttered. *Busy doing what?* a little voice whispered. The thought kept Margaret awake for a short while, but she finally managed to fall asleep.

◈

Friday was uneventful. Margaret went to work with a packed lunch full of things that would keep if anyone suggested going out. When she got to the office, she discovered that everyone else had other plans, though. She ate her lunch at her desk and finally shut her computer down not long after five. Joney had already left for the weekend. Margaret drove home feeling as if she hadn't really spoken to anyone all day.

"There's always Mona," she reminded herself as she rode the elevator to her floor. But when she got to her apartment, there was no sign of her ghostly roommate, either.

"I can talk to you," she said to Katie, who was playing with one of her toys in front of the windows.

Katie stared at her for a minute and then picked up the toy in her mouth and ran into Fenella's room. Margaret stared after her.

"Time to call Megan," she said loudly. The words seemed to echo around the apartment. Shaking her head, Margaret grabbed the phone.

"Hello?"

"Megan? It's Margaret."

"Hey, Big Sister. How are you?"

"I'm fine. How are you?"

"Busy. I'm job hunting."

"Job hunting? You have a job. You're on a paid sabbatical."

"Yeah, I know, but I've been thinking about looking around for something different."

"If you quit while you're on sabbatical, don't you lose the rest of the paid time off?"

"Well, yeah, but if the right job comes along, it would be silly not to take it."

"Surely you could wait to start looking until closer to the end of your sabbatical, though. You're supposed to be using this time to do something wonderful. Maybe you could visit your sister in another country."

Megan laughed. "I should do that. But if I wait, I might miss a wonderful opportunity."

"I thought you liked your job."

"Yeah, I do, but there are lots of other jobs out there."

"Megan, there's more to it than that. What aren't you telling me?"

Megan sighed. "I don't want you to argue with me."

"If you're making smart decisions, I won't argue with you."

"Exactly," Megan said with a chuckle. "But you think you should be the one who decides if the decision is smart or not."

"And I'm usually right."

"Not always."

"You're just trying to avoid telling me something."

"Carter and I have been talking about moving."

"Moving? Moving where?"

"I'm not sure. We've been talking about lots of options. He was living in New York City, but he doesn't want to go back there."

"So you're job hunting all over the US?"

"More or less. I'm looking at jobs that interest me and then looking to see where they're located. Would you come and visit me in Idaho?"

"I don't know."

Megan laughed. "You could at least say yes and then just always find excuses not to bother. But I'm your sister. You'll come and visit me wherever I am."

"Of course I will. But Idaho?"

"The job sounds really interesting. And Carter can work from anywhere."

"And how long have you been dating Carter?"

"A couple of months, but we both feel like we could be together for a long time."

"Is he still flying back and forth to New York regularly?"

"Yeah. He's there now, actually. He was supposed to call me an hour ago, to let me know he'd landed safely, but he hasn't called yet."

"Did you check on his flight? Has it landed?"

"I don't know what flight he's on."

"Why not?"

"He didn't say, and I didn't want to be nosy. It doesn't really matter. He'll call when he lands or when he gets to his hotel or wherever he's staying."

"You don't know where he's staying?"

"No, because I'm not nosy enough to grill him every time he goes away. I trust him."

"And I don't. Are you sure he's gone to New York?"

"Of course I'm sure he's gone to New York. He has to be in the office a few days each week. Otherwise, he can work from anywhere."

"It's Friday. Surely he doesn't have to work on the weekend?"

Megan was silent for a moment. "He probably has some weekend meetings," she said eventually. "Like I said, I trust him."

"Is he still staying with you?"

"Yes, and it's working out great, thanks. We really enjoy each other's company, and he kills spiders for me."

Margaret sighed. "You know I don't like that he's staying with you."

"I know, and when I told Carter that, he offered to move out. The problem is, he doesn't want to stay here long term. He doesn't want to sign a lease and be stuck here for months, especially not if I find my dream job and move away."

"Surely he could go back to staying with his fraternity brother friend."

"I think he might have worn out his welcome a bit there. He was only supposed to stay with them for a few days and then he met me. He ended up staying with them for over a month before he moved in here."

Margaret swallowed a sigh. She knew she needed to choose her words carefully. "Don't lend him any money. Don't invest in any incredible investment opportunities he offers you. Don't get pregnant."

"Is that it?"

Margaret laughed. "I could keep going, but I thought that was enough for today."

"I know you mean well, Big Sister. I do. But I'm old enough to make my own decisions, and smart enough not to get scammed. I won't be lending Carter any money. He has far more of it than I do. I won't be investing with him, because he only works with clients with high net worth. And I won't get pregnant. I don't even want children."

"And does Carter know that?"

"It hasn't come up."

"It should if you're talking about being together long term."

"I'm sure we'll work it out. But how are you? What's new on the island?"

Margaret told her about the fire and about Ted's cold case.

"Okay," Megan said when Margaret was finished. "Tell Ted to arrest Boris and Victor. I'm ninety percent certain that Boris set the fire. I'm only fifty-fifty on Victor, but he sounded not very nice."

"I liked him better than Trent."

"Okay, he can arrest Trent, then. I used to date a guy named Trent, though, and he was wonderful. I wonder what ever happened to Trent. If I can remember his last name, I'll have to look for him on social media."

"Just don't let Carter catch you looking for old boyfriends."

"Oh, he won't mind. He trusts me, too."

They chatted for a short while longer before they finally ended the call.

"You need to come and visit," Margaret said.

"Maybe I'll surprise you one of these days."

"I hope you do."

She put the phone down and then looked at the clock. "Where's Ted?" she muttered as her stomach rumbled. Ten minutes later, her phone buzzed.

> Sorry, I got held up at work. Want to meet me in Port St. Mary for dinner? That's where I ended up today.

> Why not?

Ted gave her the name and address for a hotel near the beach that had a restaurant that did good food.

> I'll be there as soon as I can.

She gave Katie her dinner and then got ready to go out, grabbing the keys to Mona's fancy sports car as she went. She didn't usually drive it because she knew how much it was worth, but it would make the trip to the south of the island faster and much more fun. The engine purred when she started the car. She was parking outside the hotel what felt like only moments later.

"I love that car," Ted said as he stood up from a bench overlooking the beach.

"I love it, too," she replied.

"Is that what I think it is?" an older man who was walking past asked.

"Probably," Margaret said.

The man, who appeared to be around seventy-five, sighed. "Do you know how many of those were made? It isn't a big number. I've only ever seen one of them before and it wasn't in this sort of condition. This one looks as if it's barely been driven. It's stunning."

"It isn't mine. It belongs to my aunt, but she lets me drive it."

"If it were mine, I wouldn't let anyone anywhere near it."

Margaret shrugged. "I try to take good care of it."

The man nodded as he slowly walked around the car. "I've always wanted to have a car like this. I worked with the very wealthy my entire life, but I never made enough money to afford something this special."

"What do you drive?" Margaret asked.

The man laughed. "I live in Canada. I have a very sensible four-wheel drive SUV. I'm also old enough to know that I'm too old to drive a car like that, even if I could afford one. What I'd really like to do, though, is sit behind the wheel, just for a minute. Would you mind terribly?"

Margaret looked at Ted, who appeared amused by the entire situation.

"Sure, why not?" she asked.

She unlocked the door and opened it for the man. He slid behind the wheel and gripped it tightly.

"Vroom, vroom," he said, grinning broadly. After a minute, he sighed and then slowly climbed back out of the car. It took him a moment to manage it.

"My knees don't work as well as they used to," he said. "The SUV is a lot easier to get in and out of. But thank you so very much for that. That was a thrill I never expected to get, especially not tonight."

"It was no problem," Margaret said.

The man bowed slightly. "And now you must let me buy you dinner to thank you. Both of you, of course."

"Oh, no, we can't do that," Margaret said. "It's not at all necessary."

"But I would like to do it anyway. I hate eating alone. I love to travel now that I'm retired, but I hate being alone whilst doing so. It's a terrible conundrum."

"We'll join you for dinner, but we'll pay, to thank you for visiting our lovely island," Ted offered.

"We can argue about that when the check comes," the man suggested. "I was planning on eating here," he added, nodding at the hotel. "I'm told the food is excellent."

"I was told the same thing," Ted said. "I've never been here before."

The trio walked into the hotel and then turned left into the small restaurant. They were shown to a table near the windows that gave them an excellent view of the beach.

"Before we go any further, I'm embarrassed that I haven't introduced myself," the man said. "I'm Jeremy Olson. This is my first visit to your lovely island. I'm retired now after spending a lifetime working in the hotel industry, most of it managing a luxury resort in Canada."

Margaret stared at the man. *Mona, what have you done?* she wondered.

"I'm Ted Hart. I'm a police inspector here on the island. At the moment, I'm working with the police in Canada on a cold case. I assume you remember Joel Ward?"

Jeremy flushed. "Of course I remember Joel. He wasn't the only guest who passed away at a property that I was managing over my career, but he was, fortunately, the only one who was murdered. I was thinking of trying to speak to someone from the local police while I was here, but I wasn't certain anyone would be interested in talking to me."

"I'm very interested in talking to you," Ted said.

"Then this was serendipitous," Jeremy replied.

"This is my girlfriend, Margaret Woods," Ted said after a short silence.

Margaret shook her head. "I'm sorry. I was so shocked to meet you that I forgot to introduce myself. I've met many of the people involved in the investigation over the past week. I never expected to meet you."

"It's an odd bit of timing," Jeremy said. "I've been planning to visit the island for decades. I always enjoyed talking with guests about the places where they had their homes. Joel always spoke very highly about the island, as did Trent Walsh and a handful of other guests. In the years when I was working, I never traveled. After being at a resort all day, every day, I was always happy just to stay home for a week or more when I took time off. But I started making plans to see the world as soon as I'd earned my first paycheck. The day after I retired, I started traveling."

"How wonderful for you," Margaret said.

"Where have you been?" Ted asked.

"I started with the US. I wanted to visit all fifty states. I drove myself from one side of the country to the other, moving north to south and back again while slowly progressing from east to west. I spent at least one night in every state and once I reached the west coast, I drove up to Alaska. It's beautiful there."

"What about Hawaii?" Margaret asked.

Jeremy grinned. "The first time I was ever on an airplane was when I flew to Hawaii. After a few days in the sun, I was ready to fly home again."

"Now I want to visit all fifty states," Ted said. "I've never been to the US."

"It was an adventure, and one that I thoroughly enjoyed. After Alaska, I drove back across Canada to the east coast. Then I started making plans to see more of the world. I spent a year exploring South America, partly by car. After that, I headed for Europe."

"Do you speak other languages?" Margaret asked.

Jeremy nodded. "I grew up in Quebec, so I learned both French and English as a child. I studied Spanish and German in school. I love languages and I find that I seem to pick up the basics in a new one fairly easily. I wouldn't consider myself fluent, but I can get by in Italian and even Russian."

"I wish I were better at languages," Margaret said.

"Where did you go in Europe, then?" Ted asked.

"Everywhere, really. I've been traveling for years. I even spent a weekend on the island about three years ago. I enjoyed seeing some of the places that guests had told me about over the years. I told myself after that visit that I'd come back one day."

"And here you are," Ted said.

Jeremy nodded. "I now divide my time between a small apartment just outside of Toronto and traveling. I wasn't planning on going anywhere this month, but after I recently spoke to the police about Joel's untimely death, I found I couldn't stop thinking about the Isle of Man. My previous visit had been short. I decided to come back for a longer stay so that I can really get to know the island."

"Are you ready to order?" the waiter asked. "I can take your drink order or both food and drink if you've had enough time with the menu."

"I haven't even looked at mine," Jeremy said. "I'll have a glass of wine, though."

He and the waiter had a lengthy discussion about the various wines that were available by the glass. Margaret was starting to wonder if Jeremy would ever choose one, when he suddenly became very excited.

"I've never been to a restaurant that had that particular wine by the glass," he said to the waiter.

The man shrugged. "It's the owner's favorite. He likes to offer it by the glass because that means we almost always have an open bottle on hand. Most nights, he drinks whatever is left in the bottle with his dinner."

Jeremy laughed. "That's something I would do," he said. "I'll have a glass of that, please."

Margaret and Ted both ordered soft drinks.

"We're both driving," Margaret said as the waiter walked away.

"I don't drive on the, um, other side of the road," Jeremy replied. "I learned my lesson the hard way the very first time I visited the UK. I very nearly drove my rental car into a huge line of oncoming traffic on the second morning I was there. After that, I decided that taxis were a much safer way to get around."

"So you've been traveling extensively since you retired," Ted said.

"I have. I never married. My job wasn't particularly compatible with long-term relationships. The hours weren't good for short-term relationships either, really. For a few years, I felt very much as if I was missing out on something. Then I watched several friends get their hearts badly broken, and I decided that I could be perfectly happy on my own. That means now I have only myself to please."

"Are you ready to order?" the waiter asked as he delivered their drinks.

Margaret quickly opened her menu and chose the first thing that sounded good. After Ted and Jeremy had also ordered, the waiter walked away.

Jeremy sat back with his glass of wine. He took a sip and smiled at Ted.

"I knew nearly all of the suspects. Would you like to hear what I thought of the various men and women who might have murdered Joel Ward?"

13

Ted nodded. "Yes, very much."

"Of course, I know I'm a suspect, too," Jeremy added. "I find that idea amusing. The only possible motive I can assign to myself is that Joel was a difficult person with whom to deal. That is very true, but he was by no means the only difficult person I encountered over my years in the industry. Killing all of them would have been an impossible task. And if I had decided to start eliminating the worst of them, Joel would have been at least tenth or eleventh on my list."

"There are other reasons why you might have wanted to get rid of him," Ted said.

"Such as?" Jeremy asked.

"Ideas that require some imagination, really," Ted replied. "Perhaps you were in love with Joel's wife. Maybe you thought she'd fall in love with you if you got rid of Joel, or maybe you simply thought that she was being mistreated and wanted to save her."

Jeremy stared at Ted for a moment and then laughed. "That's a ridiculous notion. I never ever got involved with guests. I was always very well aware that they existed on a different level to mere ordinary mortals like me. I never once gave any thought to how Joel treated either of his wives. If there had been any serious problems between them, I might have heard. It's difficult to keep secrets when staff outnumber guests at resorts like that. I could tell you stories about unhappy marriages, physical and emotional abuse, affairs, open relationships, all manner of things. None of them apply to Joel, though. As far as I know, he and Lynda were happy together. I believe he and Donna had been happy when they'd been married as well."

"Except they got divorced," Margaret said.

Jeremy nodded. "It was obvious, the last time they visited the resort together, that they were having serious problems. It might not have been obvious to Donna, but everyone who worked at the resort could see what was coming. But we'll talk about Donna in a moment. I'm curious what other motives you can imagine for me."

Ted shrugged. "Someone suggested that you might have been doing something illegal or immoral and that Joel found out about it."

Before Jeremy could reply, the waiter arrived with their food. After he'd delivered all of the plates and walked away, Jeremy sighed.

"I should have thought of that one myself. And I've no way to prove that I never did anything illegal or immoral in all of my days. I'd be lying, actually, if I claimed that, because I've driven over the speed limit, and I once had a relationship with someone who was married to someone else at the time. Is that immoral? It probably is."

"The question is, did Joel know about anything illegal or immoral that you'd done?" Margaret said.

"Not as far I know," Jeremy said with a small smile. "Anything is possible, of course, but I can assure you that I didn't kill Joel because he saw me speeding one afternoon. The relationship happened years after Joel's death."

"This isn't my case," Ted said. "Howard Reed is in charge of the investigation, but for what it's worth, you've always been at the bottom of my list of suspects."

Jeremy smiled and gave Ted a small nod. "I appreciate that. I have the advantage of knowing that I didn't kill him, of course."

"Someone suggested that Joel might have simply been in the wrong place at the wrong time," Margaret said. "Maybe he wandered into a drug deal or something similar."

"No," Jeremy said flatly. "No drugs were flying in or out of Collins Airfield. I'm certain about that. I suppose he could have found himself in the middle of some sort of fight or something, but he was sitting in darkness in his plane when he was killed. Anyone coming to the field that night wouldn't have even known he was there."

"So that leaves us with a short list of suspects," Ted said.

"Where should I start?" Jeremy asked.

"Who do you think killed him?" Margaret asked.

"I've thought about that a lot over the years. I've always come back to the same two suspects."

"Victor and Trent," Margaret guessed.

Jeremy chuckled. "You have been talking about the case, then. Yes, Victor and Trent. They seem the most obvious for a lot of reasons."

"Tell me about Victor," Ted said.

Jeremy took a sip of wine. "He was no different to the others. Wealthy, spoiled, full of ego. He used to bring a different woman to the resort every time he stayed. Sometimes he'd tell her that he'd never brought a woman there before, which was amusing. He was never a favorite guest of mine, but he was by no means the worst, either."

"Can you see him killing Joel?" Margaret asked.

"Perhaps, which isn't a satisfactory answer, I know. But it's the best I can do, I'm afraid. Again, the question is motive. I understand that he received some money from an insurance policy after Joel's death, but I doubt it was enough money to make much difference to Victor. He was already a very wealthy man."

"He did marry Joel's widow a year later," Margaret said.

"Yes, but I saw them together on several occasions when Joel was still alive, and I never once detected anything between them. They were friendly, but when you work in the industry, you learn to spot signs of people who are secretly involved. It's very helpful to know that two people might be sneaking off to spend time together behind their partners' backs. As I said, I never got the sense that Victor and Lynda were anything more than friends before Joel's death."

"So if Victor did kill Joel, do you think it was for the money?" Margaret asked.

Jeremy shrugged. "Perhaps. Or maybe Victor was simply tired of

Joel and decided to get rid of him. Such things do happen, although I would find that a very unsatisfactory ending to the story if it were true."

"What about Trent, then?" Ted asked.

"Another man with money and ego," Jeremy said. "He was never any more difficult than Joel or Victor, but he was never pleasant, either. He also used to bring different women every time he visited the resort."

"How likely do you think it is that he killed Joel?" Margaret asked.

"Again, it's difficult. I know he had a large insurance policy on Joel's life, but that's standard practice for business partners. I can't imagine any other motive for him, though. Not unless there were problems in the business about which I'm unaware."

"Nothing came to light after Joel's death," Ted said.

"It might be interesting to know that both Joel and Trent were guests at the resort, but they were never there at the same time. I mentioned that to Joel once and he laughed and said that one of them had to keep the business running while the other was on holiday, but I found it odd that they never took a holiday together. That might just be me, though."

"That does seem odd," Margaret said. "I'd have thought they could have at least worked it so that their vacations overlapped by a few days once in a while."

Ted shrugged. "Perhaps they were less close than we've been led to believe."

"But that doesn't mean that Trent killed Joel," Margaret said.

"I did wonder if Trent was ever involved with either of Joel's wives," Jeremy said. "As I said, they were never there at the same time, so if Trent had an affair with either of them, I was unaware."

"Donna said something about Victor asking her out after her divorce. She never mentioned Trent doing the same," Margaret said.

"It might be worth asking her about Trent, just to be certain," Jeremy suggested.

"What about pudding?" the waiter asked, handing them each a small menu.

As he cleared their empty plates, Margaret read through the

options. After they'd ordered, the waiter walked away, carrying the carefully stacked plates and flatware.

"Where does that leave us?" Jeremy asked. "Trent and Victor are at the top of my list. That's partly because I find it impossible to believe that a woman shot Joel. I know that I'm being naïve in that regard, but I can't help the way I feel."

"Tell me about Donna and Lynda," Ted said.

"They were both much nicer than Joel when it came to how they treated the staff at the resort," Jeremy said.

"Which one do you think is more likely to have killed Joel?" Margaret asked.

"Lynda," Jeremy said without hesitation.

"You're very definite about that," Ted said.

"Joel and Donna were divorced. I'm certain Donna was angry and bitter. From everything I know of the couple, she had been very much in love with him. I never thought they'd stay together forever, though. Over the course of several visits, it became obvious to me that Joel was losing interest."

"Surely that gives her a motive," Margaret said.

"I suppose so, but I don't really see it," Jeremy said.

He paused as the waiter put their desserts on the table. After the waiter walked away, Jeremy cleared his throat.

"If Joel had turned up dead somewhere within a year of the divorce, I might have suspected Donna. As it was, though, she'd had several years to get over her anger. I can't imagine why she'd have suddenly decided to kill the man."

"Maybe her resentment just kept growing," Margaret said. "Maybe she hated watching him with Lynda. Maybe, when she found out that he was taking Lynda to the resort where she and Joel used to escape, it became too much for her."

"Maybe," Jeremy said with a shrug. "But I doubt it. Lynda, on the other hand, had a much stronger motive. I still don't think she did it, but she might have if she'd started to worry that Joel was growing tired of her."

"Was he?" Margaret asked.

"If he was, he was hiding it well. I said earlier that it was obvious to me when he and Donna started having difficulties. I didn't get that same feeling about his relationship with Lynda. They seemed just as happy on their last visit to the resort as they'd seemed on their first visit."

"So you'd put Lynda above Donna on your list. What about Aaron Crawford?" Ted asked.

Jeremy frowned. "Do you remember earlier when I said if I'd started killing difficult guests, Joel wouldn't be at the top of the list? That spot belongs to Aaron Crawford."

"What made him so difficult?" Margaret asked.

"He was arrogant and rude, not just to the staff, but to the other guests. If things weren't done the way he thought they should be done, he'd scream at everyone he could find until he got his way. I know for a fact that we lost customers because of him. There were certain guests who would call and ask when Aaron was next visiting so that they could plan their trips to avoid him. Of course, we couldn't tell guests when other guests were expected. In some cases, that led to people simply finding other vacation destinations rather than risk being at the resort with Aaron."

"That's awful," Margaret said.

"Where does he come on your list of suspects?" Ted asked.

"I'd love to say that I think he did it. I'd like nothing better than for you to arrest him and put him in prison for a long time, but I can't really imagine him killing anyone. Not himself, anyway. If he did want someone dead, I suspect he'd hire someone to do the job for him."

"Maybe that's what happened," Margaret said.

Jeremy shrugged. "As far as I know, the only time Aaron and Joel ever met was at the airfield when they'd both just arrived. They had an altercation, yes, but that wasn't unusual for Aaron. He had another shouting match with someone over dinner that evening and then called me, demanding that I have a guest removed from the property while having a drink in the bar a few hours later."

"What a horrible man," Margaret said.

"He was an only child raised by incredibly wealthy parents who never said no to him," Jeremy said. "That doesn't excuse his behavior, but it helps explain it."

"Did he continue to visit the resort after Joel's death?" Margaret asked.

"He did. He might still be visiting regularly, for all I know. Once I retired, I stopped caring about the place. It got all of my love and attention for a great many years. Now it is someone else's problem."

"Was he any different after Joel's death?" was Margaret's next question.

"Not that I noticed. He was enraged in the days immediately after the murder when he was forced to speak to the police on more than one occasion. He was also infuriated that he'd been told he couldn't leave the resort. He'd only just arrived for what he'd booked as a two-week stay, but as soon as he was told he couldn't leave, he suddenly wanted to cancel the rest of his vacation and go back to LA."

Margaret frowned. "He lived in LA?"

"He had properties all over the world, but after Joel's murder he kept talking about wanting to be in LA. I believe that was simply because California was as far away from the resort as he could easily get."

"Is there anyone else that you thought, at the time or in the years since, should be a suspect in the murder?" Ted asked.

Jeremy shook his head. "There were dozens of guests and hundreds of staff at the resort that evening. I suppose we all belong on the list of suspects, but I want to believe that murder requires a strong motive. I'm not aware of anyone else who had a motive, strong or otherwise."

"This has been fascinating," Ted said as the waiter cleared away their dessert dishes.

"I'm glad we had a chance to speak," Jeremy told him. "I hope what I've said has been helpful."

They paid the checks and then walked outside.

"Is there a taxi rank nearby?" Jeremy asked. "I came down on the train and then walked for ages. I think I'd rather just get a taxi back to Douglas."

"Where are you staying?" Margaret asked.

Jeremy named a hotel that was only a short distance from Promenade View. Margaret looked at Ted. He shrugged.

"I can give you a ride back to Douglas, if you want," she offered.

Jeremy's face lit up. "In that?" he asked, pointing at Mona's car. "I really should have paid for your dinner. I'd love a ride in that car, even if you simply want to drive me to the end of the street and back again."

Margaret laughed. "I don't live far from your hotel. You'll have to walk from the parking garage under my building, though."

"I won't complain. You can leave me anywhere. Are you certain you want to let me ride in your car?"

"Like I said, it isn't even my car."

Margaret gave Ted a quick kiss.

"I'll see you at your flat shortly," he promised.

Margaret unlocked the doors and then waited until Jeremy was safely buckled into the passenger seat before she walked around to the driver's door. As she slid behind the steering wheel, Jeremy sighed happily.

"I can't wait to hear the engine," he said.

Margaret turned the key. The car roared to life and then settled into a contented purr. Jeremy made a similar noise. Margaret chuckled and then put the car into gear. Jeremy was silent until Margaret pulled the car into its space in the garage under her building.

"That was amazing," he said. "One of the best experiences of my entire life."

"Really? It's just a car," Margaret said.

Jeremy shook his head. "This car is magic. I can't tell you how much it means to me to have been allowed to ride in it. Thank you so very much."

"It wasn't a problem."

Margaret got out of the car. Jeremy took a few quick pictures, including a selfie, before he followed suit. After he shut his door, Margaret made sure the car was locked. Then she led Jeremy to the elevators.

"You can get off on the ground floor and simply exit the building through the lobby," she told him.

He nodded but he didn't really seem to be paying attention. When the elevator car arrived, they walked inside. Jeremy waved at the car as the doors slid shut. When they reached the ground floor, Margaret got off and led the man to the doors that led outside. Ted was just pulling into a parking space across the street.

"Thank you, again," Jeremy said before he walked away with a small bounce in his step.

"You made him very happy," Ted said when he reached Margaret.

"It's just a car."

Ted laughed. "I'm not that interested in cars, but even I know that your car is something special."

"It's Aunt Fenella's car."

"And it's very special. How about a stroll on the promenade, then? I was going to suggest that we walk along the beach in Port St. Mary, but you offered Jeremy a ride home."

"That would have been nice, too. I'm sorry."

"It doesn't matter. We can walk here."

He took her hand as they crossed the road to the promenade.

"Let's go to the right for a change," Ted suggested.

"Let's. We can walk through the sunken gardens. Everything should be in full bloom."

The walk to the gardens didn't take long. As they started down the handful of steps, Margaret could hear raised voices.

"...you're accusing me of," a man said.

"I'm not accusing you of anything," a woman replied. "I was just asking you a question."

"It was a loaded question," the man said. "One that sounded as if it were an accusation."

Ted and Margaret took a few steps forward and then stopped. They were hidden from the arguing couple by a row of hedges. Ted peered around the row and then took a step backward.

"What's wrong?" Margaret mouthed.

Ted pulled out his phone. He made a show of putting it into silent mode and then sent a text. Then he gestured for Margaret to do the same.

She pulled her phone out of her purse and switched it to silent mode. Ted watched and then sent another text. Margaret's phone vibrated. She read the message silently.

Harry and Tara, Neil, Cassie and Boris

"Mum, can we please not have this conversation?" a voice asked.

"Cassie?" Margaret mouthed at Ted.

He nodded.

"It was a simple enough question." Now Margaret recognized Tara's voice.

"How I feel about Cassie is between her and me." The man sounded angry.

"Boris," Ted whispered.

Margaret nodded.

"Unless you started the fire in order to force her to move back in with you."

It took Margaret a moment to recognize Neil's voice.

Boris laughed. "Are you seriously accusing me of starting the fire? That's pretty rich coming from a man with a criminal record."

"I don't have a criminal record," Neil snapped.

"Maybe not, but you have a lot of friends who do. Which one of them started the fire?" Boris shot back.

"None of my friends had any reason to start the fire," Neil argued. "The only person who is better off now is you."

"I hope that Cassie is better off," Boris said.

"She's not. She's stuck staying with you because otherwise she'd be sleeping on the floor in a hotel room. She's just using you right now, though. As soon as Mum and Dad have a better place to stay, she'll move back in with them, and you'll be alone again." Neil was practically shouting.

"No, she won't," Boris said. "We're starting over and trying again, aren't we?"

"Yeah," Cassie said with a marked lack of enthusiasm.

"She's clearly thrilled," Neil said with a laugh.

"Cassie? I thought you were happy being back with me," Boris said.

"I'm not unhappy," Cassie replied.

"That isn't what I want to hear," Boris snapped.

"I'm trying to be happy," Cassie said. "It isn't easy. We broke up for a lot of reasons. Nothing has really changed."

"I've changed. I'm trying harder," Boris said.

"Let's just leave it," Cassie said.

"I'm not just going to leave it," Boris told her. "I want to know how you really feel. I thought we were trying again. I want to rebuild our relationship."

"We are trying again. I'm just not certain it's working," Cassie said.

"I was going to ask you to marry me." Boris sounded both angry and sad.

"Marry you? We tried that, remember? It was a disaster. I'm happy to try to make our relationship work again, but I'm not interested in getting married again."

"But I love you."

"And I care about you, but I think we're better off just being boyfriend and girlfriend."

"I want us to be together forever."

"We might be, if we can work through everything."

"I'll do anything to make it work." Margaret could hear the intensity in Boris's voice.

Ted was on his phone again, sending and receiving texts.

"Anything?" Neil asked. "What would you do? Would you walk through fire for her?"

"I'd walk through fire to save her if she was in danger. I'm not going to walk through a fire just to prove a point, though," Boris replied.

"You should have been there when the fire started," Neil said. "If I hadn't been there with a fire extinguisher to fight the blaze, we all might have died."

"It was only a small fire," Boris said.

"You say that as if you saw it," Neil said.

Boris chuckled. Margaret thought he sounded uneasy. "It couldn't have been too bad. You all got out safely."

"We were lucky," Neil said. "If the smoke detectors had taken an extra minute to wake me, we'd all be dead."

"It wasn't that bad," Boris said.

"Actually, it was that bad," Cassie said. "If Neil hadn't fought the fire, we never would have been able to escape. He saved all of our lives."

"I find that hard to believe," Boris said.

"Why?" Neil asked. "Because you thought you'd only started a small fire? Because you were trying to drive us out of the flat, but you never intended to kill anyone? Save that for the judge. I don't care what you were planning. The truth is you nearly killed my parents and my sister. And they obviously mean more to me than they do to you."

"I love Cassie more than you do," Boris shouted.

Neil shook his head. "I didn't see you fighting that fire. That was all me. You were too busy running home to hide the evidence of what you'd done. I wonder when the police are going to get the search warrant to search your house."

"Search warrant? The police can't search my house," Boris said.

"They can if they think you started the fire," Neil said. "And I can't believe it will take them long to come to that conclusion. We've all already reached it, haven't we Cassie?"

There was a long silence before Boris spoke again.

"Cassie? Do you think I started the fire?"

"That's one possibility," Cassie said, her voice so low that Margaret struggled to hear her.

"There are others," Boris said.

"No, there really aren't," Neil said. "And you'd probably be better off confessing. The police are probably working on getting a search warrant right now."

"They won't find anything," Boris said. "I was too careful..." He trailed off and then sighed. "I mean, they won't find anything. There isn't anything to find. I didn't do anything wrong."

"You started the fire?" Cassie demanded.

"It was an accident," Boris said.

"An accident?" Cassie echoed.

"I came to talk to you that night, remember?"

"Yes, of course. You wanted to remind me that you'd always care for me and that you'd always be there for me if I ever needed you."

"It needed saying. I knew you'd been seeing other people. I didn't want you to forget about me."

"I question the timing," Neil said. "You come and tell Cassie that you'll always be there for her if she needs you. A few hours later, the flat where she's staying catches on fire. Does anyone else think that's suspicious?"

Margaret found herself nodding. Ted chuckled silently.

"I spilled something on the kitchen floor while I was there," Boris said.

"What did you spill?" Neil asked.

"A flammable oil. It was something I'd been trying out at the restaurant for making flambés. I had the bottle in my pocket. It slipped out and somehow came open, but it left a puddle behind."

"And you left a puddle of highly flammable liquid in our kitchen and just went home?" Tara demanded.

"I thought I'd cleaned it up. I must have missed some."

"You need to talk to the police," Cassie said. "I should say you need to confess to the police."

"I didn't mean to start a fire," Boris said.

"Even if the kitchen was completely covered in flammable liquid, nothing would have happened if someone hadn't lit a match," Neil said.

"I had matches in my pocket, too," Boris said. "They must have fallen out of my pocket when I was leaving."

"Matches don't strike themselves," Cassie said dryly. "Why don't you just admit what you did? You poured a flammable liquid in the kitchen and then lit a match on your way out. I can't believe that someone loved me so much that he was willing to start a fire to get me back."

"Cassie," Tara said, sounding anxious.

"What? I know it's been a huge inconvenience for all of us, but it's also kind of romantic. No guy has ever done anything so dramatic for me," Cassie said.

"I did it for us," Boris said. "I want us to be together. I made a lot of mistakes when we were married, but I want to try again. I love you."

"How much? Did you really start a fire for me?" Cassie challenged.

"It was only supposed to be a small blaze, just enough to force you to move out for a few days. I thought that you'd spend them with me and then decide to stay forever."

"Someone ring the police," Neil said. "Boris just confessed to arson."

"It wasn't supposed to be a big deal," Boris said. "I didn't realize just how flammable the liquid I used was."

"Tell that to the police," Neil said.

"We don't have to ring the police," Boris said. "No one has to know. They'll close the investigation eventually. We just have to keep quiet until they do."

"I'm not keeping quiet," Neil said.

"You will if you want your sister to be happy," Boris said. "You don't want the man she loves to go to prison, do you?"

"I'll worry about that when she finds someone to love," Neil replied.

"She loves me!" Boris shouted.

"I doubt that," Neil replied.

"You do love me, don't you?" Boris asked.

There was a long silence before Cassie replied. "You could have killed me. You could have killed my parents. I can't believe you set my home on fire."

"I told you, it wasn't supposed to be a big fire," Boris said.

"But you still set it and then walked away. I could have died."

"I didn't know how bad the blaze was going to get. I never wanted to hurt you. I'm very sorry."

Margaret watched as several uniformed police constables moved into positions around the garden.

"Sorry isn't enough," Cassie said, sounding sad. "It's over. I'll get my things and move back in with Mum and Dad."

"You have to give me another chance," Boris said. "I did it for you."

"Did what?" Ted asked as he walked around the hedges and into the garden.

"Nothing," Boris said.

Margaret was right behind Ted. Boris had been sitting on a bench next to Cassie. Now he jumped up and started to walk away from Ted.

"He confessed to starting the fire," Neil said.

"He's lying," Boris shouted over his shoulder as he started up the steps out of the garden.

"Then why are you running away?" Neil demanded.

"I have an appointment somewhere," Boris replied before he started walking at a rapid pace toward the road.

He was stopped almost immediately by a uniformed constable. When Boris tried to get away, another constable joined the first. Boris shouted something and then turned and ran straight into a third constable who'd come up behind him. As Boris fell to the ground, cursing loudly, Neil started to laugh.

"This is going to take ages to sort through," Ted said to Margaret. "Why don't you sneak away now? I can get your statement tomorrow."

"Are you sure?"

"I'm sure."

He gave her a quick kiss before she walked away. When she reached her building, she kept walking, enjoying the fresh air while she tried to process what she'd just witnessed.

"...and then Ted asked him what he'd done," she concluded a short while after she'd returned to her apartment.

"Very good," Mona said. "Now we need a similar outcome to the murder investigation."

"I can't see that happening, but it would be nice. How did you get Jeremy Olson to the island?"

"He'd been planning a return visit for years. But do tell me what he had to say about the case."

Margaret filled her great-aunt in on her dinner conversation.

"You should have asked more questions on the drive back to Douglas," Mona said when she was finished.

"He was too busy listening to the engine to talk to me."

"She does have a lovely purr."

"The only person I haven't met is Aaron Crawford. I can't wait to see how you get him here."

Mona chuckled. "That might be too ambitious, even for me. I suggest you solve the case with the information you already have."

"That sounds as if you think you know who did it."

"I have a good idea."

Mona faded away before Margaret could reply. Margaret stared at the spot where her great-aunt had been for a moment before she looked at Katie. "She's bluffing," she said. "She has to be."

14

When Margaret woke up the next morning, Mona's words were still on her mind. "If she thinks she knows who killed Joel, then she knows something I don't," she concluded as she made herself some breakfast.

Ted called at nine. "I need to take your statement before we do anything else. Is now a good time?"

"Now is fine."

The words were barely out of her mouth before someone knocked on the door.

"You called from the hallway?"

"I decided I didn't want to just knock, in case you'd decided to have a lie-in," he explained before he kissed her.

"I hope you don't treat all of your witnesses that way," she teased after the kiss.

Ted laughed. "I can assure you that I didn't kiss any of the other witnesses in this particular investigation."

It took Margaret only a few minutes to give Ted her official statement on what they'd overheard the previous evening.

"I probably don't need this," Ted said as he put his notebook away. "But I'll get it typed up and have you sign it anyway. Boris gave us a pretty comprehensive confession last night when we got him down to the station, though. Things didn't go exactly the way Neil described them, but Boris was able to tell us precisely how he started the fire."

"Oh? I would have expected him to deny everything."

"He tried that, but then he broke down crying about how much he loves Cassie and how heartbroken he was when she left him."

"Setting her home on fire is a funny way of showing it."

"He was desperate to get her back. I truly believe that he didn't mean to cause anywhere near as much damage as he did. I think he thought that the fire would burn out quite quickly. He wanted to do just enough to force the family to move out for a short while. He never wanted to hurt anyone or put anyone in real danger."

Margaret shook her head. "It was such an incredibly dangerous thing to do."

"Let's talk about something more pleasant. It's Saturday. We have the whole day to enjoy together. What do you want to do?"

"What about a trip to Ramsey? We could do some shopping and have lunch there. They have some different shops."

"That sounds good. After lunch, maybe we could go over to Mooragh Park. We could walk around the lake, play some crazy golf, maybe hire a pedalo for half an hour."

"Perfect."

Margaret drove Mona's car again. Ted sat in the passenger seat, wearing an expression that was not unlike the one Jeremy had worn the previous evening.

"What is it with men and cars?" Margaret asked as she drove into one of the parking lots near the main shopping street in Ramsey.

Ted shrugged. "It isn't all cars. This one is very special."

Margaret parked and then they walked the short distance to the shops. When they started to get hungry, they stopped at a convenient pub for lunch. Then they walked over to Mooragh Park. Ted beat Margaret at crazy golf before they took a pedal boat out onto the small boating lake.

"I could sit here all afternoon," Margaret said when they stopped pedaling near the middle of the lake.

"It's lovely and peaceful," Ted said. "But we only paid for half an hour."

Margaret laughed. "We probably need to pedal back, then, don't we?"

"In a minute."

"My legs are tired now," Margaret said as they walked back to the car.

"I can drive, if you're too tired."

Margaret laughed. "If it was my car, I'd happily let you, but it's Aunt Fenella's car. I know she added me to her insurance before she went away, but I'm not sure we'd be covered if you were driving."

"And I can't afford to replace the car if anything happened to while I was driving it."

"Neither can I. It's worth more than I could make in many years."

It was nearly time for dinner by the time they got back to Douglas. Margaret parked in her spot in the garage and then they took the elevator to the ground floor.

"What sounds good?" Ted asked as they walked outside.

"I'm not all that hungry. I ate a lot at the pub, and then we had ice cream."

Ted nodded. "Let's walk for a bit and then think about dinner."

They walked to the far end of the promenade and then slowly strolled back again.

"Now I'm hungry," Ted said.

"I could eat." She named a nearby restaurant.

"Perfect."

The restaurant was on a short side street that ran perpendicular to the promenade. An hour later, after a delicious meal, they emerged from the restaurant.

"It's a beautiful evening," Ted said, taking her hand.

"It is lovely."

"I feel as if we should enjoy it, but I'm also tired. We did a lot of walking, and pedaling, today."

"We did. Maybe we should just go to the pub."

They'd only taken a few steps when Ted stopped. "What about

trying a different pub?" he asked, nodding toward the one on the opposite side of the road.

"Why?" Margaret demanded.

Ted chuckled. "I just saw Victor and Lynda King walk into that pub. I thought it might be interesting to keep an eye on them."

"It doesn't look like the sort of place that they'd normally visit."

"Exactly."

They crossed the road and entered the pub. The large room was very dimly lit. Margaret blinked several times as her eyes struggled to adjust to the darkness. Ted took her arm and led her to a booth along the back wall. As she slid into her seat, Margaret noticed that Victor and Lynda were in the next booth. They were talking and didn't appear to have noticed Margaret and Ted.

Ted went to the bar and brought back soft drinks for them. He sat down next to her, leaving the bench seat on the opposite side of the table empty. Margaret took a sip and then leaned close to Ted.

"Are we eavesdropping?" she whispered.

He shrugged. "That did some good last night, but I can't imagine we'll have the same luck tonight. I was just curious what they were doing here. If nothing happens in the next few minutes, maybe we'll say hello."

A minute later, the pub's door opened. Margaret slid down her seat as Trent Walsh walked into the room. He glanced around but didn't seem to notice her and Ted. He quickly walked over and joined Victor and Lynda.

"You always choose the most interesting places to meet," Victor said tightly as Trent sat down.

"It's one of my favorite pubs," Trent replied.

"Why am I not surprised?" Lynda asked.

Trent laughed. "How are you? Surviving the new investigation into your first husband's untimely death?"

"I'm fine," Lynda said. "Hoping against hope that this time the police will find Joel's killer, of course."

"Oh, of course," Trent said.

"This is weird," Margaret whispered. "Why are they meeting?"

"What do you want?" Victor asked after a long pause.

"I just wanted to see my old friends. It's been a while," Trent said.

"We were never friends," Victor said.

"Ouch," Trent replied with a laugh. "Lynda and I were friends, though. Weren't we?"

"You and Joel were friends. I put up with you for his benefit."

"That really hurts," Trent replied, sounding amused. "I thought we had something special."

"I have no control over what you think," Lynda said coolly.

Trent laughed. "Now I'm wondering why I wanted to see you."

"We're wondering the same," Victor said.

"Maybe I wanted to raise a glass to our dear friend, Joel," Trent said. "It's been thirty-five years since his passing. I still miss him."

"We all do," Lynda said after a pause.

"Do we?" Trent asked. "I suspect Victor doesn't miss him at all."

"If you've brought me here to accuse me of murder, please don't bother," Victor said.

"I would never accuse you of anything," Trent said. "But someone did kill Joel. I wonder if the police are any closer to finding that person than they were thirty-five years ago."

"I'm not interested in speculating about the investigation into my husband's death," Lynda said.

"We could talk about island politics, then," Trent suggested.

Margaret swallowed a sigh as the trio began to discuss the relative merits of one of the members of the House of Keys. Ted frowned.

"What did Trent say about Victor when you spoke to him?" he whispered to Margaret.

She frowned as she tried to think back. "I'm getting everything muddled up in my head. I think it was Aaron that he said might have been mad enough to jump on the wing and wave a gun around, not Victor. I'm not sure I remember what he said about Victor, though."

Ted went very still. "Say that again," he said in a low voice.

"That I'm getting muddled? I'm sorry."

"No, say exactly what you said about Aaron again."

"I said that I think it was Aaron that Trent suggested might have been angry enough to jump on the wing and wave the gun at Joel. He suggested that Aaron hadn't wanted to kill Joel, just frighten him."

"And he said 'jump on the wing?'"

"I think so. It was something like that."

Ted pulled out his phone and sent a text.

"I told you all of this before, didn't I?"

He shook his head. "Not in those exact words, anyway."

At the next table, the discussion was still centered on local politics. When the door to the pub opened, Margaret wasn't surprised to see two uniformed constables walk in. Their entrance made the entire room go silent.

As they walked over to join Margaret and Ted, Margaret could see every single person in the room watching their progress. When they stopped next to their booth, Trent got up and looked to see who had attracted police attention.

"Oh dear," he said. "You didn't tell me there was a police inspector in the next booth," he said to Victor and Lynda.

"We didn't know," Victor said. "Are you quite certain you didn't set up this entire thing?"

Trent laughed. "You think I arranged to meet here so that we could sit next to the police, and I could what? Get you to confess to murdering Joel?"

"It does seem a bit odd, the police being in the next booth," Lynda said.

"Where they can hear our every word," Trent said.

Ted slowly slid out of his seat and stood up. Margaret followed. The two constables stepped back as Ted moved closer to the other table.

"Good evening," he said.

"If Trent arranged this, you mustn't believe anything that he told you about us," Lynda said.

"Trent didn't arrange anything. Margaret and I just had dinner at the restaurant across the road. When we came out, we fancied a drink," Ted told her.

"So why the constables?" Trent asked.

Ted shrugged. "I have a few additional questions for you. The constables can take you down to the station. We can talk there."

"Questions for me?" Trent asked. "I'm afraid I don't have any answers."

"Something has happened," Lynda said. "Some new evidence or something."

Victor laughed. "New evidence? It's been thirty-five years. There isn't going to be any new evidence, not after all this time."

"Mr. Walsh? If you'd be so kind," Ted said.

Trent shook his head. "I don't think so. We had a long conversation just a day or two ago. I answered all of your questions then. I have nothing else to say."

"What have you learned?" Lynda demanded. "Do you truly think that Trent killed Joel?"

"He hasn't learned anything," Trent said. "He's just trying to ruin our evening."

"I can assure you that I'm doing nothing of the kind," Ted replied.

"Now I'm trying to remember everything that was said when Trent first arrived," Victor said. "One of us must have said something suspicious. Do you want to interview me or my wife?"

Ted hesitated. "Not at the moment."

"Ah, so it's only Trent who is under suspicion. Interesting," Victor said.

"I can't possibly be under suspicion," Trent said, waving a hand. "Not unless one of you said something before I arrived. If that's the case, then you need to know that they were lying," he told Ted.

"We can discuss it at the station," Ted said.

"Discuss what at the station?" Trent demanded. "I just gave you a statement. And it was essentially the same statement that I gave the police thirty-five years ago. I was in New York City when Joel died. I don't know what happened to him, but we were friends and I still miss him terribly."

Ted nodded. "Noted. Please come with me."

Trent looked past Ted. He smiled at Margaret. "Do you know what this is all about?"

Margaret shrugged. "I think you should do what Ted has asked."

"Of course you do. But I'm not going anywhere without an explanation," Trent replied. "I was simply having a drink with some friends. Surely I can't be arrested for that."

"You aren't being arrested," Ted said. "Not as long as you cooperate."

Trent raised an eyebrow. "Does that mean that if I refuse to leave with you, you'll arrest me?"

"I'd rather not get to that point."

"I think that's a yes," Victor said, sounding happy at the prospect.

Trent frowned. "I probably need to ring my advocate. Even better, let me borrow your solicitor," he said to Victor.

Lynda laughed. "Norman was worse than useless when he was here. He's back in London now, probably trying to work out how he can charge us even more money for his uselessness."

"He's gone back to London?" Trent repeated.

Victor nodded. "There seemed no point in continuing to pay for his time, his hotel, and his meals. As Lynda said, he was fairly useless when it mattered."

Trent frowned. "It does appear as if I'm going to need a solicitor."

"You're welcome to ring Norman," Victor said. "But be prepared to be disappointed."

Trent glanced at Ted. "Maybe I need to find someone better. It looks as if I'm about to be charged with murder."

"I'm not charging anyone with anything tonight," Ted said.

"That's not terribly reassuring," Trent said.

"Is there new evidence?" Lynda asked. "Is it truly possible that you've found Joel's killer?"

"For now, I'd simply appreciate a half hour of Mr. Walsh's time," Ted said. "I have a few more questions for him."

"Come and see me on Monday," Trent suggested. "I can answer your questions from the comfort of my own living room."

"I'd prefer to have this conversation as soon as possible."

"Monday is as soon as is possible for me," Trent said. "I'm having drinks with friends tonight and then having a lazy Sunday. I'll expect you around ten on Monday."

Ted shook his head. "I'm afraid that doesn't work for me. We need to talk tonight."

"You killed Joel," Lynda said to Trent.

Trent chuckled, but it was a nervous sound. "Don't be silly," he said.

"What have you learned?" Lynda asked Ted. "You must have found out something important. Did someone see him in Canada that night? Did he have car trouble or stop for petrol somewhere? You know something."

"I might not have learned anything at all," Ted said. "I simply have a few questions for Trent."

Victor slowly slid out of the booth. "I think I've heard enough. If you did kill Joel, I hope they put you away for a very long time."

"Ha, you, of all people, should be grateful to whoever killed Joel. You made a lot of money, and you married his wife," Trent said.

"And I'd give back the money and the happiness I've found with Lynda to have Joel back," Victor said.

Trent laughed. "That sounds very nice, but we both know it isn't true."

Victor stared at him for a minute before turning and taking a few steps away. "Come on, Lynda," he said over his shoulder as he walked.

"I want to stay and hear what the police have found," she said.

"They aren't going to tell you," Victor said. "Let's go."

Lynda hesitated for a moment before sliding out of the booth. She took a few steps and then turned and stared at Trent.

"If you did kill Joel, I'll never forgive you," she said angrily before she followed her husband out of the room.

Trent sat back in his seat and smiled broadly. "Sit down, inspector," he invited. "We can have our conversation here."

Ted hesitated and then shrugged and slid into the seat that Victor and Lynda had just vacated.

"Margaret, please, join us," Trent added. "I'm fairly certain you're behind all of the fuss, anyway."

Ted moved over and patted the bench next to him. Margaret wasn't certain she was doing the right thing, but she sat down anyway.

"What did Margaret say that made you call for backup?" Trent asked.

"What makes you think it was something Margaret said?" Ted asked.

Trent shrugged. "Because nothing was said at this table that was in any way incriminating."

Ted shrugged.

Trent looked at Margaret.

"And I said something I shouldn't have when I spoke to Margaret," Trent said. "I didn't think she'd noticed. It didn't come up when you interviewed me. But it was a slip on my part."

"What was that?" Ted asked.

Trent laughed. "I'm not going to make it that easy for you. Either Margaret told you that I said something that raised your suspicions, or she didn't."

"She did," Ted admitted.

"It's been thirty-five years," Trent said. "I'm eighty years old now and it's becoming harder and harder to watch everything that I say."

"Let's go down to the station. I can take your statement there," Ted said.

Trent looked around the pub. "This is one of my favorite places on the island. I'd quite like to talk here."

Ted shook his head. "I need a formal statement from you. I can't take that in a pub."

"I miss him, you know. Joel was the closest thing I ever had to a brother. We worked well together, in the beginning. And we made a lot of money together."

Ted looked at Margaret. She shrugged.

"You must have been sorry when he died," she said awkwardly.

Trent sighed. "It was the bit about Aaron climbing on the wing that gave me away, wasn't it?"

"No comment," Ted said.

"For the first days and weeks after Joel's death, I kept expecting a knock on the door. I was certain he'd told Lynda that I was going to be driving up to the resort to talk to him. I also assumed that at least one person had seen me there. It wasn't as if I was sneaking around. I wasn't worried about being seen, not until after."

"Let's go to the station," Ted said.

Trent shook his head. "I'll talk here or not at all. This isn't a formal statement, so it isn't a proper confession. I will admit, though, that it's a relief to finally talk about all of this. Thirty-five years is a long time to keep a secret."

"There are witnesses to your confession," Ted pointed out, nodding at Margaret and the uniformed constables.

"I'll worry about that later. Right now, I'm wandering down memory lane. Joel and I were like brothers. I thought the world of him. We worked well together. And then one day I got a phone call. It was a man I knew reasonably well. Joel and I had done some business with Dale in the past. He'd called to tell me that Joel had approached him about a new opportunity. This one was such a sure thing that Joel was investing a million dollars. Joel wanted Dale to do the same."

Trent stopped and slowly shook his head.

"Are you okay?" Margaret asked as the man sat back and closed his eyes.

"It's been thirty-five years and it still breaks my heart," Trent said, swallowing hard. "Dale called me to find out how much I was investing. But Joel had never said a single word to me about the investment. When I heard the details, I could see why Joel was so excited. It was well worth the million dollars that Joel had put into it. I remember every word of the conversation I had with Dale as if it took place yesterday."

"What's Dale's surname?" Ted asked when Joel stopped for a sip of his drink.

"It doesn't matter. He passed away years ago," Trent replied.

"So what did Dale say?" Margaret asked.

Trent shrugged. "He told me all about the deal. I told him that Joel and I were still discussing it, so I hadn't committed yet. I didn't want him to know that Joel hadn't mentioned it to me. I got him to promise that we'd talk again before he gave Joel his answer. And then I called Joel."

"Was this after he'd gone to the resort?" Margaret asked.

Trent nodded. "I reached him at his cottage there. I told him that we needed to talk. I didn't mention the deal with Dale, though. That needed to be discussed in person. Instead, I made up some sort of minor emergency that needed his input. I can remember everything that Dale said, but I can't remember what I said to Joel. Isn't that odd?"

"Memories are tricky," Margaret said.

"And it didn't really matter. It was just an excuse for me to go and talk to Joel. He told me that he'd fly back down to the city in the morning, but I said it couldn't wait. I offered to drive up and meet with him as soon as I arrived. I said we could talk and then he could fly us both to the city to deal with the problem. Then he could fly us both back, and I could drive myself back to the city."

"That seems like a lot of inconvenience for you," Margaret said.

"Oh, it was, but it wouldn't have been the first time that I was massively inconvenienced for Joel's benefit. It took some doing, but I managed to talk him into meeting me at the airfield. He could sleep in his plane quite comfortably, and it meant I didn't have to disturb Lynda when I arrived."

"I'm surprised he didn't tell Lynda that you were coming," Margaret said.

"So am I. I've always wondered if he'd told her, and she's simply kept quiet about it for all these years. For a long time, I worried that she might start blackmailing me, but she never has."

"So what happened at the airfield?" Ted asked.

Trent sighed. "Joel was already there when I arrived. He was sitting in his plane, nodding off in his comfortable chair. I knocked on the window and he let me in. And then we talked."

During the long silence that followed, Trent stared into the distance, his eyes unfocused. Eventually, he cleared his throat.

"We started out talking about the problem that I'd invented as an excuse to see him. While he'd been waiting for me, he'd made a few phone calls from the phone at the airfield. He'd discovered that I'd lied."

"Was he very angry?" Margaret asked.

"He was furious. But I was angrier. He shouted at me for lying. I shouted back about the deal with Dale. It got increasingly heated until I couldn't take it any longer. I climbed out of the plane and went into the office. I knew that there was a gun there. I wasn't planning on killing anyone, though. I didn't even think the gun was kept loaded."

"Was it loaded?" Ted asked.

Trent shrugged. "It might not have been loaded. If it wasn't, then the ammunition was with the gun. I suppose I put a few bullets into it so I could shoot into the distance to make a point. Maybe I thought I'd put a hole in the plane. That would have upset Joel tremendously and made me feel much better."

"So what happened?" Margaret asked when Trent fell silent again.

"Exactly what I said happened when we were talking about Aaron. I jumped on the wing and started waving the gun around. I was as shocked as Joel when it went off. When I checked on him, he was already dead. I couldn't have done better if I'd actually aimed at him and pulled the trigger."

"How unfortunate for Joel," Margaret said.

"It was an accident, but once I'd realized what I'd done, I also realized that I wasn't sad. I hadn't meant to kill him, but I wasn't sorry that I had. He'd betrayed my trust and destroyed our friendship."

"What did you do next?" Ted asked.

Trent chuckled. "I panicked quite a lot. I was certain I was about to be discovered. I used my shirt to wipe as many fingerprints off the gun as I could and tossed the gun into the plane with Joel. Then I shut the door and climbed to the ground. I was back in my car, heading back to New York City, within minutes. I've never driven so carefully in my life, even while I was keeping one eye on the rearview mirror, fully expecting to see flashing lights the entire way."

"Carefully?" Margaret asked.

"I knew I couldn't afford to get a speeding ticket anywhere between New York City and the resort. I had a brief panic when I got to the border, and they demanded identification. Luckily for me, in those days, they only glanced at your ID and then waved you through."

"So you killed Joel because he was trying to do a business deal without you?" Margaret asked.

Trent nodded. "And after his untimely death, I went in with Dale on the deal. We doubled our money in six months. Joel should have let me in from the beginning."

"Did he give you a reason for why he didn't?" Margaret asked.

"He said something about wanting to have some business interests that didn't include me. But he was already working with a handful of others on things in which I wasn't involved. He and Victor were partners on a few things, for instance. I'm certain that this deal was the just the beginning of the end for our partnership. And it ended up absolutely being the end."

"I'd like to move this to the station now," Ted said.

Trent sighed and then picked up his glass. He emptied it and then slowly slid out of the booth. "I've been waiting for thirty-five years for this moment. In a way, it's a relief."

The two constables escorted him out of the pub. Ted and Margaret followed close behind. Once Trent was safely locked in the back of a marked police car, Ted turned to Margaret.

"I'll walk you back to your building before I go to work," he said.

"I can get home safely by myself," she replied.

"I know, but I'll feel better if I walk you home. Trent is going to demand his solicitor as soon as he gets to the station. I have plenty of time before I'm going to be able to question him."

"That was quite awful," Margaret said as they began to walk toward Promenade View.

"But we've found Joel's killer."

"We'd have found him earlier if I'd remembered what Trent had said before tonight."

"All that matters is that you did remember, eventually."

"I'm surprised that Trent made such a big mistake after all these years."

"I suspect it was deliberate. He knows he was extremely lucky not to have been caught thirty-five years ago. It's possible that he's been letting little details slip for years, but no one has caught them before now."

"I'd love to hear what Lynda and Victor have to say on the subject."

"I'm looking forward to interviewing both of them again."

"Do you think that Lynda did know that Trent was coming to see Joel that night?"

"That's one of my first questions for her. I'll let you know."

Ted walked her to her door and then gave her a lengthy kiss.

"You have to go to work," she reminded him when he lifted his head.

"I know, but Trent has been waiting for thirty-five years. He can wait a few more minutes."

"Are you going to have to work all day tomorrow?"

"I hope not. I'll ring you in the morning. I'll need a formal statement from you, too. I may have you give that to Mark or one of the other inspectors, but we can sort that tomorrow."

They kissed again, quickly, before Ted turned and made his way to the elevators. Margaret blew him a kiss as the elevator car doors slid shut.

15

Margaret was tired the next morning. She'd been up far too late sharing everything that had happened with Mona.

"I knew it," Mona had said when Margaret was finished. "I knew we could solve the case."

"I just hope, now that they know where to look, that the police can find some evidence against Trent. He's probably going to deny everything he said in his confession at the pub."

"I wouldn't worry about that," Mona had said. "Now that he's talking, he probably won't want to stop."

As Margaret got breakfast for herself and Katie, she turned on the radio, tuned to a local station.

"Breaking news, island resident Trent Walsh has confessed to the murder of Joel Ward. Joel died in Canada thirty-five years ago," the voice said. "More news as this story develops."

Margaret looked at Katie. "Mona was right," she said softly.

"Meow," Katie said.

"Yes, of course Mona was right," Margaret agreed with a sigh.

Ted rang just after one on Sunday afternoon.

"I just woke up. I was at the station until three. I need a statement from you, but it's just a formality. Trent has confessed to everything."

"I heard that on the radio this morning."

"Yeah, it's all over the newspaper's website, too. The Chief Constable put out a statement early this morning."

"I thought Trent was going to deny everything once he got to the station and had a solicitor with him."

"He tried that, but then he got fed up with the solicitor and decided it would be best just to confess. Would you mind terribly if Mark came over to your flat and took your statement? I have to talk to Lynda and Victor this afternoon."

"That's fine, but then you have to come over and tell me at least some of what they said."

Ted laughed. "That's a deal."

Margaret and Mark enjoyed tea and cookies while Margaret gave him her statement.

"Trent started out refusing to say anything," Mark confided. "It didn't take long for Ted to persuade him to talk, though. And once Trent started talking, he wouldn't shut up."

"Which is a good thing."

"Indeed."

Ted was only a few hours behind Mark. He pulled Margaret into an embrace as soon as she opened the door.

"Hi," she said breathlessly as he released her.

"It's been a long afternoon."

"Oh? Is everything okay?"

"Everything is fine, really, except Lynda knew all along that Joel was going to meet Trent at the airfield. She just didn't bother to share that information because she wasn't really sorry that Joel was dead."

"What? She was happy for Trent to get away with murder?"

"Apparently, Joel wasn't just thinking of ending his partnership with Trent. He was also planning on ending his marriage. He was still pretending that everything was fine to both Lynda and Trent, but he was making plans behind their backs."

"That's horrible."

"It is, and it got him murdered."

"And Lynda didn't tell anyone what she knew."

"Oh, she told Victor. He just told her to keep her mouth shut, though."

Margaret shook her head. "Trent should have been put in prison thirty-five years ago."

Ted nodded. "And just lately, Lynda has been regretting her earlier silence. She admitted that she's spent the last thirty-five years trying to avoid Trent because she assumed he'd killed Joel."

"At least she wasn't blackmailing him," Margaret said.

Ted laughed. "I suppose that's something. Let's go to Onchan Park and play crazy golf or something. I need to forget all about Joel Ward and Trent Walsh."

"What about a movie?" Margaret knew that Ted had been wanting to see a fairly new release.

"That sounds great. We can hold hands in the dark."

After the movie, they took a long walk on the promenade and then had a drink at the Tale and Tail.

"I'll ring you tomorrow, or I'll just turn up on your doorstep," Ted said when he walked Margaret home. "Now that the cold case is solved, I should finish work on time tomorrow."

※

The next morning, everyone at the office was talking about Joel's murder and the fire. After a lengthy conversation about both cases, Arthur, Rachel, and Margaret headed to their offices.

A short while later, Margaret stuck her head into Arthur's office.

"Do you have five minutes?" she asked her boss.

He nodded. "For you, I can spare ten."

She grinned. "I was just wondering if you knew of anyone who is hiring. Neil Mackey got himself into some trouble across, but I think he learned his lesson."

Arthur nodded. "I was thinking about him after our conversation earlier. The night manager here is thinking of moving to Bristol. Don't ask me why. Maybe Neil would be interested in the job."

"Bristol?" Margaret repeated.

Arthur laughed. "It's almost inexplicable, except I know exactly why he's going."

"Oh?"

"He met a woman on some online dating site. They've been talking for months now. Earlier this year, he went to visit her. Apparently, she's actually very much like the person she claimed to be for all those months."

"That's surprising."

Arthur nodded. "That's what I said. Anyway, last month she came over to the island to see him. She likes it here, but she has children from her first marriage and a difficult relationship with her ex-husband. She doesn't think he'd let her move the children to the island, which means either he moves to Bristol, or they end things."

"They could just stay in a long-distance relationship until the children are adults."

"They could, but the youngest is only five. I don't think either of them wants to wait that long."

Margaret nodded. "I have Neil's number if you want to call him. Or I can call him and ask him to send you his resume, er, CV."

"Give me the number. I'll ring him after lunch. If he isn't right for the job here, I know of a couple of other companies that are hiring right now. I'm pretty certain I can find him something."

Margaret went back to her office feeling better about the world. Hopefully, her efforts would help Neil with his new start. He and his family deserved some good news. As she went back to her latest batch of test results, she realized that she didn't miss her old life much at all.

"I do miss Megan," she muttered. "I hope she comes and visits soon."

MURDER AT DREEYM GORRYM POINT
A MARGARET AND MONA GHOSTLY COZY

Release date: March 7, 2025

Margaret greatly enjoys a day out with her boyfriend, Ted, his friend Mark Hammersmith, and Mark's new girlfriend, Ashley. After a brisk hike and a picnic on the beach, they start the walk back to their cars to head for home. As Margaret and Ted hike through some rows of trees, though, they stumble across a dead body.

Ted is a police inspector, and it doesn't take him long to realize that the dead man was murdered. Worryingly, the man also has a personal connection to Ashley. Margaret finds herself caught up in another murder investigation, this time one uncomfortably close to home.

While Mona's interference sometimes annoys Margaret, this time she's eager to help Ted find the killer. Mona doesn't need much encouragement to do everything she can to make sure that Margaret gets to talk to every possible suspect. Margaret just has to hope that each conversation will get her closer to helping Ted solve the case.

A SNEAK PEEK AT MURDER AT DREEYM GORRYM POINT.
A MARGARET AND MONA GHOSTLY COZY

Release date: March 7, 2025

Please excuse any typos or minor errors. I have not yet completed final edits on this title.

Chapter One

"The views are amazing," Margaret Woods said to her boyfriend.

Ted Hart nodded. "It feels as if I can see forever."

They stopped at the top of the incline and looked out over the surrounding countryside.

"In another ten minutes or so we'll reach the sea," Mark Hammersmith said.

"I hope so," Mark's girlfriend, Ashely Ellison, snapped. "We've been walking for ages already, and all we can see from here is nothing."

Margaret and Ted exchanged glances and then started walking again, following the well-worn path.

"It feels as if we're many miles away from Douglas," Margaret said after another minute.

"Too far away," Ashley said. "Hiking isn't my idea of a good time."

Then why did you come? Margaret wondered.

Ashley sighed. "Did you do a lot of hiking when you lived in the US?" she asked Margaret.

"Not really. I used to like to go to the beach and walk along the sand sometimes, but I didn't do a lot of hiking through the countryside."

"And then you moved to the Isle of Man. I don't understand why anyone would move here if they could live in the US," Ashley said.

"I came to visit my Aunt Fenella and fell in love with the island," Margaret told her. "It feels like home in a way that I'd never experienced before."

Ashley laughed. "Or maybe you just realized that your Aunt Fenella was rich enough that you could move her and live off of her money for the rest of your life."

Ted grabbed Margaret's hand and gave it a squeeze. Margaret counted to ten before she replied. "Aunt Fenella is quite wealthy, but I earn my own money," she said, choosing her words carefully.

"Margaret works hard and far too much," Ted added.

"If I were you, I'd just live off of my aunt's money," Ashley said. "Why work if you don't have to?"

"As I said, Aunt Fenella is wealthy, but I am not. I have to work."

"I wonder if your aunt feels weird about the way her aunt made her fortune," Ashley said. "Fenella inherited Mona Kelly's fortune and everyone on the island knows where Mona Kelly got her money."

Margaret inhaled slowly, counting to twenty before she spoke again.

"Mona and Max had a very unique relationship," she said eventually.

Ashley laughed. "That's one way of describing it. Max paid her to look beautiful and sleep with him whenever he wanted her. There are other words for women who sleep with men for money."

"Is that a wallaby?" Mark asked, pointing into the distance.

"I thought the wallabies kept to the Curraghs," Margaret said as they all looked in the direction he was pointing.

"They probably do. It was probably just a bird or something," Mark said. "How are things going at work?"

Margaret grinned at the man. She considered him a friend and she'd been happy to hear that he'd started dating someone new, but this was the first time she'd met Ashley and so far, she wasn't impressed with the woman. At least Mark was doing what he could to diffuse the situation. Mona's relationship with Max was far more complicated than most people realized, but Margaret wasn't about to share what she'd learned about that relationship with anyone, least of all Ashley.

"Things are good, thanks. We're working on some new formulas, which is always interesting," she replied.

"Formulas? What do you do?" Ashley asked.

"I'm a chemical engineer at Park's Cleaning Supplies," Margaret told her.

Ashley raised an eyebrow. "You're a chemical engineer? Wow. Does that pay well?"

"I'm sure it pays better in the US than it does here," Mark said with a laugh.

Margaret nodded. "That's very true, but the island is such a beautiful place to live that I feel that it's worth the lower salary to be here."

"Working for less money is never worth it," Ashley said. "But then, I really can't imagine giving up life in the US for life on a small island, either. I'd give anything to be able to live in the US."

"Why?" Margaret asked.

Ashley stared at her. "Are you serious? So many reasons."

"I think a lot of people have a romantic notion of what it would be like to live in the US," Mark said.

Margaret shrugged. "My life there wasn't that much different from my life here. I got up every morning and went to work. On the weekends, I went grocery shopping and ran other errands. But I didn't have this stunning scenery around me." She waved an arm.

"But you could go to New York City or Los Angeles or Las Vegas whenever you wanted," Ashley said.

Margaret laughed. "I didn't live within driving distance of any of those cities. Flying takes time and is expensive. And hotel rooms in any big city are expensive, too."

"Have you ever been to the US?" Ted asked Ashley.

She nodded. "My parents took me to Florida when I was a little girl. We visited all of the theme parks. It was wonderful."

"Vacations are great," Margaret said. "But real life is a lot less exciting."

"And there's the sea," Mark said as the path curved around and the sea became visible in the distance.

"Beautiful," Margaret said.

"Don't you live on the Douglas promenade?" Ashley asked. "Can't you see the water from your flat?"

"I can, yes, but I never get tired of the view," Margaret replied.

"You're living in your aunt's flat, which was Mona's flat, right?" Ashley asked.

Margaret nodded.

"And that building used to be a hotel, didn't it?"

"It was a hotel. Maxwell Martin decided to turn it into flats years ago, though," Mark said.

"Rumor has it that he designed Mona's flat himself," Ashley said. "I was told that it's the most luxurious flat in the entire building."

"I don't know about that," Margaret said. "It's a lovely apartment, er, flat, though. And it's in a great location."

They walked in silence for a few minutes. Margaret could feel herself walking faster as they approached the sea.

"How did you and Ted meet?" Ashley asked, breaking the silence.

"We met when my sister and I came to visit Aunt Fenella," Margaret said. "We'd been planning to visit ever since she'd moved to the island, but it took us a long time to actually make the trip."

"And then you fell in love with Ted? Or you fell in love with the island?"

Margaret shrugged. "I fell in love with the island, definitely. I didn't get to know Ted well enough to fall in love with him that quickly. When I left, I knew I wanted to come back, and I hoped that I'd get a chance to get to know Ted better when I returned."

"Was Ted the reason you moved to the island?"

"No. I'd just left a job and ended a relationship. I was ready for a change and when I talked to Aunt Fenella, she suggested that I consider moving to the island. The more I thought about it, the better I liked the idea, especially after I visited the island."

"What about your sister?"

Margaret frowned. "Megan visited with me, and she plans to visit again soon, but she's busy with other things, too."

Like a man that I don't trust, Margaret added silently.

"What does Megan do?" Ashley asked.

Margaret shook her head. "She's on sabbatical from her job at the moment, but that's enough about me and my life. Tell me more about you. What do you do?"

Ashley shrugged. "I work in human resources for ShopFast."

"That sounds interesting," Margaret replied.

"It isn't, though. Mostly I hire shop assistants to work at the tills. They're all young with few qualifications. But then, I used to be one of them, so I shouldn't say anything."

"You used to work as a shop assistant as ShopFast?" Margaret asked.

"Yeah, years ago. I've been working my way up ever since. They pay for me to go to school, so I've been taking a few classes here and there, too. I'm not taking any at the moment, though, because I want to spend as much time as I can with Mark."

Mark looked surprised. "I appreciate that, but you shouldn't do anything that might negatively affect your career for me. Especially since we've only been seeing each other for a few weeks."

Ashley laughed. "Don't worry, you're just a convenient excuse for me to take a semester off from my classes. I'm tired of working full-time and studying on top of that. I'm still a long way away from earning a degree that would be properly useful. Maybe I'll just stay where I am, working in HR, until I get married. Then my husband can take care of me."

Margaret counted to ten again before replying. "That's a rather old-fashioned notion," she said, choosing her words carefully.

"I don't mind if people think I'm old fashioned," Ashley replied.

Margaret glanced at Mark. His eyes were focused on the sea.

"I know someone who works for ShopFast," Margaret said after a short silence. "Do you know Tim Blake?"

"I know who he is, but we've never met. He's been working for ShopFast a lot longer than I have. And he's a senior manager. He doesn't talk to junior HR employees."

Margaret thought about defending Tim, who was one of the nicest people she knew, but decided not to bother.

"And here we are," Ted said as they reached the beach. "Dreeym Gorrym Point."

"Say that again," Margaret said.

Ted chuckled and then repeated the Manx words. Then he spelled them for Margaret.

"Dreeym gorrym," she repeated slowly.

"The first word sounds like dream, but with a bit of a rolled r," Ted told her. "I can't think of an English equivalent for gorrym. It's sort of gore-uhm, I suppose."

Margaret repeated the words again. "But what does it mean?" she asked.

"Blue ridge," Ted told her.

"Ready for a picnic?" Mark asked.

Margaret nodded. "I'm starving. Breakfast seems to have been a very long time ago."

"It's the sea air," Mark said.

Ashley laughed. "Air is air. I can never understand why people seem to think that sea air has magical properties."

"Maybe because you've always lived near the sea," Margaret said. "As someone who hasn't lived here for long, I believe in the magical properties of sea air."

Before Ashley could reply, Mark set down the bag he'd been carrying and began to unpack their picnic. Ted had another bag that he put down on the blanket that Mark unfolded and laid out on the sand. A few minutes later, they all sat down to lunch.

"This is lovely," Margaret said as she picked up a sandwich. The waves washed gently against the sand as a light breeze blew past them.

"I'd rather eat in a nice restaurant," Ashley said. "I feel as if there's sand in everything I'm eating here."

"I was very careful not to get sand anywhere on the blanket or in the food," Mark said.

Ashley shrugged. "And I'd rather be sitting in a comfortable chair than on the ground."

"So how did you and Mark meet?" Margaret asked the other woman.

"We meet in a pub. I was with some friends. We were celebrating a birthday."

Mark chuckled. "You can't stop there," he said as Ashley took a bit of her sandwich.

"You tell her the rest, then," Ashley replied, reaching for her drink.

"Ashley and her friends were in the corner of the pub, having drinks when a fight broke out on the other side of the room," Mark said. "I won't go into details about the fight, but there were half a dozen guys, and it got physical very quickly. Ashley was the person who rang 999."

"That sounds scary," Margaret said.

"It wasn't that bad. I've seen much worse, but then I used to hang out with a very different crowd of people," Ashley said. "I only rang the police because one of the guys looked as if he'd been knocked out. I thought he was probably going to need an ambulance."

"I was at the station, typing up reports, when the call came in," Mark said. "I didn't have anything better to do, so I thought I'd go along and see if I could help in any way."

"Mark ended up taking my statement," Ashley said. "And after we'd talked, I gave him my number."

Mark nodded. "That was three weeks ago, more or less."

"And here we are," Ashley said, waving a hand. "Trying to spend as much time together as we can, which isn't easy with Mark's job."

Margaret nodded. "I know what you mean."

"At least the crime rate has been down lately," Mark said. "I've been putting in far fewer hours than normal, really."

"That's very true," Ted said. "And we were both able to get the same day off today. That doesn't happen very often."

"I'm not sure we'll be able to do that again in the future," Mark said. "So we need to enjoy today."

"It is the weekend," Ashley said. "You both should be off on the weekend."

"And we usually are, but one of us is usually on-call," Mark said.

"And we both usually have active investigations that we're conducting, which means we're often still taking phone calls and maybe conducting a few interviews, even on our days off."

"At least I always get weekends off," Margaret said.

Ashley made a face. "I usually get weekends off, but a few times each year we have big hiring fairs over a weekend. I have to work those weekends, and I hate them."

"I'm glad things are quiet at the station," Margaret said after a short silence. "I'd be happy if you never got any busier than you are right now."

Mark shrugged. "If the crime rate stays this low for much longer, I think the chief constable might start thinking about reducing staffing levels."

Ted shook his head. "That's not going to happen. Crime rates rise and fall all the time. The chief constable isn't going to cut our workforce just because things are quiet at the moment."

"James left," Mark said.

Ted nodded. "But he was just here on secondment. And he left because there were issues back in Liverpool, not because we no longer needed him here."

Margaret frowned. "James? Are you talking about Inspector Stout?"

"Yeah, he was supposed to be here for longer, but he ended up going back to Liverpool last week," Mark said. "I didn't find out he was going until after he'd gone."

"It was a surprise to everyone," Ted said. "Three of his colleagues in Liverpool suddenly needed time off, so the decision was made to recall James. When the chief constable agreed, they asked James to return as quickly as he could."

"What happened to his three colleagues?" Ashley asked.

"One had a heart attack. He's on the road to recovery, but apparently it's going to be at least a few months before he can return to work. Another gave his notice. He's going to work for a private security firm. The third also turned in his notice. His wife was offered a job in Manchester, so he's planning to take a job there once they get moved."

"I take a few days off and I miss everything," Mark said.

Ted grinned. "You've had more than a few days off recently. Have you met Michael yet?"

Mark frowned. "I have not."

"James left on Thursday and Michael arrived on Friday," Ted said. "And you were off both days."

"Who is Michael, then?" Mark asked.

"Inspector Michael Madison. He's here on secondment from Derby."

"Is he here to replace James?"

"Not specifically, although it turned out to be good timing that he arrived right when James left. He's part of a new rotational program that's being trialed in the UK. The chief constable signed up to be part of the program, but at the moment there aren't any plans to send anyone from the island's constabulary anywhere else. We're just a host constabulary," Ted explained.

"So we're going a bunch of inspectors from all over the UK over here on short visits?" Mark asked.

"Not necessarily short visits. Michael is supposed to be with us for six months."

"So was James. Tell me about Michael, then."

"You'll meet him on Monday. He's in his mid-forties. Married. Two kids who are nearly teenagers. He said he never would have considered anything similar to this secondment when the children were smaller, but he reckons they are now old enough that they shouldn't be too much work for his wife while he's away from home."

"He's going to be here for six months?" Margaret asked. "That's too much work for his wife."

Ted chuckled. "He's going home on weekends, at least twice a month. And his family is going to come and visit him here as well. They've already booked a hotel for when the kids are on Christmas break and for the February half term."

"It's still a lot for his wife to deal with on her own," Margaret said.

"But it's a great experience for Michael," Mark said. "These sorts of programs are often fast tracks to promotions."

"Remember, I spent two years on mine," Ted said. "And while it

A SNEAK PEEK AT MURDER AT DREEYM GORRYM POINT

didn't get me a promotion, it did get me a ton of great experience that I never would have been able to get on the island."

"I keep thinking about doing something similar to what you did," Mark said.

"I'm not sure the chief constable is going to send anyone anywhere while Daniel is away," Ted replied.

Mark made a face. "Leave it to Daniel to marry a millionaire and then take off on a year-long honeymoon. I can't believe the chief constable actually thinks Daniel is going to come back. Now that he and Fenella are married, they'll probably want to keep traveling, not come back to the island."

"Aunt Fenella definitely wants to come back to the island," Margaret said. "And the last time I talked to her, she said that Daniel is already starting to miss his job."

"I wouldn't miss it," Mark said. "Not if I was married to one of the richest women on the planet. I'd thoroughly enjoy traveling all over the world and living a life of leisure."

"Sorry, darling, but I can't give you that," Ashley said with a laugh.

"I don't think Aunt Fenella is one of the richest women on the planet," Margaret said.

"She's a lot richer than anyone here, anyway," Ashley said. "Of course, some of the people here are in line to inherit a fortune one day, at least."

Margaret flushed. "I don't know that I'm going to inherit anything. What Aunt Fenella does with her money is her business."

"She's in her fifties and childless," Ashley said. "Of course she's going to leave her fortune to her favorite niece."

"She and Daniel might decide to adopt a child or two," Margaret said. "Or maybe Aunt Fenella will leave everything to her cat. It's her money. I would never assume that I'm going to get anything from her."

"Ted? Did you know that? And does that information change how you feel about Margaret?" Ashley asked.

Ted laughed loudly. "I am not involved with Margaret because I think she's going to inherit a fortune from her aunt. Even if we both knew that Margaret was going to be one of Fenella's heirs, Fenella isn't that much older than I am, and as far as I know, she's in excellent health. Margaret would probably have to wait for decades to get any inheritance. And by that time, Fenella might blow every penny of the money on trips around the world."

"I hope you're going to be at work a few days this week," Ted said teasingly to Mark after an awkward silence.

"I was only off for two days last week," Mark replied. "And the chief constable approved the time off. You know I was house hunting."

Ted nodded. "How is that going?"

Mark shrugged. "I don't know. I found a few places that were close to what I want, but they were both missing at least one of the things I really wanted. And they were both out of my budget, too."

"I told you we should go house hunting together," Ashley said. "If we buy a house together, we can spend a bit more."

"That's a conversation for the future," Mark said.

"But you know I'm rather desperate to get out of my current living situation," Ashley said. "And I'd love to get a foot on the property ladder."

"Time for dessert?" Margaret asked as she gathered up the empty plates.

"We have dessert?" Mark asked.

Margaret laughed. "We brought cupcakes from the bakery near my building."

"They do wonderful cakes," Ashley said. "I'm not sure what a cupcake is, though."

Margaret opened the box that contained a dozen cupcakes.

"Oh, fairy cakes," Ashley said.

Margaret nodded. "I must remember to call them that. It's such a wonderful name for them."

"Are they all the same?" Mark asked.

"Not at all," Ted said. "That would be boring. There are four varieties. Chocolate sponge with chocolate icing. Vanilla sponge with vanilla icing. Chocolate sponge with a caramel center and vanilla icing. And vanilla sponge with a raspberry cream center and raspberry vanilla icing."

"I'll just have one of each," Mark said.

"Let's let Ashley and Margaret take what they want first," Ted said. "And then we can fight over whatever is left over."

Margaret took one each of the two chocolate cake options. Ashley stared into the box for several seconds before taking one of the vanilla and raspberry cakes.

"I don't often eat sugary sweets," she said, casting a disapproving look at Margaret's plate.

Mark laughed and then took one each of the different options. Ted selected three cupcakes and then shut the box with the last two cakes inside.

"I really do want to move," Ashley said as everyone started eating.

Mark nodded. "I know. I'm sorry that you're living situation is less than ideal."

Ashley laugh was bitter. "That's not how I'd put it."

"I was hoping things were getting better," Mark said.

Ashley sighed and then shook her head. "If anything, they're getting worse. But you know I don't like to complain. That's why I haven't really said anything to you about it lately." She looked at Margaret and Ted and then shrugged. "Sorry, you have no idea what we're talking about."

"I don't, but I'm sorry," Margaret said.

"You'd be even more sorry if you knew," Ashley replied. "The thing is, I live with the worst flatmate ever."

"That's a shame," Ted said.

"She seemed so nice when I went to look at the flat," Ashley said.

"She's always very nice to me when I'm there," Mark said.

Ashley made a face. "She knows you're a policeman. She's very careful to be nothing but wonderful in front of you. Maybe you should just move in with me. I don't know how long she could continue to pretend to be sweet and kind if you were living there, but it would be fun to watch her try."

"Are you looking for another flat?" Margaret asked.

Ashley shrugged. "I would be, if I hadn't just signed a lease for an entire year. She was smart enough to make me sign the lease with her, even though she'd already rented the flat in her name. She could have just rented out a room to me, but by putting my name on the lease, she knows I can't leave before the year is out."

"There isn't any sort of get-out clause?" Margaret asked. "Most rental properties in the US allow you to pay a penalty if you want to break the lease early."

"There might be something like that in the lease, but I can't afford any sort of penalty. I can barely afford my rent, really. Living on the island gets more expensive every day."

"The flat is in a good location, at least," Mark said.

"Yeah, it's a great location. I can walk to work and I'm not far from your flat, either, but everything about the place is horrible aside from the location."

"I don't think that's fair," Mark said. "Your bedroom is spacious, and you have your own en suite."

"Yeah, but I still have to share the rest of the flat with her. And most of the furniture is hers. I hate the couch."

Mark looked surprised. "It's very comfortable."

"But it's blue."

"I don't think that's a bad thing," Mark said.

Ashley shook her head. "I do."

"The last two times I was there, she wasn't even home," Mark said after a moment.

"She's been spending a lot more time with her boyfriend lately," Ashley said. "Which is great, of course, because it means she's not home as much, but when she is home, she still nags constantly."

"Nags?" Margaret echoed, flushing when she realized that she's spoken out loud.

Ashley nodded. "She has ridiculously exacting standards of cleanliness. I should have realized when I went around the flat that everything was spotlessly clean, but at the time I was too busy looking at the space I would be getting. I never imagined that every time I put anything down in the sitting room, I'd get nagged to take it to my room."

"That must be difficult," Margaret said.

"And don't get me started on the kitchen," Ashley said. "I don't dare leave a few dirty pots and pans around the place for more than an hour or two or I get nagged until I've done the washing up. She always insists that she's worried about attracting bugs or even mice, but I can't believe leaving a pot unwashed for a few days is that much of a problem."

A few days? Margaret thought. That would be a problem for me.

"Honestly, how many stray socks are in your sitting room right now?" Ashley asked Margaret.

"Stray socks?" Margaret echoed.

"Yeah, you know, socks you've taken off and just dropped somewhere. Socks you'll get around to picking up sooner or later."

"I have a cat," Margaret said. "I can't leave stray anything anywhere or Katie takes it." Not that I would leave stray socks lying around anyway.

Ashley shook her head. "Maybe I should get a cat. Maybe a cat would give Lelia something else to worry about besides the little bit of clutter I sometimes make."

"Maybe you should have stayed in your old flat," Mark said.

"I would have, if I could have," Ashley said. "Or rather, I would have if people would have communicated with me more clearly."

Margaret raised an eyebrow. She sort of wanted to hear the story, but she didn't want to appear nosy.

"What happened?" Ted asked.

"It was a big flat with four bedrooms," Ashley said. "One guy had his name on the lease and then he rented out the bedrooms to the rest of us. I'd only been there about six months when he told me that he was not renewing his lease and that we all had to find new places to stay. And we only had six weeks to get moved out, too."

"That isn't very long," Margaret said.

"Exactly," Ashley said. "I had to rush around, looking for another place to live super-fast. I never would have moved in with Lelia if I'd have enough time to look properly. And then, after I'd signed the lease at my new place, the guy at my old place told me that he'd changed his mind and signed another lease. The other two people who were renting rooms from him hadn't found anywhere else to go, so they both stayed where they were. In the end, I was the only one who moved out."

Interesting, Margaret thought.

"The new flat is in a better location," Mark said.

"And it's nearly twice the price that I was paying before," Ashley said. "I really think we should talk about moving in together."

"But you said you can't break your lease," Mark said.

"I said I can't afford to pay the penalty for breaking it, but if we decided to live together, then maybe you could help me out with that little thing," Ashley replied, smiling at Mark.

"That isn't something we need to decide today," Mark said.

"It's something we need to discuss soon, though," Ashley replied. "I don't know how much longer I'm going to be able to live with Lelia Dodson."

Mark nodded. "Let's get everything packed up. It's a long walk back to the cars."

Ashley sighed deeply. "I don't suppose there's any way you can go and get the car and collect me from here?"

Mark looked around. "There aren't any roads out here."

"I'm just tired," Ashley grumbled as Margaret and Ted began packing up the leftovers.

When they all stood up, Mark picked up the blanket and shook as much sand out of it as he could. Then he carefully folded it and put it back into its bag.

"There must be a shortcut back to the car," Ashley said as they began to retrace their steps.

"I don't know that it's a shortcut," Ted said, "but there is another path."

He gestured to the left. Ashley quickly shook her head.

"We can go back the same way we came," she said.

"Let's go the other way," Margaret suggested. "Once we get away from the sand, it looks as if there are a lot more trees in that direction. It might be nice, walking through a small forest."

"I don't think that qualifies as a small forest," Ted said. "But there are a few trees, anyway."

"No, let's just stick to the other path," Ashley said.

Mark shrugged. "It might be nice to walk back a different way."

233

Ashley shook her head. "I'm going back the way we came," she said loudly. "You can do what you want."

As she strode away, Mark looked at Ted and shrugged.

"I should go after her," he said.

"You should," Margaret agreed.

"She's usually very nice," Mark said before he rushed off after Ashley.

"I'm not sure I believe that," Margaret said quietly as she and Ted watched Mark catch up to his girlfriend.

"I've met her once or twice before," Ted said. "She seemed nice enough on those occasions."

"Do you want to follow them?" Margaret asked as Mark and Ashley turned and started to walk away.

"Not really. Let's take the other path. I don't think it's much farther than the one we took on our way to the beach and now what we've eaten nearly everything my bag isn't too heavy."

"I can take a turn carrying the bag."

"I've got it. You can hold my hand, though."

Margaret took his hand, and the pair began to stroll slowly back along the alternate path toward the parking lot. It wasn't long before they reached the wooded area.

"This is lovely," Margaret said as they walked along a row of pine trees.

"Just hang on there a minute," Ted said.

Margaret stopped. "What is it?" she asked.

"Hopefully, nothing," Ted replied.

He gave her hand a squeeze and then released it. Margaret watched as he walked around the last of the trees in the row. As he turned back and started walking along the other side of the trees, she spotted what he'd seen.

"What is it?" she asked again, unable to take her eyes off the large dark shape on the ground under one of the trees.

"I need to call this in," Ted said. "We need a full crime scene team. I just hope they can get all of the equipment they need out here without too much trouble."

A SNEAK PEEK AT MURDER AT DREEYM GORRYM POINT.

ALSO BY DIANA XARISSA

The Isle of Man Ghostly Cozy Mysteries

Arrivals and Arrests
Boats and Bad Guys
Cars and Cold Cases
Dogs and Danger
Encounters and Enemies
Friends and Frauds
Guests and Guilt
Hop-tu-Naa and Homicide
Invitations and Investigations
Joy and Jealousy
Kittens and Killers
Letters and Lawsuits
Marsupials and Murder
Neighbors and Nightmares
Orchestras and Obsessions
Proposals and Poison
Questions and Quarrels
Roses and Revenge
Secrets and Suspects
Theaters and Threats
Umbrellas and Undertakers
Visitors and Victims
Weddings and Witnesses
Xylophones and X-Rays
Yachts and Yelps

Zephyrs and Zombies

The Margaret and Mona Ghostly Cozies

Murder at Atkins Farm
Murder at Barker Stadium
Murder at Collins Airfield
Murder at Dreeym Gorrym Point

The Isle of Man Cozy Mysteries

Aunt Bessie Assumes
Aunt Bessie Believes
Aunt Bessie Considers
Aunt Bessie Decides
Aunt Bessie Enjoys
Aunt Bessie Finds
Aunt Bessie Goes
Aunt Bessie's Holiday
Aunt Bessie Invites
Aunt Bessie Joins
Aunt Bessie Knows
Aunt Bessie Likes
Aunt Bessie Meets
Aunt Bessie Needs
Aunt Bessie Observes
Aunt Bessie Provides
Aunt Bessie Questions
Aunt Bessie Remembers
Aunt Bessie Solves
Aunt Bessie Tries
Aunt Bessie Understands

Aunt Bessie Volunteers

Aunt Bessie Wonders

Aunt Bessie's X-Ray

Aunt Bessie Yearns

Aunt Bessie Zeroes In

The Aunt Bessie Cold Case Mysteries

The Adams File

The Bernhard File

The Carter File

The Durand File

The Evans File

The Flowers File

The Goodman File

The Howard File

The Irving File

The Jordan File

The Keller File

The Lawrence File

The Moss File

The Newton File

The Markham Sisters Cozy Mystery Novellas

The Appleton Case

The Bennett Case

The Chalmers Case

The Donaldson Case

The Ellsworth Case

The Fenton Case

The Green Case

The Hampton Case
The Irwin Case
The Jackson Case
The Kingston Case
The Lawley Case
The Moody Case
The Norman Case
The Osborne Case
The Patrone Case
The Quinton Case
The Rhodes Case
The Somerset Case
The Tanner Case
The Underwood Case
The Vernon Case
The Walters Case
The Xanders Case
The Young Case
The Zachery Case

The Janet Markham Bennett Cozy Thrillers

The Armstrong Assignment
The Blake Assignment
The Carlson Assignment
The Doyle Assignment
The Everest Assignment
The Farnsley Assignment
The George Assignment
The Hamilton Assignment
The Ingram Assignment

The Jacobs Assignment
The Knox Assignment
The Lock Assignment
The Miles Assignment
The Nichols Assignment

The Sunset Lodge Mysteries

The Body in the Annex
The Body in the Boathouse
The Body in the Cottage
The Body in the Dunk Tank
The Body in the Elevator
The Body in the Fountain
The Body in the Greenhouse
The Body in the Hallway

The Lady Elizabeth Cozies in Space

Alibis in Alpha Sector
Bodies in Beta Sector
Corpses in Chaos Sector
Danger in Delta Sector
Enemies in Energy Sector
Fires in Flux Sector

The Midlife Crisis Mysteries

Anxious in Nevada
Bewildered in Florida
Confused in Pennsylvania
Dazed in Colorado
Exhausted in Ohio

The Isle of Man Romances

Island Escape
Island Inheritance
Island Heritage
Island Christmas

The Later in Life Love Stories

Second Chances
Second Act
Second Thoughts
Second Degree
Second Best
Second Nature
Second Place
Second Dance

BOOKPLATES ARE NOW AVAILABLE

Would you like a signed bookplate for this book?

I now have bookplates (stickers) that I can personalize, sign, and send to you. It's the next best thing to getting a signed copy!

Send an email to diana@dianaxarissa.com with your mailing address (I promise not to use it for anything else, ever) and how you'd like your bookplate personalized and I'll sign one and send it to you.

There is no charge for a bookplate, but there is a limit of one per person.

ABOUT THE AUTHOR

Diana has been self-publishing since 2013, and she feels surprised and delighted to have found readers who enjoy the stories and characters that she imagines. Always an avid reader, she still loves nothing more than getting lost in fictional worlds, her own or others!

After being raised in Erie, Pennsylvania, and studying history at Allegheny College in Meadville, Pennsylvania, Diana pursued a career in college administration. She was living and working in Washington, DC, when she met her future husband, an Englishman who was visiting the city.

Following her marriage, Diana moved to Derbyshire. A short while later, she and her husband relocated to the Isle of Man. After ten years on the island, during which Diana earned a Master's degree in the island's history, they made the decision to relocate again, this time to the US.

Now living near Buffalo, New York, Diana and her husband live with their daughter, a student at the University at Buffalo. Their son is now living and working just outside of Boston, Massachusetts, giving Diana an excuse to travel now and again.

Diana also writes mystery/thrillers set in the not-too-distant future as Diana X. Dunn and Young Adult fiction as D.X. Dunn.

She is always happy to hear from readers. You can write to her at:

Diana Xarissa Dunn
PO Box 72
Clarence, NY 14031.

Find Diana at: DianaXarissa.com
E-mail: Diana@dianaxarissa.com

Printed in Great Britain
by Amazon